DEAD PRIEST AT GATOR'S POND

by

J. C. Quinn

This book is a work of fiction. Names, characters, places and incidents are either the product of the author's imagination or are used fictitiously. Any resemblance to actual persons, living or dead, or to actual events or locales is entirely coincidental.

DEAD PRIEST AT GATOR'S POND
Copyright © 2013 J. C. Quinn. All rights reserved, including the right to reproduce this book, or portions thereof, in any form. No part of this text may be reproduced, transmitted, downloaded, decompiled, reverse engineered, or stored in or introduced into any information storage and retrieval system, in any form or by any means, whether electronic or mechanical without the express written permission of the author. The scanning, uploading, and distribution of this book via the Internet or via any other means without the permission of the publisher is illegal and punishable by law. Please purchase only authorized editions and do not participate in or encourage electronic piracy of copyrighted materials.

The publisher does not have any control over and does not assume any responsibility for author or third-party websites or their content.

Cover Designed by Telemachus Press, LLC

Cover Art:
Copyright © iStockPhoto/8206485/pateilers

Published by Telemachus Press, LLC
http://www.telemachuspress.com

ISBN: 978-1-939337-89-4 (eBook)
ISBN: 978-1-939337-90-0 (Paperback)

Version 2013.06.06

Printed in the United States of America

10 9 8 7 6 5 4 3 2 1

OTHER BOOKS BY J.C. QUINN

To Kill a Fox

Triple Murder

*Heroes: Stories, Letters, and Thoughts of
A Catholic Man*

ACKNOWLEDGEMENTS

I would like to thank my good friends—John Stout and Tom McGreal—for their assistance in the writing of this book. They continued reading *Dead Priest at Gator's Pond* as it progressed from chapter to chapter sharing with me their valuable insight along the way. Thanks guys. I would also like to thank Jack O'Connell for his expert computer advice relative to the story concept involving flash drives. Jack, it was a great help. And I cannot forget to thank the people at Telemachus Press for their assistance, especially the unflappable and ever competent Steve Himes. And to Karen Lieberman, my editor at Telemachus Press goes a special thanks. Karen thanks so much. You made another one of my books that much better. Finally, I save my greatest appreciation for my wife, Kathy, who has made writing books become a reality for me. Honey, I could not have done it without you. And to all those readers out there who have read my books: Thank you so much. You are a part of every story.

J. C. Quinn

"Because of his affliction he shall see the light in fullness of days; through his suffering, my servant shall justify many ..."

Isaiah 53: 11

This book is dedicated to:
Our Lady of the Rosary

DEAD PRIEST AT GATOR'S POND

CHAPTER ONE
ST. ANNE OF GOD RECTORY

FATHER ANDREW BOOK experienced a sharp pain to his lower abdomen. Clutching his stomach, he looked at the man seated across the table from him. Father Miguel's dark eyes glared back. They revealed nothing. Father Andrew wanted to say something. He started to but decided against it. What good would it do, he thought. The deed was done.

Jaw muscles suddenly tightened. Stiffness invaded the back of Father Andrew's neck. A peculiar metallic taste filled his mouth. Poison. There was little doubt. The beef stew must have been laced with it. Two hours earlier Father Miguel had left the rectory saying he would be late for dinner. And that Father Andrew should begin dinner without him. Unsuspectingly, Father Andrew had fallen into the spider's trap. A black spider tattoo now appeared plainly on Father Miguel's upper right arm. These past many months it had been kept hidden. Apparently, the charade was over. And the man posing as Father Miguel wanted his true identity known.

"I am not feeling well. I had better go upstairs and lie down for awhile," Father Andrew said without looking up. A weak, sick feeling had accompanied the pain. There was a tightening in his calf muscles along with a cold sweat that came all at once. Doubled over, Father

Andrew took small steps to gain the stairs. He half-turned upon reaching them.

"Who are you?" Father Andrew asked with a quivering lower lip and shaken upper body.

"I am Father Miguel of course. You must be seriously ill to be asking me such a question," the dark-haired man with the brown face and black, hairy mustache answered. He did not bother getting up from the table.

"No you are not," Father Andrew responded. "You may be a lot of things but you are not a Catholic priest."

Father Andrew locked the bedroom door behind him before falling onto the bed. The priest's trembling right hand reached underneath the pillow for his rosary beads. He started to pray. But a sound coming from outside the bedroom door stopped him. He observed the doorknob being turned. There was a hard push against the door. Metal scraping metal could be heard. No mistaking it. Someone was picking the lock on the bedroom door. Father Andrew had just finished putting his rosary beads back underneath his pillow when the door opened.

"I have been waiting for you," Father Andrew said to the man who was standing in the doorway holding a knife in his right hand.

CHAPTER TWO

ARMY RANGER CAPTAIN Frank Book undid the seat belt and settled back. He was fortunate to have been assigned a seat next to the emergency door exit. Later in the flight the extra leg room would allow him to stretch out his six-foot-two frame and prevent any unused muscles from becoming cramped. The flight from Columbus, Georgia, to Miami, Florida, had a scheduled stopover in Atlanta. But it had already been announced that the passengers on board would not be permitted to disembark. So for Book that meant more idle time sitting on an airplane.

At 0600 hours, dressed in civvies, he had caught a ride on an army transport truck out of Fort Benning to Columbus Airport arriving only minutes before his Miami flight. The speedy ride to the airport had conformed to his recent pattern. For the past few days, the army ranger captain had been either running to catch a flight or sitting curled up in some uncomfortable airplane seat dealing with cramped legs and tightened back muscles. Book had endured the many endless hours in the air by staring through the plane porthole, gazing at the never-ending darkness outside. He would sometimes nod off awakening to rub unused calf tendons so that blood could get back to flowing within once again. It had been an inexhaustible monotony to say the least.

It had started with his occupying a constricted seat on the flight from Jalalabad Airport in Eastern Afghanistan to the stopover for refueling at Ramstein Air Base outside of Frankfurt, Germany. And it continued with the hours spent traversing the Atlantic Ocean to New York City where Book had to wait an additional half-a-day in LaGuardia Airport for his commercial flight to Columbus, Georgia. After two years of fighting in Afghanistan, it had been a welcome sight indeed to see the army driver and car waiting for him outside the Columbus Airport terminal. And here he was the next day on another airplane taking off again. However this flight to Miami had nothing to do with the army. It was personal and could not be more so. Book was flying into the city of Miami to find out why someone had murdered his brother.

"Would you like a tuna fish sandwich? I made it especially for you."

The older woman seated next to Book had unwrapped the cellophane and was offering him a tuna on wheat bread. Book first looked at the sandwich before taking in the face of the woman holding it. She appeared to be in her sixties with shiny, gray hair and eyeglasses to match while a questioning smile formed her face. The woman was wearing a white dress that had a variety of colored flowers imprinted upon it. It lent the look of a garden sprouting.

"For me?" Book asked, not believing what he had heard.

"Well, for whoever was sitting next to me. I do this every trip. My daughter lives in Miami and I visit her often and whenever I do I always make two sandwiches, one for me and one for whoever is seated next to me. So you see; I made it for you."

"That's awfully good of you but I ..." Book started to say but the older woman did not let him finish.

"The stewardess wouldn't have let me sit in this seat if it wasn't for you because there is no way that I could hope to open that emergency door on my own. But you're so big and strong she knew that you would have no trouble so she let me sit here. I am so glad you took the window seat because the aisle seat is the one I prefer. And they don't feed you on this flight, that's why I always make sandwiches. Oh dear, I hope you like tuna fish."

"No, tuna's fine. And thank you ma'am." Book took the sandwich and observed the woman as she unwrapped another one just like it for herself. Smiling, she began eating the sandwich while watching to see if the man seated next to her followed in turn. Book suddenly realized that he had not eaten since the previous evening. It had not dawned on him until now that he was actually hungry. Taking a bite of the sandwich, he smiled his appreciation for the woman to see.

"I am so glad you like tuna," she said while dabbing at her mouth with a napkin. "It will keep you from getting hungry."

Book finished the sandwich before allowing himself to lean back in the seat to stretch out his long legs. He peered through the plane's porthole content to settle his gaze on the endless stream of white clouds going by, while the steady hum of jet engines resonated. The sound of the engines soon became enmeshed in the collected chatter of the passengers around him. It served to free the army ranger captain's mind, allowing him to contemplate on the last couple of days. He had just finished two years of U.S. Army Ranger service in Afghanistan fighting the Taliban where the insurgents attempted to conceal themselves in the high mountains and remote areas of the country. Book and his men had been assigned to the most inhospitable terrain on earth. Only the specially trained army rangers had any chance at all of being effective. And Book's mountain warriors proved up to the job. More of the enemy had been killed during the spring offensive than during any other similarly planned operation in Afghanistan.

And then he had come home to Fort Benning to learn that his brother had been murdered in some place called Gator's Pond,

Florida. The letter notifying him of Andy's death had been secreted in a pile of other unopened mail that had finally caught up to him. It was only after his downing several beers that Book eventually came across it. The letter from Andy's religious superior was notoriously short on facts. The Franciscan abbot stated in the letter that he had made several attempts by phone to notify the next of kin, Captain Frank Book, regarding his brother's death. But he had been unsuccessful. The Franciscan Order proceeded to have a funeral Mass for their deceased member and ended up burying Andy on the grounds of a monastery in Newberry, Connecticut. The abbot enclosed a Xeroxed copy of a sketchy police report revealing that Andy had been murdered during some sort of homosexual dispute. The report was handwritten and its last line difficult to read. It took considerable effort on Book's part to decipher what someone apparently had hastily inserted on the final line of the police report. It indicated that a man had been arrested for Andy's murder but later hanged himself in the police lockup.

Book immediately telephoned the abbot. The priest was cordial over the phone while sounding sympathetic to Book's loss. But he was reluctant to discuss anything concerning Andy's murder even to the point of lapsing into silence whenever pressed by Book for more information. Book could not help but feel that the facts surrounding his brother's death were of no great concern to the abbot. An allegation of homosexuality involving a Catholic priest might have been the underlying reason. It would seem logical that the Franciscans did not want a national scandal at a time when there were already too many accusations of homosexuality damaging the Church's reputation. But Andy was not a homosexual. Frank Book would never be dissuaded from that fact. No matter what anyone said to the contrary. The army ranger captain thanked the abbot and hung up the phone before reaching into the cooler for another beer.

It was two beers later that Book came upon Andy's letter. It had been addressed in Andy's own handwriting to Captain Frank Book, Fort Benning, Georgia. Book used two shaking hands to open the envelope. The feel of warm tears swelled his eyes. The first thing he observed was the *June 5th* date written at the top of the page. Book noted that the letter had been written one day prior to Andy's murder.

Dear Frank:

I am sorry that I have to write this letter and get you involved in what I feel is a dangerous situation, but I have no other choice. There is so much that I want to say and am unable to say it with the way things are here at Gator's Pond. The telephone wires to the church rectory were cut last night and my cellphone is showing no signal so the only way that I can reach you is by mail. And today is Friday so that means there will be a beer delivery at the Gator's Pond Bar and hopefully a way of getting this letter to you. I know the beer truck driver and if I can get him alone to give him the letter then I'm sure he'll agree to post it for me as soon as he gets to Naples. The only U.S. Postal slot here at Gator's Pond is inside the police station, and I can't trust the police.

Frank, for a long time I have been suspicious of Father Miguel Santiago, my associate priest from Mexico who arrived here more than a year ago. He keeps to himself and politely refuses to have anything to do with me even when it comes to Church matters. I thought he was a priest who had lost his faith. I tried everything to engage him in talking about Jesus and the Church, but he has refused all conversation with me. For a while now I have come to the conclusion that he is not a priest and is masquerading as one. Last night he left the rectory and I was able to access his bedroom where he keeps his computer. I was able to confirm my suspicions. He is not a priest, and he has come to Gator's Pond to inflict a terrible evil upon the world.

I downloaded the implicating evidence from his computer onto a flash drive. This morning I hid the flash drive in a place that should be safe. I don't want to divulge its whereabouts should this letter fall into the wrong hands, but I know that you will find it should something happen to me. God bless you, Frank, and remember what St. Bernard said of Our Blessed Mother: "In dangers, in doubts, in difficulties, think of Mary—call upon Mary. Let her name never depart from your lips and never let her out of your heart."

Your loving brother,
Andy

Book felt a touch to his left shoulder. He turned to observe that the passenger seated next to him had placed her head contentedly upon his shoulder. The tuna fish lady's eyes were closed. She was breathing softly and appeared to be quite comfortable, not evidencing a care in the world. The army ranger captain dared not move his upper body fearing it might disturb her. For a man who had witnessed so much violence, so much death, and now to have to deal with the sorrow of losing his only sibling to more violence, more death, the sleeping head on his shoulder was most welcome. If only the rest of the world could possess the woman's heartfelt innocence, her easy smile, her peaceful look. How much better it would be. How much less pain it would have to feel. Book looked once more out the jet plane's porthole window. There was a sadness inside him that would not leave. Andy's face appeared and the thought of his kid brother took over. Memories Book had not entertained for years came back stronger than ever. Frank and Andy were boys again. And as always, Frank was there to take care of his younger brother. It was the Book brothers against the world.

The Books had grown up in the slums of Detroit where the two boys stuck out like white patches of snow on an asphalt street. Frank was four years older. He was the adult child who had seen their father walk out on him, Andy, and their mother. All because Harold Book one day had decided that he did not want a family anymore. The nice house in the suburbs became lost to them. The comfortable life they had come to know was lost as well. Theresa Book had to get a job cleaning downtown office buildings late at night in order to pay the rent on a one-bedroom apartment in East Detroit. That meant thirteen-year-old Frank and nine-year-old Andy would no longer be attending a suburban school. They would attend Carver, a Detroit public grammar school.

The huge, red-brick building covered nearly an entire city block. It had been built in the 1920s when the eastside consisted of mostly immigrant Irish and Italian blue collar workers. The men worked in one of Detroit's many auto assembly plants while the women stayed home taking care of the children. And the children either attended a neighborhood Catholic grammar school or went to the monolithic Carver. But in the 1970s three local Catholic grammar schools had been forced to close their doors and were eventually torn down. That left Carver the only remaining grammar school for the east side of Detroit. It had an almost entirely black student body other than for a handful of Hispanics. The school had not seen a white student attending in nearly a decade. But that all changed the day Frank and Andy Book came to Carver.

"We don't want no white boys at Carver," the fifteen-year-old, black thug warned the brothers on their first full day of school. The gangbanger's real name was Prescott Thigpen. People called him Corny because he liked to wear his greasy, black hair in corn rolls. Corny had been in and out of juvenile court since he was ten years old. He had committed crimes ranging from strong-arming other kids for nickels and dimes to breaking into houses in search of money and guns. The Detroit police had been actively looking for Corny. It concerned the robbery-murder of a pizza delivery man just two nights previous.

Frank Book and his younger brother Andy stood by staring blankly into Prescott Thigpen's sneering black face. They had said nothing to warrant his outburst. Both boys were shocked into silence by the unprovoked threat. The Book brothers, Corny, and two of Corny's black accomplices stood outside the main entrance to Carver Grammar School. A few black students hung around watching, but for the most part no one paid much attention to the two young, white boys being confronted by the older, black gangbangers.

"Don't ever come back to our school if you know what's good for you," Corny said before grabbing Andy and throwing the youngster down onto the ground. He placed the barrel of a shiny 32 caliber revolver into the boy's mouth.

"Leave him alone," Frank yelled while trying to pull away from Corny's two accomplices, who had the thinly built, not more than a hundred-and-ten-pound boy pinned to the sidewalk.

Corny laughed a high-pitched laugh. He spat in Frank's face. The gangbanger took the gun barrel out of Andy's mouth tucking the gun inside his pants belt. The gun butt became hidden underneath a brand-new, Michael Jordan tee shirt. Grinning, Corny walked away. His two accomplices let Frank go to follow Corny down the street.

It was still dark the following morning when Frank Book hid a baseball bat in a large bush outside the main entrance to Carver Grammar School. He then went home to tell his brother Andy that he would not be taking him to school that day. Afterward Frank walked the four blocks back to Carver School. He did not have to wait long before observing the three gangbangers. They were marching down the street shoulder to shoulder. Corny held the middle. His two cohorts walked either side of him. Big as you please, they were. Taking over the sidewalk, the gangbangers pushed whoever got in their way into the street.

Frank was standing next to a large bush outside of Carver's main entrance. Seeing the skinny, blond-haired, white boy, the trio quickened their pace. The gangbangers' faces were showing smirks. *Hurry, hurry* ... their minds raced.

"Do you believe that?" Corny muttered under his breath. The black thug could not believe what he was seeing.

Corny felt the resentment building in him. While standing not more than a few feet away was the cause for his resentment. All three thought for sure that the boy would run. And when he did not, Corny became suspicious. He reached underneath his Michael Jordan tee shirt for the 32 caliber gun. That is when a baseball bat fell across his right wrist. Another swing of the bat broke Corny's nose. Another dislodged his front teeth. Succeeding blows broke his arms. Corny's two accomplices stepped back in horror. They stood frozen. Both gangbangers watched the white boy walk by them into the Carver School. Frank Book kept a tight grip on the baseball bat. He did not release his grip until well inside the front door entrance.

After Corny's beating no one bothered Frank and Andy. Word had spread to leave the two white boys alone if you did not want to end up in the hospital like Corny. Mr. Johnson, Carver's black principal, called Frank into his office a couple of days after the beating incident. The principal thanked the boy for ridding the school of a cancer that had been plaguing the student body for too long. But not everyone felt the same. There were those who had become outraged over Corny's month long stay at the county hospital.

The white assistant principal, Mrs. Trout, was one. She felt that Frank should be expelled from school labeling him racist and sadistic. A smiling Mr. Johnson told his assistant principal to keep her mouth shut. He further instructed the former ACLU secretary to leave the boy alone. Frank graduated from Carver Grammar School the following spring. He went on to the district public high school where the student body consisted mostly of black and Hispanic students with a sprinkling of whites. Frank Book was no longer the slight, thinly-built boy who had confronted Corny two years prior. He had grown considerably, showing muscular arms and shoulders to match. In addition, he had obtained a reputation for not backing down from anyone. Playing fullback for the varsity football team, Frank started all four years of high school and ended up graduating with honors. He would later laugh about his graduating with honors citing the fact that the majority of his graduating class could not read. The day after graduating from high school Frank Book enlisted in the United States Army.

"You couldn't wait to get away from me could you, Frank?" his mother had said to him the night before he was to leave for the army. It did not happen often but tears came to fill the eyes of the eighteen-year-old, solidly built, Frank Book. He looked down at his mother who was staring up at him. Theresa Book showed tears of her own.

"You know that's not true," he told her. "I have to get away from Detroit because there's no future here for me. It's you and Andy who I'm going to miss."

He hugged his mother. The next morning Theresa Book watched her first-born walk away for the last time. She died three months later. Her dead body was discovered in a bathroom on the twelfth floor of an office building that she had been cleaning. An autopsy later revealed the woman had sustained a ruptured aorta resulting in her bleeding to death. Theresa Book was thirty-eight-years-old.

Fourteen-year-old Andy was sent to live in a boy's home outside of Detroit run by the Franciscan Order. Theresa Book had been a devout Catholic who instilled that same devotion and faith in her two sons. So it was only natural for Andy to go and live with the Franciscans. The younger Book soon discovered a serenity and purpose that imbued the everyday life of the gray-clad Franciscans. Six years later he took his first vows joining the Order. After four more years, Andy Book became a Franciscan priest.

Frank Book decided to make the army his chosen career. He finished nine weeks of basic training at Fort Jackson, South Carolina, before undergoing army ranger training at Fort Benning, Georgia. The tough kid from Detroit's eastside took to the in-your-face, take-it-or-leave-it ranger way. The harder the training, the greater the challenge, the more Book flourished. He was grouped with young men like himself who were told to give it their all. Yes, you have reached your mental and physical limit but give more, dig down, find it somewhere because we want more. There were no timeouts like in high school football. Book readily discovered that army rangers never asked for timeouts. And if you wanted to be an army ranger you did not ask for them either. He found it to be one of the finest fighting forces in the world. If called upon, Book would claim the finest. The army rangers wanted winners and accepted nothing less. They found a winner in Frank Book.

Colonel Henry Blake held the rank of captain when he saw Book for the first time. The then private occupied a twenty-by-twenty-foot boxing ring. The ring had been erected in the middle of a rehabbed warehouse on the outskirts of Birmingham, Alabama. The lanky, army ranger was fighting a tough marine heavyweight who had a good twenty pounds on Book, not to mention years more ring experience. It was the last boxing match on the night's card. It concluded the charity event that had been co-hosted by the U.S. Army and U.S. Navy. Blake had not planned on staying for the entire card. Later he was glad that he had. The young army ranger fighting in the ring was showing a lot of heart. He had no quit in him no matter how hard the big marine could punch. The kid's face was bloody, his legs wobbly, but he had not gone down even after taking a terrible shellacking for two rounds. It was now into the final round. Blake felt that if the kid could stay on his feet until the bell rang it would be a victory of sorts. The kid might have lost the fight but at least he hadn't been knocked out. Blake was entertaining that very thought when the big marine unleashed a flurry of punches. The young army ranger landed hard on the canvas floor.

Blake felt his heart sink inside him. He had hoped that the kid could have lasted through the final round. The referee was counting when Blake got out of his seat. He started up the aisle heading for the exit door. An excited roar from the crowd stopped him. Blake turned back around to find himself staring in disbelief. The young fighter had somehow come to his feet and was now pummeling the older marine with a combination of lefts and rights to the head. Soldiers in the crowd were cheering madly. Blake knew the final bell would be ringing at any moment. He started to yell, cheering the army ranger on. A colossal roar soon enveloped. It rose to fill the entire building. The big marine had fallen to the canvas. He was not getting up. Blake stood watching open-mouthed with nothing coming out. The referee started counting ten showing finger after finger until finally waving the fallen marine out. He went over and raised the winner's right arm, which brought another clamor from the crowd. Blake could not get over the feeling of exhilaration. It had taken possession, consuming every part of him. Turning to the officer next to him, Blake shouted so that the man could hear him above the roar of the crowd.

"Who the hell is that kid?" he asked smiling while feeling as though he had won the fight and the crowd was cheering for him.

****

Two days later Private Book was standing in Henry Blake's office. Blake was seated behind his desk staring up at the uniformed soldier who had a young man's face topped by a blond crew-cut. The army captain liked what he saw. There was intensity in those blue eyes looking back at him. There was confidence as well without the glare of arrogance so many young men his age evidenced. Blake stood and went around his desk. He extended his right hand. Private Frank Book readily took it.

"That was some performance the other night," Blake said with eyes burning, displaying their own intensity. Book was nearly nineteen, tall, and muscular while Blake was thirty-nine, small, and wiry, but it was the army ranger captain who exuded physical dominance. Frank Book could see it, feel it. The hard-set jaw and hawk-like nose accompanied by the litheness in how he moved portended a strength about Blake. It suggested, yes, you might kill me, but I'll kill you as well before I die. Book felt himself overwhelmed by the man.

"Thank you, sir."

"No, it is I who thank you, Private Book. You are a credit to the rangers and I most certainly give you thanks on their behalf. Now let's get down to your future. Are you making the army your life's work?"

"Yes, sir. I am."

"Good. I was hoping you would say that. Book, I want to help you if you will let me. The country needs men like you and right now they are far and few between. Will you let me do it?"

"Of course, sir. I would appreciate any …"

"Appreciate it after you get it. From this moment on I will be taking a personal interest in your career. Keep in the back of your mind Officer Candidate School. I will help in arranging college classes for you and future work assignments. That's all for now. Good luck to you, Private Book."

"Yes, sir." The army ranger private saluted and the captain returned his salute. Book was opening the office door to leave when Blake stopped him.

"Book tell me one more thing before you go. It has been nagging at me for the last two days. You were done, finished when that marine knocked you down in the last round. I would have bet a year's pay that they would have had to carry you out of the ring, that's how bad it looked. What made you get up? Why did you get up?"

Book looked across the room at Blake who was seated behind his desk waiting for an answer. The army captain did not have to wait long. Book's response came without any forethought.

"Captain, I had to. I didn't have any other choice."

Henry Blake's face was blank until an inching smile gradually took it over. His gray eyes widened to a fostering glint. He nodded to the young man who was standing in the doorway.

"Thanks, Book," Captain Blake acknowledged before lowering his gaze to a report he had picked up off his desk. "You will definitely be hearing from me."

Frank Book went on to follow Henry Blake's lead. And under the older man's tutelage gained promotion and stature in the U.S. Army Rangers. Blake, through the years, was able to achieve the rank of lieutenant colonel while Book obtained captain. The two men forged a bond which grew only stronger over time. Those around them often said the older Blake and the younger Book had somehow been carved out of the same hardwood tree. It was as though they had sprung from the same DNA. That's how much alike they appeared before the eyes of the other rangers. The men witnessed how the lieutenant colonel and the captain interacted with one another. And with their witness came the father-son appraisal. Soldiers might have talked about it. Henry Blake and Frank Book came to experience it. Married with three nearly grown-up daughters, the fifty-three-old Blake, saw in the thirty-three-year-old Book the son he had always wanted. The feeling of fatherly pride swelled up inside him whenever he watched Book excel in the army ranger life. Blake saw the respect other soldiers gave to the once raw kid who years ago had told him that after being knocked down he had to get to his feet because it was the only thing to do. It was a genuine father's pride that Henry Blake felt for Frank Book.

Something only a father can feel for his son. It had become a part of the two men's spiritual DNA, a bonding of souls set down before either had been born. It was an emotional attachment the army ranger colonel told himself that he would never reveal to anyone.

Book discovered in Henry Blake the father image, the manly emulation, the end goal of who he wanted to be and how he was going to get there. He wished to duplicate the honor, the integrity of one Henry Blake. One tour of fighting in Iraq followed by two tours in Afghanistan had given Book the opportunity to display the courage, leadership, and commitment to his fellow soldiers that enabled him to gain the honor and integrity he had been seeking. He devoted his every day to what was important in life, adhering to the words of Henry Blake who had stressed it through the years without letting up. "God, family, and country in that order is how you place priorities in your life," Blake had repeated over and over again. "Nothing else is important. When all else is said and done, that is what we will be judged upon, that and that alone."

And here he was on a flight to Miami in an attempt to find out about his brother Andy, the only family that had been left to him. Someone had killed Andy. Frank Book had to know why. Colonel Blake had granted him an extended leave. Book was going to use that time to learn why a man would murder a Catholic priest. And then hang himself after confessing. Book also wanted to know what made a Franciscan abbot so hesitant to discuss the details concerning the murder of a priest under his authority. And then there was the letter from Andy written the day before he was killed. It mentioned a pretender priest who was planning some terrible evil. Book could not help but feel that something was wrong concerning the police investigation. What was it that actually led to Andy's death? The army ranger captain knew that if he did not get to the bottom of it there would never be any peace left for him.

The jet plane vibrated briefly during its approach into Miami Airport. Book felt the head resting against his shoulder begin to stir. The fish lady was wakening up. He looked down and saw two light green eyes looking up at him. Book could not help but smile at the sleepy eyes and the gray eyeglasses turned to the side. He saw the woman smile back.

"Thanks for the shoulder," she said to him with her head coming up. "Maybe we will be on the same flight going back." She commenced to pat at her ruffled gray hair with a right hand while straightening up in her seat. Turning to him she added, "I certainly hope you like chicken sandwiches."

"My favorite," Book answered while wondering what the future days would bring.

CHAPTER THREE

THIRTY MINUTES LATER Book's plane landed at Miami's airport. After fifty minutes he was outside the terminal tossing his green duffel bag into the back seat of a taxi. Dressed in a long-sleeve blue shirt and dark slacks, the ranger captain told the driver to take him to the Miami-Dade Medical Examiner's Office. Book jumped into the taxi's back seat and immediately felt the tension starting to build inside him.

He had an open appointment with Dr. Nigel Simon, the pathologist, who had performed Andy's autopsy. The army ranger captain was not looking forward to hearing the grim details surrounding his brother's death. Book had talked to Dr. Simon over the phone and had been unable to obtain anything more than generalities. Andy had died from multiple stab wounds and poisoning. That was about all Book could get out of the man. Hopefully, he would find out more in a face-to-face meeting with the Miami-Dade pathologist.

Dr. Simon's office ended up being nothing more than a cubicle consisting of four metal walls and a door. It was situated at the end of a long line of cubicles abutting a narrow hallway. Upon entering Book felt as though he had stepped into a 15 by 15 metal box in which someone had decided to cut out a door. Dr. Simon was seated behind a large wooden desk that took over most of the room. It left little space for anything else including the 6-foot, 2-inch, 225 pound Frank Book. Peering from behind a pair of wire-rim glasses, Dr. Simon recognized his visitor's questioning gaze.

"Yes, it is a doctor's office but unfortunately not much of one, I know. But then again the patients I get don't care what kind of office their doctor has. They are beyond caring about anything anymore."

Book smiled. "Then again, it's not like you're out there trying to solicit more customers, now is it doctor?"

"No, Captain Book, it certainly is not. The Miami-Dade County Medical Examiner's Office has an unabated flow of dead bodies coming through here with causes of death ranging from gunshot wounds, stabbings, beatings, to whatever cruelty one man can possibly inflict upon another. You name it, and this place has seen it."

Dr. Simon came out of his chair. Leaning over his desk, the doctor shook hands with Book. He then motioned for Book to take a chair that had stacks of loose leaf papers covering it. The doctor's face betrayed his annoyance.

"Please, put them on the floor," he said with a gesturing right hand before sitting back down. "I don't usually get many visitors, but when I do I rarely see them in here. I try to make arrangements for a reserved table downstairs in the cafeteria. In your case I wanted things more private."

Book took in the disheveled, hunched over man at his desk. The elongated, thin face presented a pallid look, somewhat illogical for someone residing in Florida. The gray, balding head glistened underneath the bright light, while gray eyes behind wire-rimmed glasses stared across the desk at Book, appearing tired, battle weary to say the least. The army ranger picked up something else from the doctor but could not grasp it. Maybe it was the hint of nervousness that formed in the tight corners of the man's mouth, or perhaps the incessant tapping of the doctor's right hand on the desktop. Something was there. The man appeared agitated.

"All right, Captain Book. You requested this meeting and here we are. Now, what exactly do you want to know concerning the death of your brother?"

Book slid the chair closer while bringing his upper body forward. The army ranger's dark blue eyes took on a hard penetrating glare. Dr. Simon immediately took notice. It caused the doctor to shift further back in his chair.

"I want to know everything. And I don't want you to leave anything out."

"I already told you over the phone that the cause of death was due to multiple stab wounds and poisoning. A man was arrested and he killed himself. Why can't you leave it at that? What good can come of going over morbid details that will change nothing?"

"How many times and where on his body was he stabbed? What kind of poison and by what means? Everything, doctor. I didn't come here for a lecture. I want to know exactly how my brother was killed, and I'm not leaving until I get it."

Dr. Simon removed his eyeglasses. They were set down on the desk in front of him. The doctor then rubbed his eyes using the palms of both hands before putting the eyeglasses back on.

"As you wish, Captain. I only wanted to spare you the pain. But yes, I will supply you the information you seek. But what I am going to describe is most terrible, something I haven't seen since my early days while working for the Red Cross in the Sudan. There was an aid station outside of Khartoum and it often received victims from the tribal violence that used to spring up from time to time. Captain, have you ever heard of the phrase, 'death by a thousand cuts'?"

Book nodded while keeping his steady look centered on the man seated in front of him.

"Well I haven't seen another human being desecrated in such a manner in more than twenty-five years until the day your brother's body was brought in here. There were so many lacerations inflicted on his body that I could not be accurate in my count. None of them were post-mortem. He was alive and felt every one of them. The stab wound to the heart was the only fatal wound while the rest were superficial and inflicted to cause pain and tremendous anguish. Captain Book your brother had been forced to sustain horrible torture at the hands of someone who was quite good at keeping his subject alive so that the torture could be extended over a period of time. No arteries had been cut and the threat of his bleeding to death kept to a minimum so conceivably the ordeal could have lasted for several hours."

Frank Book kept a somber look. But below the skin, where a person lives and breathes, it was quite different. His heart raced while his stomach churned as the nightmarish picture described by Dr. Simon formed in his mind. He tried to keep Andy's face out of his thoughts so that he could think clearly. The doctor was looking at him. Book forced himself to concentrate on the man's troubled face.

"How about the poison, Doctor?" Book asked.

"There was enough Strychnine in his blood to have killed him, but it would have taken a day or two for a fatal reaction to have occurred. Beforehand it would have left your brother weak with considerable abdominal pain and unable to defend himself. He was in excellent physical condition so I would venture to say the poison was administered in some covert manner in order to leave him helpless and no threat to his killer. In effect your brother was rendered defenseless so that he could be tortured to death."

Book had heard enough. He stood up. Dr. Simon did likewise. The two men looked at one another. Neither man spoke but there was a sharing of sorts. Andy's last moments of life had to have been terrible. Both men together had revisited that time. Book could now understand Dr. Simon's reluctance to detail the manner in which Andy had been murdered. He could also understand why the Franciscan abbot did not want to discuss the murder of a fellow priest over the phone. It had been painful in the telling not only for Book but for the doctor as well.

"Thank you, doctor," Book said extending his right hand. Dr. Simon took it stepping around his desk.

"I'm sorry Captain for being the one who had to give you this information about your brother. I hope you can remember him in better times when you were both happy together. Try and do that. Maybe then you will be able to put this ugly picture out of your conscious mind."

"I don't think that's possible," Book said. "Andy was the only family left to me and the death he underwent is one that I didn't think could have taken place in this country, especially to a Catholic priest who had never harmed another soul in his entire life."

"One minute, Captain," Dr. Simon said remembering something and reaching back to his desk for a piece of paper. "I nearly forgot to give this to you. Florida Assistant Attorney General Robert Collins phoned this morning and told me to give you this message. He wants to see you before you leave Miami. His office is only a few blocks from here and should be easy for you to find. I wrote the address and directions down."

Book took the paper from Dr. Simon. He put it in his front shirt pocket. The army ranger captain had every intention of seeing the assistant attorney general. Collins was a West Pointer and friend of Colonel Henry Blake. Before leaving Fort Benning, Blake had told Book that he would attempt to arrange a meeting with Collins.

"Thanks again, Doctor," Book said turning toward the door. Dr. Simon walked behind Book placing a right hand on his guest's shoulder. They faced one another in the doorway.

"The man who killed your brother in such a terrible way is dead so try and let it go, Captain," Dr. Nigel Simon said in his most consoling tone. "Try and forget about what has happened."

The doctor observed a hardened look appear where earlier no emotion had been shown. Book had revealed nothing even after hearing the gruesome facts concerning his brother's death. Dr. Simon realized that the man had only been concealing his feelings.

"And it's a good thing that he's dead," Book said, "Because I would have made sure of it."

"Goodbye, Captain Book." Dr. Simon said, not feeling comfortable with the change he saw in the man.

Prior to walking away Book told him, "Yes, goodbye doctor and thank you for your time."

CHAPTER FOUR

BOOK FOUND THE offices for the attorney general on the building's seventh floor. And he did not have to wait long in the reception area before a smiling Bob Collins came out to meet him. Book could tell the man was former U.S. Army. He possessed a short grayish haircut, trim build, and bright hazel eyes that looked right at you without wavering. The ranger captain could understand why Henry Blake had said of Collins, "Frank, he's one of the few men I have ever trusted."

"Captain Book, I've heard so much about you from Colonel Blake that I feel I already know you." Collins gripped Book's extended right hand. The two men shook. Collins then escorted the army ranger captain through an opened door and down a carpeted hallway to where the assistant attorney general's office occupied an entire corner suite.

The view of the Atlantic Ocean captured Book's attention the moment he stepped into Collins' spacious office. Bluish-green, white-capped water stretched as far as the eye could see until it became a part of the cloudless, blue sky on the horizon. Collins' corner office had a full-tinted glass window extending the entire length of its east wall. It presented a breathtaking panorama for any visitor.

The office itself was surprisingly sparse in décor. It consisted of a medium-size desk with a computer along one wall while in the center of the office floor was an oblong-shaped, conference table showing six brown-padded chairs. A freshly made pot of black coffee rested at one end of the table. The coffee pot was sputtering out its last few remaining drops of hot brew.

Book noticed there was nothing displayed on any of the walls except for the space directly behind Collins' desk. It showed a framed photograph depicting a group of U.S. Army Rangers huddled together in full-battle gear. The caption underneath the photograph read, *Mogadishu, July 2, 1993*.

"I'm the dumb looking guy in the back row on the left, and the intelligent looking fellow to my left is your commanding officer Henry Blake," Collins volunteered after noticing Book's interest in the photograph. "We were a lot younger back then and as tough as they come. That photo was taken after the fighting at Mogadishu, Sudan. The battle was aptly portrayed in the book *Black Hawk Down*, but like most things in life you have to live it in order to know what it really was like. Henry and I fought back-to-back there. Neither one of us thought we would come out of it alive. But then Frank, I don't have to tell you about that, now do I? Colonel Blake has told me all about you. There are not too many soldiers awarded the Silver Star along with all the other achievements that have been accredited to you."

"Thank you, sir, but right now I would just like to find out about my brother."

Collins tapped Book on the right shoulder directing him to the conference table. The two men sat down opposite one another while the assistant attorney general immediately went for the coffee pot. He poured hot, black coffee into two white mugs before handing one of the mugs to Book.

"I can't tell you who killed your brother, but I can tell you who didn't kill him," Collins said before taking a sip of coffee and putting down the mug. "A down and out alcoholic by the name of Charlie Steed was arrested for your brother's murder and supposedly signed a written statement implicating himself. Steed reportedly told the police that he and your brother were having a homosexual affair and your brother began seeing other men behind his back."

"I don't believe a word of it," Book said, shaking his head.

"Neither do I, but let me finish so I can tell you why I don't believe it. Supposedly Steed became enraged over the idea that your brother was having sex with other men so he killed him. First he tortured him, then he killed him. Most conveniently after signing his confession, Steed hangs himself in the Gator's Pond police lockup using his own belt.

"Frank, Charlie Steed was illiterate and could barely sign his own name. He could not have read and understood the statement that he had signed. We know that from his sister who had to go with him every time Steed bought a car or had to sign any legal document. Secondly, he had been married twice and had obtained legal divorces from both women. We have written affidavits from Steed's former wives stating that he was not a homosexual. Charlie Steed was made into a convenient scapegoat. Between you and me, the man was murdered by someone in the Gator's Pond Police Department in order to cover up the identity of your brother's killer."

"But why?" Book asked finding it difficult to comprehend what he had just been told him. "Why would the police do such a thing?"

"For the obvious reason," Collins said falling back in his chair. "The real killer is important to them and they wanted him protected. And with Charlie Steed out of the way and blamed for your brother's murder there would be no reason for any further investigation to be conducted by this Office or the Florida Department of Law

Enforcement. The case would be just another homicide cleared and closed and filed away with no questions asked."

Frank Book looked into Collin's face observing its sincerity. It told Book that the man could be trusted. He was someone who would not let you down in the clinch. Nevertheless, there was something more. The assistant attorney general's eyes seemed to be saying to him, "*Yes, you can trust me, Frank Book, but I can't tell you everything. There are some things I cannot reveal to you.*"

Book knew Collins' heart would always be army. And he would not deliberately lie to him. But what was the assistant attorney general not telling him? What was he leaving out? Andy was not and never had been a homosexual. Of that Book was certain. And apparently Charlie Steed who had been blamed for Andy's murder had not been one either. Someone in the Gator's Pond Police Department had concocted their relationship in order to cover up the actual motive behind Andy's murder. Book would need more information before going to Gator's Pond. Otherwise he would be walking in blind. There was only one person who could give him what he needed. It was the man presently staring intently across the table at him with a coffee mug in his right hand.

"Bob, you know that I stopped here on my way to Gator's Pond, and that I'll be there tomorrow at the latest. Don't make me the guy who's walking point with a blindfold on and not knowing what I'm walking into. You have to tell me everything. What is it about Gator's Pond that you're leaving out?"

Collins came abruptly out of his chair. He moved to the glass window behind him where his gaze settled. The former army ranger and now Florida state prosecutor appreciated the endless stretch of water and the serenity of its waves rolling to meet the shoreline. Hordes of barely-clad sun bathers decorated the sandy beach, while a cadre of windsurfers with yellow and blue sails streaked pell-mell across blue-green water. Collins stood watching until the windsurfers and sails became tiny specks in the distance.

"Frank, I promised Henry Blake that I would do my best to keep you from going to Gator's Pond," Collins said while not removing his eyes from the scene outside his office window. "I could have lied to you and said the murderer of your brother hanged himself in the police lockup. End of story. Case closed. But I couldn't do that to a guy who has done three tours of duty between Iraq and Afghanistan and was wounded twice. You deserve better."

Collins turned around and placed the palms of both hands down on the table in front of him. He leaned forward counteracting Book's intense look with one of his own. Each man held the other's gaze.

"Bo Wiley runs Gator's Pond and everything in it. His sugar and cattle plantation covers more than two hundred thousand acres which on three sides abuts the Everglades. And with the Everglades you have more than twelve hundred square miles of trees, swamp, and basically one of the most inhospitable places anywhere in the world. Every year, Wiley brings in hundreds of immigrants to work his plantation, most of them coming from South America and Mexico. They're kept in line through brute force. He keeps his own police department with his brother Cash running it for him. His sister Evelyn's two boys, Turk and Tank Thompson, are two of his deputies. They're big, sadistic thugs who do whatever Bo and Cash want them to do. Two years ago Turk and Tank got into it with a tourist from Michigan who was drunk and started trouble in the Gator's Pond Bar. He was found the next morning hanging in a lockup cell with his own belt tightened around his neck. Sound familiar? There was a state investigation which netted nothing. Frank, you could end up the same way if you go poking around asking questions. That's why I told Henry Blake that I would do my best in talking you out of going. Your brother's murderer will be caught, but it is going to take time."

"I have to go," Book said coming to a standing position. "Andy was the only family I had. I have to find out what happened to him and who killed him. Not to go to Gator's Pond would be like leaving behind someone in your unit because you might get hurt going back for him. You would never do that Bob so how can you ask me to?"

"Okay, go then," Collins said while looking across the table at Book who reminded the assistant attorney general of himself twenty years prior. "But first I am going to tell you something that, if it got out that I told you, might end up costing me my job. Maybe even get me arrested on an official misconduct charge."

"I didn't come here to middle you," Book conceded. "Andy was my brother not yours."

"Just shut up and listen to me, will ya?" You're too bullheaded to realize what you're walking into at Gator's Pond so listen to what I am going to tell you. Approximately two years ago the U.S. Internal Revenue Department was all set to take Bo Wiley's plantation away from him because he owed millions in back taxes. But a couple of days prior to the confiscation, Wiley somehow came up with the necessary money to pay back all the tax money owed. How he came up with the millions to do it no one knows. But he did it.

"And right about that time a Federal Drug Enforcement agent who had been working undercover at Gator's Pond came up missing. He had been investigating the smuggling of Middle Eastern heroin into the United States. That DEA agent has not been heard from and not a trace of him has ever been found. My people and the Florida Department of Law Enforcement went into Gator's Pond along with the DEA and came up with nothing. The Feds now have a standing order for us to keep away from Gator's Pond because they have something going on there and don't want us getting in the way."

"So you're saying Bo Wiley is involved in the heroin trade and that's what this is all about?"

"Yes, and who knows what else he might be involved in. You can't bring millions of dollars of smuggled heroin into the country without some kind of an organization behind you. Wiley must have partnered with a well-connected entity that has the means to get rid of large quantities of heroin on the open market. And Frank you can bet that they will kill to protect their arrangement."

"Do you think that was why Andy was killed?" Book asked.

"Yes, I do. And he wasn't just killed, he was tortured to death. Your brother must have had in his possession something belonging to someone else and they wanted it back. And his being a Catholic priest didn't protect him the same as your being a captain in the U.S. Army won't protect you. But I would think that Wiley would be somewhat hesitant to kill you outright after your brother's recent murder. Undoubtedly, it would end up bringing a full scale federal investigation into his back yard, and right now I don't think he wants that kind of heat."

Book reached into his back pants pocket and took out Andy's letter. He handed it to Collins. "Andy wrote that letter the day before he was murdered." Book watched Collins unfold and begin to read the letter. He added, "Bob, I want you to keep it, and if anything should happen to me I want you to use Andy's letter to start up that investigation you were talking about."

"Do you have any idea where your brother might have hidden the flash drive?" Collins asked while briefly taking his eyes off the letter to look at Book. "Because he writes here that he knows that you will be able to find it. Frank, what did Andy mean by that?"

"I don't know," Book answered. "But he ends the letter with the quote from St. Bernard. Something about going to Mary. I think it's more than just a Catholic priest invoking help from the Mother of God. I feel that Andy was trying to tell me where to look for the hidden flash drive. It's location has something to do with Mary. Maybe a statue of her either in the church or in his room. I have to get to Gator's Pond to find out."

"Before you leave I have something to give you," Collins said putting the letter in his coat pocket and walking over to a door on the other side of the office. Book observed the assistant attorney general opening the door and reaching in to remove a brown cardboard box. Collins carried the box back to Book. "Here," he said handing the army ranger captain the box. "It's a gift from Henry Blake that arrived this morning. The Beretta 9mm. might be from Henry, but the five loaded ammo clips are from me. Call it a combined strategic effort on our part."

Book opened the box and removed the gun. Holding the gray-steel Beretta in his right hand, Book liked the feel. He balanced the gun's weight on an open palm before tightening his grip. Collins looked on with an approving smile.

"Good luck, Frank," the assistant attorney general said putting his right arm around Book. "I wish you all the best."

"Thanks, Bob. And thanks for the gun and ammo. It might come in handy at Gator's Pond."

CHAPTER FIVE

JOE LUERA COULD not recall ever stopping at Gator's Pond. That was what made the stop so unusual. Luera had been driving a Sunshine Bus for more than twenty-one years with the last ten of those being the Miami to Naples run across Alligator Alley. The run crisscrossed the Florida Everglades through hundreds of square miles of endless swamp. It was listed on the bus manifest as an express, which meant no stops. But this trip had an unscheduled stop penciled in for Gator's Pond. The bus stop itself amounted to nothing more than a crossroads where a hand-painted sign indicated "Gator's Pond 5 miles." The upper portion of the sign showed a red arrow pointing south down a gravel road. Luera had never been to Gator's Pond nor had he known anyone who had. So it was strange for him to note that someone wanted to go there.

Sixteen passengers had paid in full for their tickets. That meant the company would be losing money this trip. Eighteen was the break even number. Putting on his seat belt, Joe Luera was all set to pull out of the Miami terminal when he abruptly removed the seat belt from around him. He got out of the bus and went back into the office to double check the Gator's Pond stop. The veteran bus driver wanted to be sure no one was pulling his leg and trying to put one over on him. He soon learned from a smiling female clerk that the manifest sheet was accurate. The Miami to Naples run called for a stop at Gator's Pond. One passenger out of the sixteen wanted to be dropped off in the middle of the Everglades where the heat index was well above one hundred degrees. And crazier still, he intended on walking the five miles to Gator's Pond.

"Are you sure that you want to get off here mister?" Joe Luera said two hours later to the man carrying a green duffel bag and exiting the front door of the Sunshine bus.

"Is this the stop for Gator's Pond?" Book asked looking back. Luera stared into a pair of dark sunglasses underneath a blond crew-cut. The bus driver could not help but think military.

"Yeah, if you want to walk five miles down that road. It ain't safe around here mister. There's snakes, alligators, and every kind of bug born to bite out there."

"As long as it gets me to Gator's Pond I don't care," Book said walking away.

Joe Luera shook his head before throwing the bus into gear. He told himself that no matter how long he drove a bus there would always be that one person who left him dumfounded.

****

Deputy Angela Valadez was the first to observe the stranger. She caught sight of him while sitting behind the steering wheel of her marked police car parked under the shady sycamore tree in front of Willie Stump's bait shop. Valadez had an unobstructed view of the only road into Gator's Pond. It allowed the twenty-five-year-old deputy the opportunity to see whoever came in and out of town. That was why Chief Cash Wiley had ordered his only female deputy to sit four hours of every shift under the same sycamore tree.

"I want to know the minute you lay eyes on anyone you haven't seen before. Do you understand what I'm sayin', Angie? Not after you go to the bathroom or check your hair. The exact minute you see 'em."

Deputy Valadez reached for the portable police radio on the seat next to her. She had every intention of informing Chief Wiley about the stranger's presence in town, but for some unknown reason changed her mind. She told herself that Cash Wiley could wait. Angela wanted to see more of this man walking down the middle of town with a green duffle bag across his right shoulder and purpose in his step. She could tell that he had walked a long way in the searing heat and beating down sun. His long-sleeved white shirt showed heavy staining under both arms, while his black slacks were spotted white from the gravel road's turned up dust. He had on dark sunglasses and his close-cut blond hair shone wet with sweat in the sunlight. But it was the tall build and squared shoulders and the easy way he moved that caused the Gator's Pond deputy to sit up straighter and lean forward. What would a man like this be doing in Gator's Pond, she thought? She could not help but feel that his presence meant trouble. Cash Wiley did not like strangers coming to town. No one in Gator's Pond did. Angela reached out for the police radio on the seat next to her.

****

Deek Stram was bent over the juke box in Gator's Pond Bar looking for any song by Charlie Rich. He happened to look up and, through the front glass window, observed a stranger walking down the middle of the town's only street. It took a while for Deek's eyes to adjust to the bright afternoon sunlight and for his fogged-over brain to stem off the effects of drinking ten bottles of beer. But soon enough the scraggily-haired, bony-thin man made out the tall figure carrying the green duffel bag. Deek let out a whoop and banged the top of the juke box with his right hand.

"Looky here what I see," he yelled without taking his eyes away from the glass window in front of him.

Oil Can Carter soon joined Deek at the window. He pressed his bulbous black nose against the window glass before grabbing Deek's right arm to keep from falling over. Oil Can too had been drinking beer all afternoon. Gator's Pond Bar was the only place in town with air-conditioning other than a few places where window air-conditioners blowing full blast might just barely put a dent in the outside smothering heat and humidity. That was why Deek and Oil Can tried to spend as much time as possible in Gator's Pond Bar.

"Who is he?" Oil Can asked with more than casual interest. Seldom did strangers come to Gator's Pond. And whenever they did Deek and Oil Can took notice. Both men were escapees from a Georgia chain gang where they had killed a prison guard in making good their escape. Bo Wiley kept them gainfully employed. There was no fear from the law with Bo's brother Cash being the chief of police.

"Think he's the law?" Oil Can asked turning to Deek who did most of thinking for the two of them.

"You get dumber every day. Think he's the law? What would the law be doin' walkin' down the middle of town in this heat, you idiot?"

"Don't call me an idiot, Deek. You know I don't like it," Oil Can said backing away from the window. The big-chested goliath reached for the black handle of the knife protruding from the sheath attached to his right side. Deek slapped the top of the huge man's hand.

"But you are an idiot if you think that's the law."

"Who are you talking about?" Maria Carrera questioned. The proprietor of the Gator's Pond Bar came out from behind the bar going to a different window. She looked out in time to observe the tall stranger walking past her. Maria had not seen many strangers in town since the tourists had gone back up north. And that was only the occasional few who would stop by the marina for fuel or Willie Stump's bait shop to buy bait. They would sometimes come to the Gator's Pond Bar for a drink and sandwich before taking their boats back into the swamp.

Maria watched the man as he walked in the direction of the police station. He had to be going there, she thought. There was nowhere else for him to go. Other than maybe the marina. And Maria did not see the man as a tourist. He most certainly did not look like one. And if it were the police station, what could he possibly want with the police? The proprietor of Gator's Pond Bar did not take her eyes from the stranger until she saw him walk through the police station door.

****

Twenty-eight-year-old Deputy Tank Thompson did not bother to look up from the newspaper sprawled out in front of him. Angie had told him over the police radio about the stranger headed for the police station. And Thompson was in no mood for small talk especially with some stranger. The old broken down air-conditioner in the front window was maintaining a steady ninety-degree temperature. That left the temperature inside the police station only ten degrees less than what it was outside. Tank Thompson's gray police uniform was soaked with sweat and sticking to him, while his forehead felt raw from his repeatedly wiping it. The large, big shouldered deputy had gulped down six cans of cola in less than two hours. And it had accomplished nothing. He was still thirsty and the cola machine was empty. So after hearing the police station door open and then close, Tank Thompson had every intention of making the stranger wait.

Tank knew that eventually he would have to talk to the man. Chief Cash Wiley had a policy of wanting to know about any stranger coming to Gator's Pond. And he already knew about this one. After Angie had radioed, Tank went and told Wiley about the new guy in town who was walking down the middle of Gator Pond's only street.

"Tell me who he is and what he wants as soon as you get rid of him," Cash Wiley had said while chewing on an unlit cigar stub. "And Tank, don't mess with him. I know what a rotten son-of-a-bitch you can be, and this ain't the time for it. Find out what he wants and send him on his way."

The piece of paper brushed Tank Thompson's nose before settling down onto the table in front of him. "If you're looking for something to read, read that," Book said.

Thompson glanced up. He observed the stranger removing his sunglasses. It was then that the deputy saw the squinting blue eyes along with the tightened jaw muscles. Thompson also caught the look one man shows another whenever he wants to get the message across that he will not be pushed any further. Tank Thompson picked up the piece of paper.

"Wait here," he said getting up. "I'll have to show this to the chief."

In less than three minutes Tank Thompson came out the chief's office door with Cash Wiley behind him holding the piece of paper Thompson had given him.

"Howdy, I'm Chief Cash Wiley. I take it you're here about the dead priest who was murdered. This here letter says you're his brother. If that's right let me see some ID."

Book removed a brown leather wallet from his back pants pocket. He opened the wallet before handing Chief Wiley a U.S. Army identification card.

"That piece of paper that I gave to your deputy is a letter of introduction from my commanding officer at Fort Benning, Georgia," Book said. "I'm Captain Frank Book, the brother of Father Andrew Book who was murdered in your town."

Chief Wiley stared at the identification card he was holding in his right hand. He glanced up to look at the face of the man who had given it to him. At the same time Wiley removed the cigar stub from his mouth tossing it on the floor.

"Yep, it looks official all right. And it says here, you're army rangers. I thought all you boys were fighting some place or another. How is it you got left behind?"

The police station door opened before Book could answer. A uniformed deputy entered. The ranger captain thought he was seeing things. He quickly turned to look back at Deputy Tank Thompson. He noticed the smile on the deputy's face. Chief Wiley's fat belly started to shake. His fleshy jowls puffed out. The chief let loose with a loud burst of laughter.

"That's Turk the other half of the Thompson twins," Chief Wiley said still laughing. "If you could see your face army ranger you'd be laughing too."

Frank Book's gaze went from the uniformed deputy who had just walked into the police station to Tank Thompson who was standing next to Chief Wiley. The two men were identical twins. They looked like a pair of farm boys who after years of tossing bales of hay had been given deputy uniforms and 9mm. handguns.

"I can't keep track of them myself," Wiley said. "Some citizen comes in here beefing on one of them and after he sees the two of them together can't decide which of them did him wrong. I have to throw the whole complaint out because there's no way it can be proven which one done it. These boys could get away with robbing banks as long as they didn't do it together."

"What's he doing here?" Turk Thompson asked going to the cola machine and finding it empty.

"He's here about that dead priest," Tank told him knowing how his brother could be when it came to dealing with strangers.

"Is he now? You got to wonder what would bring a man out in this kind of heat just because some faggot priest got himself killed by his faggot lover?"

"Hold on Turk," Wiley said holding up his hand. "This guy's a captain in the U.S. Army Rangers and the priest was his brother." Looking at Frank Book, Wiley added, "Nothing personal here Captain. Turk is the one who found the guy who killed your brother hanging in his cell back in the lockup. The boys here had to remove the belt from around the man's neck and it didn't set too well with them. You can understand that."

"Why did he have a belt in the first place?" Book asked not taking his eyes from Turk. "It should have been confiscated before he was placed in the cell."

"I guess that I just forgot," Turk said showing a smile on his face.

"Yeah, the boys do get lax at times," Chief Wiley relinquished. "You're right Captain Book the man's belt should have been taken from him, but it did happen to save the state of Florida a ton of money with him hanging himself. He had your brother's blood on his shirt and shoes and the boys here found the knife that he used to kill your brother under the mattress in that shit hole of a place he called a house over in Indian town."

"And he confessed too, chief. Don't forget that," Tank Thompson chimed in while duplicating the smile on his brother Turk's face.

"That's true enough the son of a bitch did just that. It was a first rate job of interrogation by you boys and I'm mighty proud of the two of youse. Captain Book you can thank these boys for bringing in the murderer of your brother."

"Why did he kill him?" Book asked while making eye contact with each of them. "I haven't heard yet why a man who had never been arrested before suddenly decided on killing someone."

"You know about Charlie Steed then?" the chief questioned.

"I know a lot about a lot of people," Book said while not attempting to hide the disdain in his voice. "I stopped in Miami and talked to Dr. Simon who conducted the autopsy on my brother. He said Andy's body was loaded with Strychnine and had been tortured terribly before being stabbed in the heart. Now why would a down and out drunk do something like that to a Catholic priest?"

"Because he was a faggot who got jealous after finding out that your brother was seeing other men behind his back. He told us so. He even signed a confession before going back into the lockup and hanging himself. Charlie knew all about what they do to faggots in prison."

Turk Thompson moved closer to Book. There was no mistaking the man's resentment and challenge. Book chose to ignore it.

"My brother was not a homosexual," Frank Book said matter of factly.

"The hell he wasn't," Turk retorted.

"Hold on here," Chief Wiley moved his rotund body between the two men. "Let's not rub salt in any open wounds. Turk, you'll never be nothin' more than a deputy on a small town police department until you learn how to deal with the public. I know you're good at bringing in the bad guys, but you sure as hell don't know how to talk to people. And Captain Book I understand your feelings sir. Nothing is more important in this world than family and the loss of your brother must have been devastating to you but we cannot change the facts of this case even though we would like to do nothing else. Isn't that right boys?"

The chief looked directly at Turk. He motioned with his head for the deputy to leave. Turk turned and walked out the police station door slamming the heavy door behind him. Tank Thompson saw the chief pointing a finger at him. And then at his office door indicating where he wanted Thompson to go. Tank immediately went where directed. He slammed the Chief's office door behind him. It left Chief Wiley and Captain Frank Book standing facing one another. A smile appeared on Wiley's portly face.

"It's lucky we have any doors left in this place," the chief chuckled. "Now, this is better with just the two of us discussing your brother's case. You have been given the facts Captain Book and though you might not care for them they are not going to change. What more do you want from me?"

"I would like to spend the next couple of days talking to people who knew Andy and get things straight in my mind. There was another priest who worked with my brother. I would like to talk to him and anyone else who could help me make sense out of what happened."

"That would be Father Miguel," Chief Wiley said. "He is the other priest at the church. The best time to get him is in the morning after that he's usually out and about visiting folk. And as far as talking to people who knew your brother I could have one of my deputies show you around."

Chief Wiley caught the change in Book's facial expression.

"No Captain," Wiley said laughing. "It won't be Turk or Tank. Deputy Valadez will be just right for the job. We call her Angie and she's a sweetheart. I would imagine that you will be staying at the Gator's Pond Inn because it's the only place in town. You must have passed it on your way in."

Book remembered seeing the motel after first coming into Gator's Pond. He had thought the place was abandoned. It had a dozen or so attached single units in terrible condition. The doors on a couple of the units were missing and their roofs caved in.

"I know the place," he replied.

"Good. I'll instruct Deputy Valadez to come by for you in the morning around seven o'clock. Before then you can get breakfast at the Gator's Pond Bar. It ain't nothin' fancy, but it'll have to do because there are no other restaurants in town. And Captain, do me a favor, will ya? Tell Cornelius at the Gator's Pond Inn to get over here and clean this place. It's starting to look like a pig sty."

Book nodded before picking up his green duffel bag and walking out the door.

****

Book walked in on a grizzled, unkempt, black man in his early sixties who was seated behind a counter in what passed for the Gator's Pond Inn office. Travel brochures were strewn about the countertop. They advertised ocean cruises to the Hawaiian Islands along with excursions to the vineyards of France. In addition there were picturesque boat rides along the canals of Venice. There was also a bottle of Jim Beam on the countertop. The bottle had a half-filled glass next to it. The man's right hand held the glass and he appeared intent on raising it. Apparently Book's coming into the office had precipitated a change of mind.

"Yes, sir," the man said shoving the travel brochures to one side and putting the bottle and half-filled glass underneath the counter. "Welcome to the Gator's Pond Inn."

"Are you Cornelius?" Book asked while looking into two wet black eyes. The oval-shaped eyes were locked inside a creviced face that lent the appearance of dried out leather. Book thought the face to be consistent with something that had been sunbaked or windblown for too many years.

"Cornelius Jackson at your service, sir. If you're looking for accommodations it's fifty dollars a night and with it you get ham and eggs and a side order of hash browns at the Gator's Pond Bar in the morning."

"I'll take a room for at least two nights," Book said before throwing down a hundred dollar bill. "And before I forget, Chief Wiley said for you to come by the police station and clean the place."

Cornelius Jackson smiled. The army ranger watched the lined, leathery face spread out into an easy grin. The two wet black eyes looked back at Book. They showed an amused glint.

"The chief must have a pile of those chewed up cigar butts of his all over that police station floor if he wants old Cornelius to come by. That's what I do when I'm not running this fallin' down shithole. I clean up the white man's police station so he has a nice clean floor to throw his cigar butts down on. But I ain't complainin' none. It keeps this nigger in Jim Beam and cornbread and chitterlings and that's all he cares about. Mister you can write your name and address on this here registration form. Then I'll get you your key."

****

Book figured he had paid fifty dollars too much for the room. Cornelius Jackson had been correct in describing the Gator's Pond Inn as nothing more than a shithole. Book's unit had four cracked walls, a sagging mattress in what might pass as a queen-size bed, and a small wooden desk that had a metal backed chair pushed up against it. An undersized, narrow bathroom exhibited a leaky toilet while both shower and sink were covered in some kind of dark green mold. And to add salt to the wound, the unit conspicuously lacked both television and radio.

A pungent smell filled the room. Book tried but could not identify it. It caused the army ranger to think of bivouacking in a Georgia swamp during a heavy rain while lying on the wet ground soaked to the skin. He turned the knob to high on the window air-conditioner before letting his duffel bag drop onto the bed. Reaching into the bag, he removed the Beretta and one of the ammo clips. Book slid the metal magazine into the gun, jacking a round into its chamber before placing the Beretta on the floor under the bed.

He had not slept in nearly thirty-six hours. It was starting to show on him. The thought of closing his eyes edged everything else out. Book told himself that he would need sleep if he was to deal with whatever Bo Wiley and his brother, Cash, had in mind for him. But he would have to first secure the motel door. The army ranger captain came off the bed. Taking the metal back chair, he lodged it between the doorknob and floor. Book made sure that the chair was firmly braced before settling back onto the bed. It was then that a fully clothed Frank Book closed his eyes and fell asleep.

CHAPTER SIX
Nuevo Laredo, Tamaulipas, Mexico
(Across the border from Laredo, Texas)

GABRIELLA LOPEZ SIPPED the glass of Tequila before placing the nearly empty glass back down onto the table. The sun was beginning to set. That meant the late afternoon crowd which frequented the Café Monte would soon be gone. The well-dressed, working men and women who had stopped off after work for a couple of drinks with co-workers were already starting to leave. Gabriella sat alone at a center floor table. She was watching a short, heavy-set man sporting a white sombrero and black three-piece-suit with silver buttons streaming up and down both sides of his pants play his guitar. The older man had been singing popular ranchero love songs in a low, captivating voice. Gabriella listened intently, waiting to hear the words, *Eres la chica que me encanta.* You are the girl I love. Then she would know that they were coming for her. That her 'would-be' abductors had taken the bait. It was the signal Shadow had devised to give her warning. It would signify that the abductors had left *La Zona*—Boy's Town and were only minutes from the café.

Gabriella had committed herself to the plan in the hope that it would save the life of her sixteen-year-old sister Aleena. The girl had been abducted from the same café just two weeks prior. She had come to it with her boyfriend directly from a rock concert on the outskirts of Nuevo Laredo. Shadow's face surfaced in Gabriella's mind. It was a strong, handsome face that gave the young woman comfort. Especially while she waited for the guitar player's warning.

Gabriella had met Shadow after Aleena's abduction. The meeting had taken place in a dark corner of a restaurant in Laredo, Texas. Gabriella had contacted an acquaintance in the U. S. Drug Enforcement Agency who arranged the meeting.

"I can give you nothing more than my code name. You will only know me as Shadow."

Gabriella nodded her head while staring into the dark, brown eyes looking across the table at her. She had talked to two DEA agents prior to meeting him. He was different than the other two. This man calling himself Shadow seemed to be probing her inner mind, intently checking out the person inside, analyzing, appraising. Was she good enough? Could she handle what was sure to come her way? Gabriella had been a Laredo, Texas, police officer for three years. She had dealt with men in law enforcement on a daily basis. But she had never come in contact with anyone quite like this man. Shadow had a confidence and strength about him that Gabriella could not recall seeing in other men. There was also the threat of danger evident in the light brown, clean-shaven face. Twenty-six-year-old Gabriella fastened her brown eyes onto the man seated across from her. While she leaned forward to better hear the sound of his voice.

"They told you everything and you agreed. The microchip will be embedded in your upper right arm giving off a continuous signal which I will monitor from a good distance away. That means you'll be on your own dealing with scum who will probably rape you. No one in DEA told you that, but I will. The abductors will be looking at you as nothing more than a piece of meat that they're taking to market in order to sell. And along the way you will be something they can have a good time with. There's not a female agent working in DEA who would take this assignment. That's why it has never been tried before. Gabriella, don't do it. Tell me you changed your mind, and you're going back to being a Laredo police officer. You can't help your sister. Nobody can."

"I'm doing it," Gabriella said feeling the hot surge of anger rising up inside her. "My sister is sixteen years old and only a kid when it comes to dealing with men. I can only imagine what she has been through and what it has done to her. Don't try changing my mind again. I'm going through with it no matter what happens."

"Very well," Shadow said shifting his weight in the chair. "I had to try or feel guilty for not trying. But it's your decision. Your sister had a fight with her boyfriend while at the Café Monte. He left her alone and she was abducted shortly after that. When he came back she was no longer there. We'll set up the same scenario. It worked once and hopefully it will work again. You and I will put on a public show at the Café Monte of two lovers having a spat. I'll walk away leaving you alone and vulnerable for the abductors to come and grab you."

"Who are they?" Gabriella asked feeling anxious at the thought of being alone and abducted by strange men. "I mean you call them abductors but what cartel? Don't the Los Zetas control Nuevo Laredo?"

"Yes, but not La Zona. A new cartel has taken over the red light district. They call themselves Las Arañas Negras, *The Black Spiders*. Their leader is known as the Black Spider, and he has made a pact with Los Zetas for control of all prostitution and narcotics trade inside La Zona. He and his cartel are behind the abductions of young women. They kidnap unsuspecting girls, the younger the better, and bring them to a place in the U.S. where they are then sold to buyers in the Middle East and Europe. It's worth millions of dollars to Las Arañas Negras. Hopefully if all goes as planned the signal from the microchip in your arm will reveal where the girls are located and help us to determine how the cartel plans to take them out of the U.S."

"They probably transport the women by van or truck, most likely truck, across the border and then God only knows where," Gabriella said, thinking, calling upon her experience as a police officer in a border town. "There are eighteen points of entry into the U.S. from Nuevo Laredo, and they can use any one of them."

"International Bridge Four, the World Trade Bridge, would be a good bet. It's the busiest. They have Interstate 35, which connects directly to Dallas, Texas and from there anywhere in the United States comes into play. But don't worry about where they will be taking you. That's my department. You just take care of yourself. I'll be driving alone in a newer car a mile or so behind you and the other women. They most likely will have spotters along the way watching out for anyone following, but they won't be looking for a lone driver especially someone that far behind."

"What kind of backup will there be?" Gabriella asked finding herself locked in on the man's eyes across the table from her.

"There will be two DEA swat teams following exactly five miles behind me in separate vans and in contact at all times. But remember, we will not be moving in on anyone until we are certain that we have the U.S. headquarters for the cartel and all of its main players. Gabriella that means you will be entirely on your own without any help from me or the other agents should something take place. The only advantage that you will have is that you're valuable to them. If you end up dead, they get nothing for you."

"How reassuring," Gabriella said placing an open right hand under her chin. "Shadow, you have a way of making a girl feel so good about herself."

Gabriella saw him smile for the first time. It was a nice smile. One she thought that she could easily get used to seeing.

"Remember, I did tell you not to go through with it."

"I know you did, but I have to," she said removing the hand from her chin. "But why can't you end it once we cross the border? You'll have the abducted women and whoever the escorts are. You can have the escorts tell you where they were the taking the women."

"The escorts will only be mules. The minute we do that the cartel will be made aware of it, and they'll move their U.S. headquarters. They can then start again, abducting more girls like your sister, but next time they'll know we're onto them and it will be that much harder to get someone on the inside."

"When do we start?" she asked while feeling the reality of what she had committed to resonating within.

"Tomorrow night. We'll have the microchip implanted by then. Are you alright with that?"

"The sooner the better," Gabriella answered. "Aleena needs me, I can feel it."

****

The Café Monte was nearly empty save for the singing charro and the older couple who occupied a table in the far corner. Gabriella held her empty tequila glass inside two sweaty palms. She could feel the wet on the glass, its slippery feel. The wait was agonizing for her. What if the abductors did not take the bait? Would she and Shadow try again the following night? And Shadow. Where was he? Was he somewhere close by? She and Shadow had acted out their lover's spat for everyone in the Café Monte to witness. Gabriella had done what Shadow had instructed her to do, slapping him hard across the face. Was he watching her now?

Gabriella told herself that she was ready. She would deal with *The Black Spiders*, the Arañas Negras Cartel when they came to take her. The embedded microchip in her upper right arm now proved to be a source of comfort, reassuring in its presence. Its implantation would enable Shadow to know her whereabouts at any time. With the microchip transmitter inside her arm, she would never be alone. Someone would always be there. Shadow would be there.

Gabriella stared at the man with the guitar waiting for his words of warning. She dared not look anywhere else. Part of her wanted to get up from the table and run—to forget everything. To tell Shadow that he was right and she no longer wanted to go through with it. Then she heard them. They were the words she had dreamt being said to her by a good man. But now they only brought anguish. The guitar player's voice rose and fell. It was so pleasant, so caressing, so sweet. "*Eres la chica que me encanta.* You are the girl I love."

CHAPTER SEVEN
Washington D.C.

FEDERAL DRUG ENFORCEMENT Administration Head of Special Operations Jim Garrison leaned back against his black Lincoln Continental. Garrison wished that he did not have to be spending a Sunday afternoon on the seventh floor of an East End business parking garage. But the fifty-eight-year-old, career drug enforcement special agent in charge did not have any other choice. There was a leak somewhere. And he did not want to hear about a DEA agent getting killed because the necessary precautions had not been taken. He had already lost one agent in Operation Silverback. Garrison did not want to lose another.

The tires of the black Mercedes squealed while making the turn off the up ramp onto the seventh tier of the parking garage. Garrison could not see through the Mercedes' tinted windshield but he knew who was inside. U.S. Attorney Chief Investigator Casey Blurmeister would be driving. And the U.S. Attorney for the Southern District of Florida, Vince DeWitt, would be seated next to him on the passenger side. They were coming to meet Garrison for a briefing on Operation Silverback. Garrison had tried but could not stall them any longer. However, he had been adamant on the time and place of the meeting. And he alone had decided on who would be present for it.

The U.S. Attorney General's Office, collectively, was like a pampered, over indulged adolescent. It had to have its own way with every case coming down the pipeline. Well, not this one, Garrison told himself before spotting the two smiling faces getting out of the Mercedes.

"Jim, you're getting paranoid in your old age. Meeting in a closed down parking garage on a Sunday afternoon is too much cloak and dagger even for you," DeWitt said slamming shut the Mercedes passenger door before walking over to Garrison. Blurmeister followed a step or two behind his boss. He wore the same smug grin. Both men had on light short-sleeve shirts and casual, dress slacks. DeWitt took off his sunglasses. Blurmeister left his on.

"We'll let time decide that for us," Garrison responded while reaching out to take DeWitt's offered hand. He then shook hands with Blurmeister. The DEA supervisor reached into the driver side of the Lincoln Continental to retrieve two plain manila folders. He handed each man a folder. "You are holding in your hands Operation Silverback. You are also holding the identity and life of our agent on the ground at Gator's Pond. I don't want this file downloaded into any computer, filed away in some file cabinet, or shared with anyone else in the Justice Department. It must be kept in a safe place for your eyes only. Those are my conditions. If you don't want to accept them give me back the folder."

"Take it easy, Jimbo," DeWitt said forcing a smile. "You're throwing orders around like some traffic cop out there on K Street in the middle of traffic. This is the U.S. Attorney General's Office you're talking to. You must have forgotten that while waiting for us in this out of the way parking lot. We give the orders."

"No, not this time DeWitt," Garrison shot back while snatching the manila folder from each of their hands. "Subpoena the file if you want it and I'll fight you every inch of the way. This time things have to be done differently. There's a leak either in your office or mine.

We have an agent on the ground at Gator's Pond who I don't want murdered like Agent Peterson. Bo Wiley will not be given the opportunity to kill another one of my people and hide his body in the Everglades to never be seen or heard from again."

The smile disappeared from DeWitt's face. The U.S. Attorney had not expected Garrison's response. And for DeWitt to push the issue at this time, he knew could end up getting messy. A person did not become head of the DEA's Special Operations Unit without knowing somebody. It was the premier unit in the U. S. Drug Enforcement Administration and rapidly becoming known around the country as the Navy Seals of the DEA. No, DeWitt knew that he would have to bow out graciously regardless of how much he disliked doing it.

"Okay Jim, you win. Give us back the Silverback file, and we'll play it your way. We want Bo Wiley as bad as you do so don't go forgetting we're on the same side."

Garrison returned the manila folder containing Operation Silverback to each of them.

"Friend's again," DeWitt said, smiling. "It's too bad these little disagreements have to happen from time to time. But Jim, you have my word on it. You can trust Casey and me with the file. And I can assure you that your agent's identity will be safe with us. Isn't that right, Casey?"

"That's right, sir," Blurmeister answered while not taking his eyes off Garrison.

"Alright then," Garrison said while turning to get into the driver's side of the Lincoln Continental. Suddenly as if remembering something, Garrison stopped. The DEA special agent in charge came back around to face DeWitt and Blurmeister. There was a hard look on Garrison's face that was not there before. Both men from the Justice Department recognized it.

"If for some reason my agent in Gator's Pond is placed in jeopardy because of either of you," Garrison said calmly. "There is nowhere in this world you will be able to hide from me."

CHAPTER EIGHT

BO WILEY COULD not remember being in such a miserable mood. Wearing a blue silk bathrobe, the overweight Wiley reposed painfully on the brown, leather couch. He kept his bare right foot resting on an accompanying hassock. A soft feather pillow taken off one of the many beds in the seven bedroom mansion served to keep the foot elevated. It supported an inflamed, double-sized big toe showing a deep, reddish color. The toe's unusual color contrasted strongly against the white pillowcase. Looking at it as though he were spying an enemy, Wiley grimaced, shutting his mouth to close off the groan about to emerge. Gout-ridden, the pulsating appendage burned like the dickens, compelling the sprawled out plantation owner to fight back the wave of tears forming in his eyes.

"Don't any of you walk anywhere near it. Even the air moving around it hurts like a son-of-a-bitch. Yellow Flower get me another whiskey and water and put more damn whiskey in it this time. You heathen bitch, can't you do anything right?"

The slender, twenty-three-year-old hurried to the liquor cabinet to retrieve another drink for the man who owned her. Long shoulder-length, black hair framed out a pretty, delicate featured face, while a smooth, dark complexion betrayed the young woman's Seminole Indian heritage. She had been christened Sharon Cornfield.

Bo Wiley changed her name to Yellow Flower after having bought the girl ten years earlier from her uncle. Yellow Flower filled the capacity of concubine, servant, and punching bag. It depended upon Bo Wiley's inclination at the time.

"Relax, Bo. You've gone through these bouts before and they don't last more than a day or two."

"Cash, don't tell me to relax with this damn toe of mine and everything else going on. I can hardly wait until these upcoming days are done with. July fourth can't come any too soon for me. And Maria, where's that damn Bernardo anyway? We always end up waiting for that greaser to show whenever there's a meeting."

Maria Carrera showed an amused smile. She took a sip of wine from the glass that she was holding in her right hand. The Mexican woman's brown eyes held a humorous glint. They were affixed on the sagging-jowl, gray-haired man with the protruding stomach resting on the couch in front of her. Carrera thought of a beached whale unable to move. Maria despised Bo Wiley and hated his brother Cash nearly as much. But for the time being they were necessary to Bernardo's plan. Soon the last shipment would arrive. It would then no longer be necessary for her and Bernardo to deal with the Wileys or have to worry about some U.S. federal agent discovering what they were doing in Gator's Pond. She and Bernardo would go back to Mexico where the two of them could live like royalty. They would be king and queen of their own fiefdom.

"You don't have *bolas bastante grandes*—big enough balls to say it to his face," she said mockingly. "Your kind never does."

Bo Wiley rose up in the couch only to fall back again. A look of pain ratcheted his round, fleshy face.

"You bitch. Once this damn gout clears up I'll show you who has balls," Wiley spat out. "Damn it all to hell, who would ever think one son-of-a-bitchin' toe could hurt this bad. Yellow Flower where's my whiskey and water?"

The young woman scurried to him holding between her two hands the large glass of whiskey and water. She had over-filled the glass. Some of the contents spilled while handing it to Wiley. After taking the drink from her, Wiley backhanded Yellow Flower, striking the left side of the young woman's face. The force of the blow sent her spinning backward. She ended up on the living room floor.

"You'd have gotten worse if it wasn't for this damn toe," he said to her before downing a third of the glass in one gulp. "Where is Bernardo? My brother and me don't have all night to sit around waiting for some greaser who can't tell time?"

"Good evening, Bo," Bernardo Arellano said coming out of the kitchen. "I used the back door. I hope you don't mind."

"It was double locked. How did you get in?" A surprised Bo Wiley exclaimed. He turned to see the dark-haired Bernardo standing just inside the living room. The newly arrived visitor's brown face portrayed a grin, while his two dark eyes contained a wary look. Wiley felt uneasy whenever confronting Bernardo. It was like watching a coiled snake waiting to strike.

"I'm good with locks," Bernardo answered before moving into the room. He took a seat next to Maria who held out her left hand to him.

"We were waiting for you," Bo told Bernardo before finishing off the whiskey and water. He looked to Yellow Flower who had taken a seat on the couch next to him. The young woman dutifully took his empty glass and went to the liquor cabinet to refill it. "Do you want something to drink while she's getting me one?"

Bernardo shook his head. "No, Bo, I don't want anything to drink. I want to know what you and your fat brother are going to do about the stranger who came to Gator's Pond today."

"Who are you calling fat?" Cash Wiley said coming to his feet.

"Shut up Cash and sit down," Bo told his brother, not taking his eyes off Bernardo. Sixty-three-year-old Bo Wiley was overweight, starting to succumb to physical ailments, and most definitely not the same Bo Wiley who at one time wrestled full-grown alligators for sport. But he was the same Bo Wiley when it came to craftiness, self-predicating, and the take-care-of-your-own-ass philosophy that had served to keep him out of prison when so many law enforcement agencies wanted to put him there. Bo recognized danger whenever it got too close. And he recognized it now in Bernardo's dark eyes.

"What do you want us to do?" Bo asked.

"Kill him like you did that federal agent that showed up here. And like the man you hanged in the police lockup. Do whatever you have to do just make him disappear. We have one more shipment coming in from Mexico. Once it gets here we fly that shipment out. And after the plane returns, our deal is done. You will be free and clear of the Arañas Negras and of me, as well. Our cartel gave you the money to pay off your back taxes, while you promised us safety and protection here in Gator's Pond. Fulfill your end of the agreement. Kill the stranger. We can't take any chances with the July fourth date so close."

"He came here because you killed his brother. And we took care of you with that bum we framed for the priest's murder. So don't go talkin' about fulfilling agreements. We've more than lived up to our end. We've covered for you while you've been masquerading as that Father Miguel over at the church, and we've kept people's mouths shut after they started complaining about you not being a priest. If we kill a U.S. Army captain, the feds will be down on us like flies on shit. You'll be gone, and we'll be stuck with it."

"The priest got everything off my computer. I had to try and get it back from him. But he was too stubborn and wouldn't tell me what he did with the thumb drive."

"He never talked. You tortured the shit out of him and got nothing for it. If he got that flash drive out of Gator's Pond, you can forget about your plans for the fourth of July."

"He didn't get it out. The thumb drive is still here. The priest hid it somewhere, but we can't take the chance that his brother might find it. Wiley, you kill him or I will."

Bernardo came to his feet. Maria did the same. The leader of the Arañas Negras cartel looked down at Bo Wiley who was seated on the couch with his bare foot resting on the hassock. There was no hiding the hate in Bernardo's black eyes. Reaching and grasping with a right hand, the Mexican squeezed Wiley's big toe before walking out the front door.

CHAPTER NINE

FRANK BOOK AWAKENED to a room engulfed in total blackness. He reached for the small lamp next to the bed, turning on the light. It was still dark outside and raining hard. The sound of the rain striking the tin roof overhead sounded like so many pebbles bouncing off a garbage can lid. The bouncing sound followed him as he ambled from the bed to the bathroom. Turning on the sink faucet, Book threw handfuls of cold water onto his groggy face. The wristwatch on his left wrist read five o'clock in the morning. He had slept for more than ten hours straight. Stripping down, the army ranger captain stepped into the shower ignoring the green slippery mold on the tiled floor along with the dank feel. A deluge of cold water soon took away any lingering grogginess.

Book dried himself using one of the two ragged towels Cornelius had given him at check in. Then he quickly dressed throwing on a pair of faded blue jeans over white boxer shorts before slipping into a loose-fitting, beige-colored, short sleeve shirt. Digging deep into the duffel bag, the army ranger captain came out with two rolled-up white socks and a pair of gray-colored Nike shoes. He sat down on the edge of the bed and put them on. That is when he thought of Bob Collins. The assistant attorney general had requested that Book telephone him once contact had been made with anyone from the

Gator's Pond Police Department. Book knew that he should have phoned Collins immediately after checking into his motel room. But at the time he had been too tired to even think about it.

Nobody would be in at the assistant attorney general's office at this hour to take his phone call. And it was too early for him to try Collins' cellphone. But he might not get the chance to phone later. Book decided on telephoning the assistant attorney general's office and leaving a message. He would give Collins a brief rundown of what had taken place so far. And then tell him that he would try phoning again later in the day. Opening up his cellphone, Book found that it was showing 'no signal.' Strange, he thought. Why should the cellphone be showing 'no signal?' The army ranger captain decided that he would try again later.

The rain striking the tin roof overhead had slowed to nothing more than an occasional tap. The slowdown aided Book in his decision to take an early morning walk around town. He would do it before his scheduled seven o'clock meeting with the Gator's Pond Police female deputy. There was also the already paid for breakfast awaiting him at the Gator's Pond Bar. It might be too early for breakfast but not for a morning walk.

Before leaving the motel room there was the matter of his Beretta along with the gun's extra ammo clips. He could not take a chance on being searched. If the gun should be discovered, Chief Wiley and his two deputies would confiscate it for sure. He was also cognizant of the possibility that his motel room might be checked as well. And with the likes of Turk and Tank Thompson nosing around, it probably would be given the once over. There had to be some place in the motel room where he could hide the Beretta and the extra ammo clips. But where, he thought. They would definitely empty out his duffel bag. And the bed would be tossed for sure. The desk was another place that undoubtedly would be searched. Book walked over to the bathroom. He poked his head inside. There was one possibility. He felt that it was worth a try.

Book quickly emptied the clear plastic bag containing his toiletries onto the small countertop in the bathroom. Taking the empty bag into the bedroom, he located the Beretta along with the extra ammo clips under the bed. Book placed the gun and ammo clips into the plastic bag before reaching into his duffel bag. Grasping one end of an army issue shoelace, he tied the shoelace tightly around the clear plastic bag effectively sealing it. The army ranger captain found himself left with approximately six inches of extra shoelace. More than enough for what he had in mind.

After a couple of turns the shower's metal drain cover came up easily. Book tied the loose end of the shoelace onto the metal drain cover before lowering the plastic bag with the Beretta and ammo clips down into the empty shaft. The shower's metal cover was then securely put back in place. Wanting an authentic look, Book lifted some green mold off the shower floor and set it over the metal drain cover.

Satisfied, he started to leave when another thought came to him. Book picked up the tube of toothpaste from the countertop. Pressing down on the tube, he squeezed a small dab of toothpaste onto his left index finger. After placing the toothpaste tube back on the countertop, Book walked out of the bathroom. The small desk in the far corner of the room immediately caught his attention. Book walked over to it where he placed the dab of toothpaste on the bottom desk drawer. The army ranger captain knew that the toothpaste would quickly dry and create a seal. And if the drawer should be opened, the seal would break. A broken seal would tell Book that his room had been searched.

The army ranger captain removed the metal back chair from against the motel room door and stepped outside. A wave of fresh air greeted him. It was most welcome, especially after all the hours he had spent inside the fusty motel room. Taking a deep breath, Frank Book sauntered off into the surrounding darkness of Gator's Pond.

CHAPTER TEN

CAESAR GOMEZ EASED up on the accelerator of the white panel truck before pressing down on the brake pedal and coasting to a stop. The large produce truck in front of him had already stopped as had the countless other trucks in front of that one. The line of trucks extended nearly a quarter of a mile to International Bridge #4, the commercial entry way into the United States from Mexico. It was eleven o'clock in the morning and the busiest time of day on International Bridge #4. That was why Gomez had chosen this time. U.S. customs agents would be overwhelmed with inspections while thinking of their upcoming lunch break. It would leave them less concerned about what might lie secreted behind the false wall of an incoming truck. They might not even care to look past the cardboard boxes marked plastic plumbing supplies. Who knows, Gomez mused. The U.S. customs agents might not even inspect the truck at all.

"Tell them it will be at least two hours before we reach U.S. Customs. The car on Bridge #3 should be disabled and the bomb ready to be activated precisely at the moment we are pulling up for inspection."

Gomez's passenger, Jose Herrera, nodded before calling on his cellphone to those members of the Arañas Negras cartel who had been assigned the task of creating a diversion on International Bridge

#3. Once the car explosion proceeded as planned, a portion of U.S. customs agents assigned to Bridge #4 would rush over to Bridge #3 leaving the truck inspections on Bridge #4 cursory at best. It was normal operating procedure for U.S. Customs. The Arañas Negras cartel routinely took advantage of it. If not a car bomb detonated, then a disturbance of some kind would be staged. In their many crossings, Gomez and Herrera had never been caught transporting illicit cargo into the United States. This trip would be no different.

There were fifteen young women squeezed together like sardines in a tin behind the white panel truck's false wall. All were pretty. And on the black market worth more than their weight in gold. They would be sold for many Euros to a brothel in Rome or Paris. Or sent to a city in the Middle East like Istanbul or Cairo where the young women would eventually waste away from the devastating effects of syphilis or gonorrhea. The lucky ones would be beaten or stabbed to death.

Caesar Gomez thought nothing of what might lie ahead for any of his human cargo. He instead smiled thinking of the young, pretty faces he had inspected prior to his loading the drugged women into the false front of the panel truck. Some were only girls barely in their teens. But all were beautiful. It would be difficult to choose which one to take first. But then it did not really matter because he and Jose had more than enough time to sample each of them. Caesar knew that it would take at least three days to reach their U.S. destination. That meant three nights of parking his truck in some hidden, remote area. And doing whatever he pleased to a drugged-out, naked, female body. Yes, he thought. They were all pretty faces while one was familiar to him. It was a face he had seen before but could not place. The squat, balding, forty-year-old, truck driver from Laredo, Texas, knew eventually it would come to him. Eventually, he would remember where he had seen the young woman and under what circumstances. It always worked out that way. Ask anyone who knew him and they would readily tell you. Caesar Gomez never forgets a face.

****

Gabriella could barely breathe with the duct tape covering her mouth. Whatever air the hot, enclosed space afforded came in short pants through her nose. Gabriella's hands remained bound behind her back. Her ankles fastened together. She could not move. A feeling of helplessness invaded the young woman's psyche. She looked into the encompassing blackness while the steady drone of the other women's breathing chorused about her. Drowsiness, the desire to sleep fell heavy. Gabriella fought it. She attempted to counter the effects of the drug that she had been given by shaking her head, telling herself to concentrate on the rattle of the truck. Listen to the women around you gasping for air.

Two men had come to the Café Monte to abduct her. Gabriella heard the guitar player's words of warning. She did what Shadow had instructed her to do. She got up from the table and walked to the women's restroom located at the rear of the café. Gabriella remained inside the restroom exactly five minutes before leaving. The men were waiting outside for her. She felt their rough hands grabbing her. There was the smell of their foul breath. One of them injected her left arm with a hypodermic needle. Gabriella lashed out with both hands, using pointed fingernails. She targeted the men's brown, unshaven faces. Their moans and curses came to her. It caused Gabriella Lopez to fight all the more. The Laredo City police officer continued fighting until the injected drug rendered her unconscious.

She regained consciousness prior to being loaded into the panel truck. There were fourteen others. Two girls were barely in their teens. Gabriella's heart sank after not seeing her sister Aleena's face among them. Where was she? Could there be another truck? But

Gabriella saw only the one truck. And it was parked inside a large warehouse where stacks of wooden pallets were strewn about an expansive cement floor. A lined section of large overhead doors occupied one end of the warehouse. Gabriella could tell it was daytime by the sunlight passing through the overhead skylight. She observed three Mexican men, one holding an automatic rifle standing by the white panel truck. There was a Mexican woman with them. In her forties, dirty and haggard looking, the grim-faced woman was going around with a tray of hypodermic needles giving the dazed women lying on the concrete floor another injection. The women had been stripped of previous clothing. All wore gray loose-fitting pajamas. Shoes or footwear had been removed. They were barefoot lying face down on the floor. Their wrists cuffed together behind their backs. Plastic handcuffs secured the women's ankles.

Gabriella recognized the man's face. He was one of the three Mexicans standing by the truck. Turning her head to the side, she tried to avoid his look. It was last month on a back street in the city of Laredo, Texas, that Police Officer Gabriella Lopez observed the man driving his white panel truck the wrong way on a one-way street. She activated her mars light and pulled him over. He was polite and cooperative. He said nothing to her after she had handed him the traffic ticket. But would he remember her? She had cut her hair for a younger look. And she had let the dark brown natural color come back into it. Perhaps then he would not remember the soft, brown eyes and the friendly smile and the slim figure he had watched in his side mirror as she walked up to his truck. Gabriella could do nothing more than hope.

The Mexican woman stuck Gabriella in the arm with the hypodermic needle and a wave of unconsciousness soon took over. How long has it been? She now asked herself, fighting to keep the drowsiness from her mind. She could not remember being loaded into the panel truck. Had the man recognized her? Had he remembered the young woman who had written him the ticket? Did he recall the smiling face of the police officer handing it to him and saying, 'Have a nice day?' The truck was moving, hopefully heading north into the United States. It appeared as though the plan was proceeding on schedule as Shadow had said it would. Gabriella tried to find comfort in that fact. But would she ever find Aleena? And then the jolt of fear struck her. It felt like a ton weight. Admit it, she told herself. You are afraid. You are in this dark, confining space and afraid. His strong, manly face suddenly filled her mind. Shadow. Gabriella saw only the smooth skin, the high-cheekbone face. She tried to block everything else out around her. Stay with me, Shadow, Gabriella thought. I need you.

****

A lone car was parked high on the hillside overlooking International Bridge #4. The man behind the steering wheel sat upright looking down on the long line of trucks coming from the Mexico side of the Rio Grande into the United States. Repeatedly, he diverted his attention to gaze down at the monitor on the passenger seat next to him. A steady blinking light greeted him. She was coming, he thought. Inside one of those trucks Gabriella Lopez was coming.

Shadow continued to watch the commercial trucks on the bridge. No matter how hard he tried the nagging feeling would not leave him. He had placed Gabriella Lopez in harm's way. He had devised the plan knowing the danger it involved. The implanted female agent had little, if any, chance of surviving. He knew it beforehand but still allowed Gabriella Lopez to go through with it. Now something unforeseen had happened. His plan had gone wrong. The veteran DEA agent just knew it. Gabriella Lopez was in trouble. He could do nothing to help her. Shadow looked over at the monitor once again. It was still blinking. As long as it continues to blink, he told himself. I will be able to find her. But it must stay blinking. The long line of trucks on International Bridge #4 stretched all the way back to the Mexican side. Shadow wondered which of the trucks held Gabriella. And would the Laredo City police officer be able to survive the coming days.

CHAPTER ELEVEN

U.S. ATTORNEY FOR the Southern District of Florida Vince DeWitt sat behind his desk at his Washington D.C. office. The Operation Silverback file was opened up in front of him. It had proved interesting reading indeed for a U.S. prosecutor who harbored high political ambitions. And especially for one who possessed the right family connections to make it all happen. The Florida governorship was on DeWitt's radar. The thirty-nine-year-old, Princeton ivy leaguer felt it would be the right stepping stone on his way to the ultimate goal. DeWitt closed the file before looking across at his boyhood friend and Chief Investigator Casey Blurmeister.

"A Bo Wiley conviction would put me in the governor's chair. The publicity surrounding it would reach national proportions and put us right where we want to be. Casey, it's a godsend."

"Wiley is not even charged with anything and you have him already convicted," Blurmeister said smiling, knowing how carried away his friend could be at times, especially when it came to politics.

"But he will be. This file says so. We will have him killing a man to protect the murderer of a Catholic priest. Not to mention trafficking in Middle Eastern heroin, and the best of all, his involvement in the abduction of young women for the purpose of selling them into a lifetime of slavery. Just think of the female votes that will get us."

"You're forgetting the Catholic vote with the murdered priest."

"That, too. Hell, I should skip the governorship and go right for president. And then make you my CIA director. What do think of that? Or would you prefer the FBI?"

"I think we better wait for Jim Garrison and the DEA to give us Bo Wiley and his brother Cash," Casey Blurmeister said while looking at his own copy of Operation Silverback. "There are a lot of unknowns in this case. The DEA doesn't know how the women get to Florida or how they're taken out of the country once they're there. And how is the heroin brought in? Right now, they don't know. The priest's missing flash drive is another thing. What's on it and who is this guy passing himself off as a Catholic priest, this Father Miguel?"

"I agree with you there's a lot of work yet to be done but with a DEA agent on the ground and what we have so far I feel confident that it will only be a matter of time before Bo and his brother Cash are charged. All we have to do is sit and wait for the incriminating evidence to come to us. In the meantime, I want you to download Operation Silverback into the U.S. Attorney's computer."

"Vince, are you sure about that?" Blurmeister said coming out of his chair. "You gave your word to Garrison that it would not be put into the computer. He said there was a leak, and he's not the kind to say that unless he has good reason to believe there is one."

"I am not taking orders from Jim Garrison. We have to have official standing on this case and that's why I want it in the computer. Attach a priority access code to it, but I want it in today. And I want something more from you, but I don't want it to go any further than this room for the present."

"What is it?"

"This is the chance I've been waiting for, Casey. I want to get way ahead of Garrison on Operation Silverback and have it appear as though we are running the day-to-day and the DEA is only following our direction. I want you to put together a brief that I can hand over to the Senate Committee on Homeland Security detailing the entire operation. Let it show us spearheading Operation Silverback. That way after the case breaks, we'll get the lion's share of credit for bringing down Bo Wiley and his organization. We'll grab the major headlines and the DEA will have to settle on playing backseat to the U.S. Attorney's Office."

"Vince, you're crazy. Garrison and the DEA won't stand for it. They'll scream to the high heavens and want our heads, not to mention running to the Justice Department asking for a full inquiry."

"Let them. By then I'll be the governor of Florida and you'll be my right hand man. It'll all die down like those things always do. Nobody will care anymore and the whole thing will be forgotten."

"I don't know. We're dealing with Garrison."

"Let me worry about Garrison. You just concern yourself about the brief. Put it together at your apartment and nowhere else. I don't want anybody at the office catching wind of it and then running their mouths off and it getting back to Garrison. After you're finished with it give it to me and I'll take it from there."

"All right Vince, if you say so, but Jim Garrison isn't the type of guy to screw around with. I've worked cases with him and he can be a son-of-a-bitch if he thinks you screwed him. I'm just letting you know."

"Okay, you told me," Dewitt said also standing. "And I'm going to tell you that Jim Garrison and nobody else is going to tell me what to do. Don't worry about him. I'll take care of Garrison."

CHAPTER TWELVE

A LIGHT RAIN fell in the early morning darkness. On the eastern horizon the first signs of light appeared. Book walked along the only road in Gator's Pond. He could hear the crunch of his own footsteps on the wet gravel underfoot. The lights were on down at the marina so he headed in that direction. While walking he listened to the sound of the squawking mud hens at the water's edge. And the loud splash of what Book discerned to be an alligator hunting them. The stifling humidity permeated everything, including the air a man needed to breathe.

Book knew the ground that he was walking on formed the edge of the Everglades. And out beyond the darkness were extended miles of endless water donning sawgrass, cypress, juniper, along with thousands of other trees and plants, not to mention the insects, snakes, and animals that called the formidable swamp home. He, like all army rangers, had done his training in the Everglades. In order to complete his special tactical training Book had been lowered into a remote section with nothing more than a knife and rifleman radio. He was left to survive on his own for a week. The army ranger captain walked out of the Everglades at a predetermined location seven days later. And that was after he had been secreted into one of the most treacherous environments in the world.

The Gator's Pond Marina consisted of nothing more than a rundown, white, paint-peeling, wooden shack. It displayed a ragged gray-colored canopy stretching down to the water's edge. Book figured the canopy was used to block out the hot afternoon sun. A warped, plank pier extended into the water. A couple of johnboats were tied up to it. Sitting out of the water and resting on cut cypress logs were three airboats. There were two ten-footers and a large eighteen-passenger that had its large screened-encased propeller removed. The boats appeared to be under repair. Book noticed an older man wearing greasy, gray overalls come out of the shack. He was looking in Book's direction. Book waved to him. The man did not wave back.

"Good morning," Book said showing a smile. "Saw your light on and thought I'd come down to say hello."

"We don't get many strangers here mister. What can I do you for? There's no boats for rent if that's what you want. It's out of season for rentin' boats."

"No, I'm not looking to rent a boat. Just a little information."

"Well then, that depends on what kind of information."

Book smiled appreciating the unshaven face and squinting eyes and the lit, hand-rolled cigarette dangling from the man's tight-lipped mouth.

"It's about the priest who was murdered here in Gator's Pond a few weeks back. Did you know him? He was my kid brother, and I'm trying to find people who knew him."

"No, I'm afraid I didn't," the old man said seeming to relax while taking a long drag on his cigarette. He blew the smoke off to the side staring at it for a moment before coming back to Book. "I'm not the religious kind. So having anything to do with a priest wouldn't enter into for me, if you know what I'm sayin'. But I'm sorry for your loss, mister."

"Thanks," Book said while not taking his eyes off the man. "How about Bo Wiley, does he enter into for you?"

"Mister, you're ask'in for trouble. One look and I can tell you're either in or just out of the service. I did twenty in the navy before getting out. So take an old navy man's advice and leave Gator's Pond. Don't wait, walk out of town right now because there's nothing but trouble here for you."

"My name's Frank Book and I am a captain in the army rangers. I've been given leave by my CO to find out what happened to my brother and why he was murdered. I need your help."

"You have no idea what you're askin' me."

"Yes. I think I do. I am asking an old navy man to help out a fellow service man who has lost his only brother. It might be a lot to ask, but I'm askin'. And I think I'm askin' the right man."

The old man took another drag on the cigarette just prior to tossing it in the direction of the water. He gave Book a cockeyed, measuring look. It questioned the makeup of the man standing in front of him. Whether the finished product added up to its given parts. He spat out a wad of phlegm before speaking again.

"This here pond ain't that big as far as ponds go. Over yonder there's a line of sycamores, go past them and you're in the swamp. But inside this here pond an eight-foot alligator has staked it out for his very own. Now he ain't all that big as far as some gators go, but he's the biggest thing in this here pond. And he does pretty much what he pleases. He kills and eats whatever he wants to kill and eat. If he doesn't want something in his pond, he kills it. Now I've given that gator a name. I call him Bo. Captain Book, I hope that answers your question."

"I think it does ..."

"Gus. My name is Gus Meeker, but everybody calls me plain old Gus."

Book reached out to take Gus's hand. While the two men shook, Book caught movement off to his right. He turned his head to observe an Indian dressed in green fatigues getting into one of the johnboats.

The Indian and Book's eyes met for a brief second. That was all the time it took for Book to recognize the telltale sign. The look that only someone who has killed before recognizes in another. And along with it came the sign of the hunter. The man had the look of the hunter in his eyes. He hunts down his prey prior to killing it, Book thought. But it is men that he hunts. He hunts men and kills them.

"Who is he?" Book asked Gus Meeker nodding his head in the Indian's direction.

"That's Panther. He's a Seminole hunter and trapper. And sometimes he and his two cousins do work for Bo Wiley."

"What kind of work?"

Gus Meeker shook his head. "Captain Book you can never let well enough alone can you?"

"What kind of work, Gus?" Book persisted.

"Whenever any of those Mexican wetbacks Bo Wiley has working for him on his plantation decide to take off into the swamp, he sends Panther and his two cousins after them to bring 'em back."

"What if they don't want to come back?" Book asked.

"Then they don't," Meeker answered before walking away back toward the wooden shack.

****

Book observed the lights being turned on inside the Gator's Pond Bar. Closer inspection revealed a woman behind the bar moving around in a hurried fashion. She lent the appearance of someone who was getting the place ready for another day of business. Book tried the front door but found it to be locked. The woman inside must have heard the door because she came out from behind the bar. It did not take her but a few seconds to get the door opened. A smiling Book stepped past her. That is when he noticed the pretty face and flashing black eyes along with the strong scent of lilac. She was obviously Mexican with her dark brown hair, nearly black in color, and a light brown complexion that appeared smooth and creamy in the bar's not so bright light. The shoulder strap top she wore was red as were the tight shorts she had on. The shorts clung to her backside like skin on an apple.

"The man at the Gator's Pond Inn said that I could get breakfast here," Book said while watching her go back behind the bar.

"You will as soon as I cook it," she answered without looking at him.

Book walked over to the bar and sat down on one of the bar stools. He made sure that it gave him a good view of the woman behind the bar. She must have heated up the grill because the smell of burning grease filled the air. Soon there were three eggs sizzling in an inch or more of grease along with a slab of fatty ham. A pile of hash browns came next. She plopped them down alongside the eggs. Book watched as the woman spread gobs of yellow butter onto two pieces of white bread.

"Coffee should be ready in a minute. Do you want a cup?" she asked him without turning around.

"Yeah," Book said while looking over at the grill. "But you can hold the grease. I take my coffee black."

He caught the makings of a smile lighting up the right side of her face.

"We all have to die from something, Captain Book."

"So you know who I am?" he said looking at her, wondering.

Maria Carrera turned around with a plate of eggs, ham, and hash browns along with two pieces of buttered white bread. She set the plate down in front of Book. "Of course, I do," she said. "You're the only stranger in town. Everybody's talking about you."

"Are they now. And what are they saying?" Book asked while taking the handed fork and knife from Maria Carrera. He cut into the slab of ham.

"They're wondering how long it will be before Bo Wiley has you killed," she replied while looking him straight in the face.

"And why would he want to do that? I haven't done anything to him."

She watched him swallow a piece of greasy ham before scooping up a forkful of eggs. Maria Carrera knew men. She had dealt with them ever since a girl child on the backstreets of Mexico City where she quickly learned that they give pesos to pretty girls who sell their bodies. And she recognized that this man was different from most men. Maybe it was his mocking blue eyes and perpetual grin that made him different. She could not be sure. But there was something. The man invoked both fear and titillation in her. And Maria Carrera knew that to be a dangerous combination.

"You're a stranger poking his nose around where it is not wanted. Leave Gator's Pond, Captain Book. I'm telling you for your own good."

"Not until I get the cup of coffee you promised me," Book said wiping the plate clean with the last piece of white bread. "And not until I find out why a Catholic priest was murdered and some poor slob blamed for it."

She poured him a cup of coffee plopping the brown mug down in front of him, spilling some of the coffee. He took a drink and held the mug to his mouth longer than was necessary. Their eyes met staying fastened for a brief moment. Maria Carrera did not like the feeling inside her. Bernardo was her man. There would be no other. The front door opened. Both of them turned toward the door.

"Oil Can, look who beat us in for breakfast. It's that fellow whose faggot brother got himself all cut up."

Deek and Oil Can walked inside the bar. Oil Can slammed the front door shut. The two sat down at a table not far from where Book was seated. They were close enough for Book to smell the rancid body odor wafting off them.

"What kennel did those two spend the night in?" Book asked Maria Carrera.

"They work for Bo Wiley and you better be careful," she said looking first at Book and then at the two sitting at the table. Carrera grabbed the coffee pot and two empty mugs before walking over to Deek and Oil Can's table.

"So are you a faggot like your brother?" Deek spouted while a big smirk widened his narrow face. Oil Can let loose with a boisterous laugh. His huge body rocked back and forth in the wooden chair. "What are you lookin' at," Oil Can demanded. The big black man stopped laughing after noticing that Book was staring at him.

"I'm not quite sure," Book said keeping his eyes centered on Oil Can. "Orangutan came to mind at first, but seeing how ugly you really are I'm thinking more on the line of Congo Lowland Gorilla."

Oil Can came to his feet and started toward Book.

"Stop it. Deek tell him to sit down or there will be more trouble than you two can handle." Deputy Angela Valadez was inside the bar and walking over to Book.

"Valadez get out of my way or I'll knock you down," Oil Can said hovering over the female uniformed deputy. "Deek get her out of my way."

Deputy Valadez said in a raised voice, "Oil Can sit down or you'll have to deal with Cash. He's the one who sent me over here to take this man around town. It's not me that you're going to have to answer to. It's Cash Wiley."

"Oil Can do what she says," Deek told his friend. "We'll take care of the cracker, don't you worry."

Oil Can sat down in his chair. While his two bloodshot eyes filled with hate stayed fixated on Book. The army ranger captain stared back. An amused grin came to his face.

"Captain Book it's time for you to leave," Deputy Valadez said.

"I suppose you're right," Book responded before coming off the bar stool. "The air is getting pretty bad in here." Turning to Maria Carrera behind the bar, Book tossed down a five dollar bill. "Thanks for the lube job," he said smiling.

"Captain Book leave Gator's Pond while you still can," Maria Carrera said to him before picking up the five dollar bill and stuffing it into her back pants pocket.

CHAPTER THIRTEEN

A BRIGHT MORNING haze greeted Book outside the Gator's Pond Bar. The army ranger captain instinctively took a deep breath. The morning air felt heavy. It was like someone had dropped a wet mesh over everything. Deputy Valadez's marked squad car was parked in front. The young deputy was standing by the passenger side door waiting for him. Book took in the woman's gray sweat-stained uniform, shined, black shoes, and the Glock 9 mm. handgun strapped to her right side. The police uniform did not conceal the well-formed contours and curves of the female body underneath. Her straight, brown hair looked like it had been recently cut. It topped an athletic five-foot-five frame. But it was the woman's facial expression that captivated Book. It told him that she did not want to be there. For Book, the perturbed look only served to enhance the green color in Angela Valadez's eyes, making her even more attractive.

"You're lucky that you didn't get killed in there," she said to him while not attempting to hide her displeasure. Angela wanted no part of escorting Book around Gator's Pond. The tone in her voice reflected it. She opened the squad car door before motioning for him to get inside.

Book smiled walking toward her. "You arrived in the nick of time to save the day and now I have the pleasure of your company for the rest of it. I am indeed fortunate."

"Get in the car Captain Book."

"If we're going to be spending the day together let's make it Frank. Your chief of police said yours was Angie. I prefer Angela. Can we keep it on a first name basis?"

"Fine. Just get in the car before one of those fools decides on coming out to start things all over again."

"Good idea," Book said getting in the front seat. Angela shut his passenger side door before going around to the driver's side of the squad car. She slid in behind the steering wheel, starting up the car's engine. The Gator's Pond deputy turned to look at Book.

"Chief Wiley said you wanted to talk to people who knew your brother. That would mean just about everyone in Gator's Pond, which also means Indian Town. Your brother made a point of seeing everyone no matter if they were Catholic or not. Anyone in need of help knew they could get it from Father Andy because he was that kind of a priest. So I don't really know where to start."

"So you knew him then?"

"Yes. I knew him. He was my priest. I would go to his Mass and many times stop by the rectory just to talk. Captain Book, your brother was my friend."

"Angela, call me Frank, especially seeing that you were a friend of my brother. It's nice to know that there was at least one person who Andy could consider a friend in this town."

"He had lots of friends. Everyone loved Father Andy. The people in Indian Town absolutely loved him."

"Well someone in Gator's Pond didn't because he ended getting murdered. Now what can you tell me about his murder?"

"Nothing that you don't already know. I was there when they took his body away. It was terrible what happened to him. I still have a hard time dealing with it whenever I think about how he looked and what he must have gone through. I shouldn't be saying this to you, I know, but it's just that he was so good, and nobody, especially someone as good as him should have had to go through something like that. I'm sorry Captain ..."

"Angela, do you know the other priest, this Father Miguel?"

"Not very well. He keeps to himself and doesn't have much to do with anyone. He is the complete opposite of the kind of priest Father Andy was."

"Let's start with him then. Your Chief Wiley said early morning is the best time to get him at the rectory. I also want to check out Andy's room. We can take care of that right after we talk to this Father Miguel."

****

Angela spotted Father Miguel exiting the side door of St. Anne of God's rectory. She immediately pulled her squad car around to the church's side gravel parking lot. The deputy halted the squad in front of the man dressed in a black, short-sleeve shirt and black pants. With his path blocked and red roadster parked on the other side of the squad car, Bernardo posing as Father Miguel Santiago stopped. He had no other alternative but to stand and wait for his visitors to get out of the car. The man forced an open-mouth smile. His immaculate white teeth clashed with his dark brown face and black bushy mustache. Bernardo immediately recognized Book from Maria Carrera's description.

"Good morning," he said centering his attention on Book. "I was just leaving to do my rounds. There are so many people for me to see and not enough time in the day to do it."

"Father Miguel, this is Captain Frank Book, Father Andy's brother," Angela told him while walking alongside Book. She watched the two men shake hands. There was no missing the onslaught of rigidness in Book. Does he know, she thought? But how could he?

"Captain Book, it's so nice to meet you. Your brother was a ray of hope for the poor people living here. I was privileged to have worked with him and to have him as my friend. He will be deeply missed by everyone but more so by me than any of the others. Father Andy is irreplaceable. I am lost without him."

"I wanted to meet you," Book said while looking deep into the man's black eyes. "I read the police report and it indicated that you were the last person to have seen my brother alive."

"I am sure Captain Book that you mean prior to the person who actually killed him."

Ignoring the comment, Book continued. "Andy was feeling ill and went to his room to lie down. The police report stated that you did not see him again until the following morning when you found his bedroom door open and Andy dead, lying face up on the bed covered with blood."

"Yes, I don't think that I will ever forget …"

"And you didn't hear anything all night long?"

"No, my room is in on the first floor and I sleep …"

"My brother was tortured all night long in the same house you were in and you never heard him scream?"

"The police said the killer must have placed a gag or some kind of tape over your brother's mouth and that was why I did not hear anything. I am sorry …"

"The police didn't find any gag and tape leaves residue on the skin around a person's mouth. There wasn't any residue left around Andy's mouth. Are you trying to say that the man who tortured my brother to death took the gag with him?"

"I'm not trying to say anything, Captain Book."

The two men's eyes locked. There was no mistaking what each was thinking. *He murdered my brother.* Book knew it. It was in the man's eyes plain to see. The same man Andy had called an impostor priest. Book fought back the urge rising up in him to grab the man's exposed throat and choke the life out of him. But before doing anything he had to first know why Andy was killed? What was on the man's computer that Andy found so disturbing? And why was this impostor posing as a Catholic priest?

He knows I killed his brother. Bernardo recognized the awareness in Book's eyes. But how does he know and what is he doing here at this time? In the matter of only a few more days the highly developed plan will become a reality. Does the army captain know about it as well? Does he possess what the priest downloaded from my computer?

"I must be going," Bernardo said turning to walk away.

"Not before I see my brother's room," Book said grasping Bernardo by the right shoulder. The solidly built Bernardo broke Book's grasp with an upward thrust of a right arm. "The side door is open," he spat out while a grimacing face betrayed his feeling toward Book. Both Book and Angela watched Bernardo walk away in the direction of the parked red roadster.

"Take me to Andy's room," Book said turning to Angela. "And then I want to visit the church."

Book followed the woman deputy inside the rectory. They took the stairs to the second floor, stopping outside a closed door. Angela looked up at Book. He could not help but notice the forlorn look.

"I know how hard it is for me to go back into this room. It must be doubly hard for you. Frank, are you sure that you want to do this?"

Book nodded before turning the doorknob and opening the door.

CHAPTER FOURTEEN

BOOK STEPPED INTO the room. Angela was right behind him. The large reddish-black bloodstain on the bed's mattress caught Book's immediate attention. There were also bloodspots on the white wall closest to the bed. And more on the ceiling above it. The rest of the bedroom was in shambles. Dresser drawers had been pulled out. Contents dumped onto the beige carpeted floor. Someone had smashed the wooden drawers into multiple pieces. The same had been done to the desk in one corner of the room.

Broken sections of a mirror crunched underneath Book's shoes as he walked around the room checking it out. Two religious statues had been thrown against one wall. The ceramic parts rested on the floor. They were undistinguishable as to which saints the statues might have depicted. Book bent over and picked up a photograph that had been knocked loose from its frame. The photo was of him and Andy. It had been taken by their mother when the brothers were just kids. The photo must have been shot some time before the family had moved to Detroit's eastside, Book surmised. He remembered the time. The three of them had gone on a picnic out in the country. It was far outside the city of Detroit and there were trees leading down to a lake. As best as he could recall, it had been a happy time in his life. Book folded the photo before sliding it into his front pants pocket.

"Is this how it was when you were here last?" Book asked Angela while he stared at the blood-soaked mattress.

"Pretty much. Except Father Andy was still lying face up on the bed, and there was a white sheet on the mattress covered in blood. I think Chief Wiley had Turk take it off the bed and inventory it after Father Andy's body was taken out. And I almost forgot. Here this belongs to you."

Angela went into her pants pocket to remove a string of rosary beads. "That day I found these on the floor behind the bed. They were Father Andy's. I had planned on keeping them but then found out about you being family. I know that Father Andy would've wanted you to have them."

"Thanks," Book said taking the beads. He put them in his pants pocket along with the photo. "There's nothing more to see here. I want to stop by the church. Then we can go."

Book told Angela that he wanted some time alone and asked her to wait outside while he went into St. Anne of God's Church. Respecting his wishes, Angela stayed outside. It did not take Book long to check out the two Marian statues inside the church. He could not find anywhere in or around either statue that could have been used to hide Andy's flash drive. When he came out of the church, Book found Angela standing next to the squad car fanning herself with a metal clipboard. The hot morning sun was beating down and the Gator's Pond deputy's gray uniform shirt was dark with perspiration under both arms.

"You could have waited in the air-conditioned car," Book said while walking over to her.

"I usually spend a good part of my day sitting in this car. I needed the change of pace. Besides I don't want my backside to start spreading out too much."

"From what I've seen, it hasn't started spreading out at all."

"So you have been looking?"

"A couple of times, only when I knew you wouldn't notice."

"Thanks. I don't get too many looks in this town."

"Well, you are more than welcome," Book said smiling. "Now where are you going to take me next?" He opened the front passenger door and got into the squad car. He watched Angela do the same on the driver's side. "Indian Town," she told him. "It's where I was born and raised."

Angela started up the squad car and drove out of St. Anne of God's Church parking lot. Neither she nor Book saw the two men sitting in the light-colored, late-model sedan parked a good one-hundred yards down the street. Tank Thompson handed his brother Turk the field binoculars he had been using to observe Book and Angela.

"Okay, let's go. But stay back so they don't see us," Turk said as brother Tank directed the late-model sedan down the street.

CHAPTER FIFTEEN

IT WAS A narrow dirt road cut out of the Everglades to accommodate only one car. Book wondered what would happen should another vehicle appear coming from the opposite direction. A cloud of dust trailed the police squad car as Angela maneuvered past shoulder high sawgrass and lines of hammock trees. Glancing out his passenger side window, Book caught glimpses of the black water canal paralleling the road. He observed hundreds of multi-colored birds flocking to it. While occasionally he spotted on the embankment an alligator stretched out in the hot, baking sun. Book had found leaving Gator's Pond's gravel road for the present one to be much like crossing an imaginary line, stepping out of civilization and entering the hidden world of the Everglades.

"You were born and raised out here?" Book asked looking over at Angela who was staring intently ahead.

"Not far from here. But I've been through just about every foot of these swamps. Like city kids play in the park, I played out here growing up. My father was born in Mexico before becoming a U.S. citizen and my mother was half-white, half-Seminole Indian. I guess the Seminole part kind of took over for me."

Book's attention fell upon the clasp bracelet decorating Angela's left wrist. He noticed it before but had said nothing. The bracelet looked to be solid gold, uniquely fashioned. It did not appear to be something one would expect to find on display in some jewelry store. Angela could not help but see her passenger staring at it.

"It was my mother's. It is all I have left of her. She died when I was ten and my father gave me her bracelet. And then five years ago he died, but I don't have anything of his. I don't even have a photograph of him. This bracelet helps to keep both their memories alive for me."

"No other brothers and sisters or family?"

Angela shook her head. "No, just me. After my father died, I won a four-year-scholarship to the University of Miami, obtained my degree in history and then applied for this job. And here I am taking you to Indian Town which, by the way, is where we are right now."

Book looked up to observe the cluster of chickee huts with their open sides and frond roofs. Many of the huts had fires going inside. Smoke filtered out of them encompassing what appeared to be a small Indian village in the midst of the swamp. Wood-built houses occupied the far end of the town while a large expansive tent had been erected in the middle. "Grocery Store" was printed on the front of the tent.

"I don't think Wal-Mart has too much to worry about here," Book said, not quite believing what he was seeing.

Angela responded, "Bo Wiley has basic essentials shipped in and the people trade to get whatever they can. Wiley always makes out like a bandit because the people of Indian Town live by hunting and fishing and poaching. They trade alligator skins for groceries which ends up supplying Bo Wiley with a high return on his investment." Angela pulled the squad car between two chickee huts and turned off the engine.

It was not long before a dozen or more screaming kids no older than ten or eleven descended upon the police car. Book recognized shades of red, white, brown, and black in the smiling faces of the children. Indian Town apparently was an ethnic melting pot.

"I know they're not this happy to see me," Book smiled looking to Angela who was reaching behind into the back seat of the car. "Or me either," she commented while picking up a cardboard box. "Frank grab this will you, it's pretty heavy. It's what's inside that's causing all the excitement."

Book took the box while looking again to Angela. She could not help but laugh after seeing the perplexed look on his face. "Bring it out there, put it on the ground, and then get out of the way," she said while still laughing. Book did as instructed. He barely missed the onslaught of young hands descending upon the cardboard box.

"They don't get candy very often and when they do it's a real treat," Angela said looking down at the happy kids filling their pockets with Hershey bars, Almond Mounds, Snickers Bars and a variety of other candies. "Come on, I want you to meet someone."

Book followed Angela over to a nearby chickee hut. There an old Indian woman occupied a place next to a sunken fire pit. A small coal fire burned in its center while a metal pot hung suspended over it. Book enjoyed the pleasant aroma of whatever was cooking in the pot. He immediately caught the happy smile lighting up the old woman's face the moment her eyes fell upon Angela.

"This is *Hvresse Hokte*—Moon Woman," Angela said before bending to kiss the elderly woman on the forehead. "She practically raised me after my mother died. You asked me before about family and I should've mentioned her. She taught me more about life and what it means to be a woman. I love her deeply."

Angela said something in the Creek dialect. Book watched the old woman nodding her head up and down before stopping to look up at him. Two gray-colored eyes set inside a craggy, wrinkled face peered out. They seemed to measure and dissect the tall blond-haired white man who was accompanying the young woman she viewed as her granddaughter.

"*Miko*," she said to Angela. "*Holatte torwv Ivmhe.*" Then Moon Woman pointed to Angela saying, "*Lane Torwv Fuswv.*" The old woman clasped two hands together. She started laughing while her gray eyes danced in merriment. Soon Moon Woman's happy laughter filled the air inside the chickee hut.

"What was that all about?" Book asked while seeing Angela laughing as well. "I must have missed the punch line. She looks at me and then points to you and starts laughing. I didn't know that I had that kind of an effect on people."

"No, don't take offense. She actually thinks highly of you. *Miko* is the Creek word for chief. She says that you are a chief among white people. And she has given you a new name, Blue-Eyed Eagle, because your eyes are dark blue like the sky and you are strong and powerful like the eagle."

"Why was she laughing?"

"Nothing really." Book could see Angela's reluctance in telling him what the old woman had found so funny. "Come on now. She pointed at you so you must have something to do with it."

"Moon Woman is an old woman who likes to tease me, that's all. She calls me *Lane Torwv Fuswv* which means Green-Eyed Sparrow because I have green eyes and the innocence of a sparrow."

"Okay Green-Eyed Sparrow, why was she laughing?"

"Moon Woman is a medicine woman of sorts here in Indian Town. People come to her whenever they are sick because she knows about the old cures handed down through the generations. She is also a soothsayer, predictor of what's to come. Moon Woman said you and me would one day come together as one. We would be husband and wife."

"Do her predictions usually come true?"

"Yes, nearly always."

"Well, I wouldn't be sending out wedding invitations quite yet," Book said laughing.

Angela did not have the opportunity to respond. A young woman walked into the chickee hut. Angela turned and immediately embraced her while gently touching the woman's left cheek where a deep reddish welt was visible. Yellow Flower moved Angela's hand away.

"Did Bo Wiley do this?" Angela asked her.

"Forget it. It's nothing. I must talk to you." Yellow Flower glanced suspiciously at Book. Angela took the young woman's hand and led her outside the hut where the two talked in a low tone. Book watched them while wondering what it could mean.

CHAPTER SIXTEEN

THE FOUR MEN were seated at a table in the back room of the Gator's Pond Bar. Three bottles of beer and one glass containing a whiskey and water were setting on the table. The sound from the bar's jukebox out front filtered back to them. Three of the men had their eyes fixed on the fourth man. He was reaching for his glass to finish off what was left of the whiskey and water.

"It's all settled then. We kill him tonight."

"But Bo, it's too soon after the priest's murder and Charlie Steed's hanging in the lockup. The Fed's will be down on us with both feet."

Bo Wiley stared across the table at his brother Cash. Tank and Turk Thompson sat by silently watching. They knew better than to say anything contrary to what their Uncle Bo had his mind set on. And as far as they were concerned, killing the army ranger captain was a done deal. Bo Wiley wanted him dead. That was the end of it.

"Cash, we can't take a chance on this guy Book finding out anything, especially with this thing Bernardo has going on the fourth of July. I hate the greaser's guts, but he's right about this guy. Book will be here at the bar tonight and when it's all over it'll be just another bar fight that someone ended up getting killed in. Tell Oil

Can and Deek after it's done to hide out where the women are stashed in the swamp until things blow over."

"How do you know Book will be here tonight?"

"He'll be here. He wants to ask questions about his brother and there's nowhere else at night for him to go. Did you boys see him talking to anybody in Indian Town?"

Turk said, "Just that old lady Angie knows and some other deadbeats. They checked out Charlie Steed's place but there was nothing there for him to find anyway."

"Did Angie say anything about what he's looking for? Is it the information his brother downloaded from Bernardo's computer?"

"She thinks so. He searched the priest's bedroom and she watched him while he was inside the church looking around by some statues. Angie thinks he came here to find the priest's thumb drive."

"All right then. Tell Angie I want her here tonight. She'll leave a report afterward about the fight and how she tried to break it up and the soldier boy got killed anyway. I want no mistakes, do you hear me? Make sure you tell her."

Turk nodded. "Don't worry Bo, I'll tell her."

CHAPTER SEVENTEEN

"BADGER ONE. THIS is Papa Bear how do you read me?"

"Papa Bear. This is Badger One. I read you loud and clear."

"Badger One. What's the situation at Gator's Pond? Anything about the priest's flash drive being found? Or any changes regarding the July fourth date?"

"Papa Bear. Negative. They are still searching for the flash drive and the July fourth date is still a go. But a problem has risen since our last communication."

"Badger One. What kind of a problem?"

"Papa Bear. The priest's brother has shown up in Gator's Pond and they plan on killing him. He's an army ranger captain by the name of Frank Book and he seems to know about the flash drive. He's also been asking a lot of questions about his dead brother that Bo doesn't like. Wiley wants him killed and out of the picture for good. It's set to happen at the Gator's Pond Bar tonight."

"Badger One. He's on his own. Do you read me? Don't interfere and compromise yourself. This might work out to our advantage with them concentrating on this fellow Book. It could give you a free hand to look for the flash drive. How about the DEA agent? Are either the Wiley brothers or Bernardo suspicious?"

"Papa Bear. Negative. The agent is still working on the inside but no closer to finding the flash drive than I am. I have done as you instructed and not

divulged my identity. But I think that I should make contact with the DEA agent."

"Badger One. Negative. Keep things as they are. If the DEA upper echelon can't see that both their operations are one and the same that's just too damn bad. The important thing is locating the priest's flash drive. You have got to find it. The entire plan for the fourth is on that disc and we are running out of time. If it becomes necessary for both the army ranger captain and the DEA agent to be killed in the process so be it. Just find that flash drive."

"Papa Bear. I copy you. Over and out."

CHAPTER EIGHTEEN

DEA HEAD OF Special Operations Jim Garrison fell back in his armchair. He looked up at the map covering the entire wall of the windowless cinderblock room. Garrison was inside his war room located in the basement of a federal building in Washington D.C. It was where the special operations head came to study, to go over in his mind again and again, the many highly developed plans DEA Special Operations had conceived and implemented. No one accompanied Garrison to his war room. The special operations head came alone. He called it Garrison's private strategic command post.

Hundreds of white, yellow, and red-colored pin flags dotted the map on the wall in front of him. A white flag designated a DEA operation still in the planning stage but not yet implemented. A yellow flag indicated an operation underway proceeding according to plan. However, a red flag, and there were only two showing on the wall, signified an operation underway in danger of imploding. The two red flags were what brought Jim Garrison to the war room this day. One red flag was pinned in the vicinity of southwest Florida. The other was pinned to a spot in south Texas. They were named respectively, Operation Silverback and Operation Rescue. But were they one in the same? That was the question plaguing Garrison. Bo Wiley dealt in abducted women who later were sold in exchange for

Middle Eastern heroin. The Arañas Negras Cartel abducted women from Mexico and brought them into the United States. But where were they brought to? That was always the unanswered, the unknown. Garrison checked his fact sheet on the table in front of him. The white van being used in the transporting of the abducted women was presently traveling north from Dallas, Texas. The abductors were using side roads that paralleled U.S. Interstate 35. And I-35 was the route one would take if going to southwest Florida. It could be. No, it had to be, Garrison told himself.

The special operations head picked up the Operation Rescue file and opened it. The photograph of the agent in charge was on top— Code name: Shadow—Joe Torres, 32, enlisted four years in the U.S. Marine Corp serving two tours in Iraq, DEA agent for seven years with an impressive list of accomplishments including working undercover to infiltrate the notorious Los Zetas cartel which led to a number of arrests and convictions both in the U.S and Mexico. But one fact about Torres disturbed Garrison. A female DEA agent while working undercover with Torres had been killed by the Los Zetas. The cartel had discovered her true identity. They tortured her prior to killing her. According to the supervisor's report, Torres had blamed himself for the agent's death even when there was no evidence to support it. Torres's supervisor's final recommendation was that the agent not be involved in any future undercover assignments.

Garrison put the file down. Did he have the wrong man on the ground in Operation Rescue? There was presently a female police officer working with Torres. Garrison personally had approved her undercover role in Operation Rescue. Would Torres be able to put the death of the previous female DEA agent behind him? Would he act responsibly and fulfill his duties as agent in charge? Jim Garrison wished that he knew. The special operations head told himself that he had no other choice but to wait and see.

Garrison picked up the Operation Silverback file. He did not bother opening it because every tidbit of information concerning the operation had already been committed to memory. He personally had sought out and recruited the DEA agent presently on the ground at Gator's Pond. The agent's safety and well-being were his responsibility and no one else's. The thought stayed with him. For the moment, Garrison could appreciate Joe Torres' guilt-ridden feelings at the loss of the female DEA agent in the Los Zetas operation. Torres had recruited the young woman for the undercover assignment. Her face and the faces of those like her never leave you. The same as Agent Roy Peterson's face never left Garrison.

The thought of Peterson brought back Operation Silverback and the apparent leak. Where was it? Who was responsible? Roy Peterson had been killed because of the leak. Now his replacement was in danger of being killed as well. The leak was either in DEA Special Operations or the U.S Attorney's Office. It could be nowhere else. It had to be in one or the other.

Garrison had no use for anyone in the U.S. Attorney's Office, especially Vince DeWitt. The office was loaded with lawyers who cared for little else other than furthering their own political careers or landing a big job in some prestigious law firm. DeWitt's being the former. Garrison did not trust DeWitt or his chief investigator, Casey Blurmeister. Garrison looked upon them both as two snakes sharing the same hole in the ground.

But would they compromise a DEA Special Operations investigation? DeWitt was a political games player who would use his own mother if he thought it could help him. And Blurmeister was a womanizer who might say anything to get a good-looking woman into bed with him. Garrison had both men placed under surveillance the moment he had suspected a leak in Operation Silverback. DeWitt attended nearly every cocktail party in Washington D.C. the past year.

He had left little to no time for his job as U.S. Attorney for the Southern District of Florida. And with his wife and two children living in Miami, Blurmeister leased an apartment that he used while in Washington D.C. The chief investigator frequently picked up women in bars and nightclubs bringing them back to his apartment. Had DeWitt at a cocktail party let something slip regarding Operation Silverback? Or had Blurmeister mentioned the operation to one of his pickups in an attempt to impress her?

Garrison stared at the two red pin flags on the wall. He knew that the next few days would turn out to be crucial. They would determine whether Operations Silverback and Rescue were to be a success or failure. They would also determine whether the agents on the ground survived or not. The Special Operations Head got up from his chair. Jim Garrison took one last look at the flag pins on the wall before walking out the war room door.

CHAPTER NINETEEN

GABRIELLA LOPEZ WAS not sure how long the white panel truck had been stopped. She vaguely recalled it stopping earlier for a short period of time. It was then that two men came in and took down the truck's false front wall. Afterward the men went about removing the plastic handcuffs from around the drugged women's wrists and ankles. Each woman was given a small amount of drinking water before being dragged across the hard, metal floor. Soon fifteen, gray-pajama-clad bodies were dispersed inside the panel truck's 26-foot interior. Gabriella had recognized one of the men. He was the chunky, bald-headed man she had written the traffic citation to back in Laredo, Texas. But the man did not appear to recognize her.

That happened earlier after the truck had first crossed into the United States from Mexico. This present stop was turning out to be quite different. The same two men entered through the back of the truck as they had done previously. And they wasted no time in grabbing the youngest of the women. They half-carried, half-dragged both girls out of the truck. The overhead door had been slammed shut afterward. Gabriella could now hear the men outside talking and laughing. She fought back the drowsiness, the sleepy feeling plaguing her brain. The men were speaking in Spanish. Gabriella could not make out all of their words. But the ones that she could decipher left her terror stricken.

"*Este nunca tuvo un hombre antes*—This one never had a man before."

"*No este tampoco*—Not this one either."

"*Sálvate a ti mismo mi amigo. Hay más después de estos dos*—Save yourself my friend. There are more after these two."

They were drinking tequila and talking. And laughing about the two girls they had taken out of the truck. How they would be doing the same to all the women. There was no sound coming from the girls other than an occasional soft moan. But Gabriella had no illusions as to what was happening. The youngest among them were being raped. Eventually all of the abducted women would suffer the same fate. Shadow had said as much. The reality of it was not there for Gabriella before, but now it was.

Gabriella attempted to steel herself. Fear was beginning to take over. Be strong, she told herself. You will survive this. You will come out of it intact. Aleena had to go through this nightmare. So did all the other women who had been taken against their will and brutally raped. Gabriella stretched her arms above her head. She attempted to get the feeling back in them again. The interior of the truck was dark. Slivers of light seeped in at the door's corners. The air was stuffy hot and the smell of urine strong. Gabriella's body jumped at hearing the sound of the truck's overhead door being raised.

The men tossed the girls' slender bodies back into the truck like sacks of potatoes. Gabriella was close enough to see both of their teary-eyed faces. She wanted to reach out and take each girl into her arms. To hold her. To make the hurting pain go away. To heal the young mind and body. But Gabriella could not. She had to remain motionless showing a blank stare. And pretend incoherence at what was going on around her. She observed one of the men climb into the truck. It was not the man Gabriella had written the traffic citation to. This man's shoulders were rounded and stooped. He possessed lizard eyes, black and shiny, set deep inside a pockmarked face. The man's head appeared too small for his body. It moved from side to side as though it were perched on a swivel. Gabriella could see that he was carrying a tray of hypodermic needles. Another shot. The women were to be given yet another shot of a debilitating drug.

Gabriella knew that another injection would render her completely drugged and helpless. But what could she do? She watched him bend down over a woman. He injected the woman's flaccid arm before placing the used syringe back on the tray. The man took a fresh syringe. He moved to the next woman. All the women were lying strewn about on the truck floor appearing in a near comatose state. The man was moving from body to body. Gabriella knew that it would be only a matter of seconds before he got to her. She watched him bend over to administer another shot. His back was turned. Could she get past him? Gabriella seized the opportunity. She moved. The man did not see her. Once by him, Gabriella dropped down. Her body became intermingled with those bodies already inoculated. She was hoping the gray pajamas and dark hair would render her indistinguishable. That he would not be able to differentiate her from all the others. While moving past him, Gabriella had been close enough to smell the scent of tequila off the man. She also smelled the blood from the girls he had raped.

Gabriella wondered if he would overlook her. Or would the unused syringe give her away? She watched as he inoculated the last of the women. She saw him put the used syringe down onto the metal tray. He turned around to look at the fifteen bodies lying on the floor of the truck. Gabriella could feel her heart pounding. The tightening knot in her stomach grew tighter. She observed him walking, stepping over the women's bodies. He was getting closer. The man reached her and stopped. Gabriella dared not move. She kept her head down and eyes closed. He stepped over her.

She opened her eyes in time to see him jump out of the truck. The overhead door was brought down. There followed the hard sound of the metal lock sliding into place. Darkness filled the truck once again. Gabriella felt more alone than at any other time in her life. Tears streamed her face. She closed her eyes and started to pray.

CHAPTER TWENTY
National Hurricane Center
Florida International University in Miami

PETER LOGAN LOOKED across the cluttered table at his friend and colleague Billy Burke. Saying nothing, Logan dropped the clipboard that he had been holding and jumped to his feet. The highly-respected, hurricane tracker hurried over to the huge tracking board which took over an entire wall of the spacious room. Logan pointed to the black lettering spelling out the name "Ruth." He had inscribed the name ten minutes earlier. It was located in an area directly above the island of Haiti.

"You still don't believe Ruth is coming to Florida, do you?"

"No, I don't," Burke said smiling while appreciating the intensity in the face of his fellow hurricane tracker. "I think she'll slam into Haiti's mountain range, slow down dramatically and then veer back into the Gulf of Mexico just like Hurricane Quentin did two weeks ago."

"Ruth isn't Quentin. She's already a Category three while Quentin was only a two after reaching Haiti. I've been following Ruth since she started out as a tropical wave on the west coast of Africa and then became a tropical depression three, a tropical storm, and now a hurricane. The 53 Weather Reconnaissance Squadron says she has a 25-mile-eye radius and well-defined inner core. She's spread out over close to 500 miles. No Haitian mountains are going to slow her down that much with winds as strong as 110–130 mph."

"If you're right, she should then slam into Cuba and that will slow her down even more. You're counting on her skirting Cuba's north coast and entering the Florida straits where, over warm water, she could gain more strength. I don't think that's going to happen. I think she's going to head into the Gulf and sidestep Florida."

"Well Billy boy, I wouldn't make any outdoor plans for the next week because Ruth is coming to south Florida. She's moving slow so I give her maybe two days, three at the most before she bangs into the Florida Keys. I'll bet you a steak dinner on it."

"Okay, I'll take that bet. And I'm going to win it." Billy Burke said feeling confident that this time he would finally win a bet, for a change.

Peter Logan laughed out loud.

"No, you won't, Billy. Hurricane Ruth is definitely coming to Florida. And anyone living in close proximity to the Florida Everglades is going to be in for a nasty time of it."

CHAPTER TWENTY-ONE

IT DID NOT take long for Frank Book to discover that his motel room had been searched. The dried toothpaste seal he previously had placed over the desk drawer had been broken. It told Book that some person or persons had come into his motel room and searched it sometime after he had left that morning. His first thought was that they had found the Beretta and ammo clips. Book hurried to the bathroom where he undid the shower drain cover. The gun and ammo clips were as he had left them. They were still in the plastic bag. And the bag's seal was intact. Whoever had searched his room had not discovered the gun and ammo clips. Book quickly lowered the plastic bag back into the narrow space before securing the metal drain cover once again.

Book returned to the bedroom and sat down on the bed. He removed the cellphone from his pants pocket. Still no signal. The army ranger captain had been attempting to phone Bob Collins, Florida's assistant attorney general, all day and had come up with the same result. Someone had to be jamming the signal. There could be no other explanation. Book recalled in Andy's letter that his brother had been unable to obtain a signal on his cellphone. The apparent jamming had made it impossible for Andy to call outside Gator's Pond for help. The same was happening to him. Bo Wiley did not want anyone to have outside access. If Andy's flash drive were to be found, Book would have to be the one to find it. He could not count on help from Bob Collins or any other person outside of Gator's Pond.

Book went over the day's events in his mind. Angela Valadez had dropped him off at the Gator's Pond Inn after the two of them had spent most of the day at Indian Town. Book had met a number of people who had known Andy and genuinely liked the pastor of St. Anne of God's Church. But no one cared to answer any of Book's inquiries relating to Bo Wiley or the associate priest Father Miguel. The army ranger captain tried pressing them but got nowhere. And he could not help but recognize the fear both names brought out in people's faces.

Angela had also taken him to Charlie Steed's rundown shack. She showed him where Turk and Tank Thompson said they had found Steed hiding in a closet. Steed's clothes were supposedly stained with Andy's blood. The place was nothing more than a deserted shack. It had a dirty mattress on the floor in one bedroom and a couple of chairs set against a table in the kitchen. There was nothing in the place that came back to Charlie Steed. No bills or receipts with his name on it. No evidence linked the man to the rundown shack. That was probably the reason Bo Wiley and his brother Cash had chosen Steed to pin Andy's murder on. He was a vagrant with no known residence. They both knew that the down-and-out drunk would not be missed. He had no one who cared enough about him to ask any questions.

Book was sitting on the bed thinking about Angela Valadez and wondering how she fit in with the Wiley brothers and the Thompson twins when he heard the knock at the motel room door. He was definitely not expecting anyone. The Beretta in the shower drain came to mind. But there was no time to retrieve it. Book came off the bed. He sidled up to the motel window while attempting to see who was at the door. Rain drizzle on the window muddled his view, but he did make out the pretty face and slim body. Book went to the door. After undoing the door's lock and chain, he opened it.

****

It was raining. The early evening rain had wetted her brown hair leaving dark strands hanging down. Angela used her right hand to push the wet hair to the side while the young woman's green eyes stayed fixated on Book. She showed him a questioning look. Oblivious, he stood stolid in the doorway staring back at her.

"Well, are you going to let me in or leave me standing out here in the rain?"

"Sorry," Book said catching himself and moving out of the way. "It's just that you only dropped me off a short time ago, and I didn't expect to be seeing you again so soon."

"That makes us even. After dropping you off I hadn't expected to be coming back so soon either."

Angela walked past him into the motel room. Book shut the door after her, locking it. He then watched the uniformed deputy walk directly to the bathroom and come out holding the last of Book's clean towels. Angela commenced drying her face and hair with it. Book watched as the young woman rubbed the top of her head furiously with the towel. She didn't stop until only loose strands of brown fell across her forehead. Smiling at him, Angela tossed the wet towel onto the bed.

"I parked the squad car out back because I didn't want anybody to see me coming in here. An umbrella would have really come in handy. By the way, thanks for the towel."

Angela detected the semblance of a grin forming on Book's face along with the half-turn of his head.

"No Frank, I didn't find you so irresistible all day long that I had to come back to spend the night alone with you, too. So take that silly grin off your face and get me a drink. I don't usually drink, but I need one now."

"Coming up," Book responded. "I can hardly wait to hear what brought you back to my humble abode. You had me on cloud nine there a moment ago." He went over to the green duffel bag on the floor next to the bed. Reaching in, Book came out with a pint of Jim Beam. He held the bottle up to show Angela before going into the bathroom to retrieve two paper cups.

"I don't know how long these cups have been around, but the Jim Beam should kill anything that's on them that could hurt you."

Book poured some of the whiskey into a cup and handed the cup to Angela. He then poured a drink for himself.

"So what brought you back?" he asked taking a sip of the whiskey. He watched Angela do the same and caught her wince at its going down. She fought to catch her breath.

"I'm not used to this stuff."

"Nobody gets used to it so don't feel bad."

"You have to leave and I mean right now. I'll drive you to Miami in my squad car and drop you off. If you don't go, they'll kill you for sure."

"Who's going to kill me?"

"Bo Wiley. He wants you dead and out of the way for good. Bo won't be the one to actually do it, but he's ordering it. Oil Can and Deek are the ones who will carry it out. And it's all planned for later tonight at the Gator's Pond Bar. Oil Can is going to start a fight with you. If he doesn't kill you outright, Deek is supposed to stab you with that toad sticker he keeps in his boot."

"Toad sticker?"

"A stiletto. He keeps it concealed in his right boot."

"How do you know all this?"

"Turk Thompson told me less than fifteen minutes ago. Earlier today there was a meeting between Bo, Cash, and the Thompson twins. Bo told them he wants you killed in what's supposed to look like a barroom fight. He wants me to witness the fight and later make out the police report so it all looks official. It will appear on paper that you got involved in a bar fight and ended up getting killed in the process. The plan then calls for Oil Can and Deek to hide out in the swamp until things die down. Bo and Cash Wiley are good at this sort of thing. They've been doing it for years and have always gotten away with it."

Book took another drink of whiskey. Then he poured more out of the bottle into his paper cup. He raised the bottle to Angela, but she shook her head no. So that was how it was going to be, he told himself. His thoughts went to the Beretta in the bathroom shower drain. Book found comfort in the gun's being there. He knew that he could face almost any odds as long as he had the Beretta. If it was a battle Bo Wiley wanted then so be it. The whiskey had given Book's stomach a warm feeling. It had gotten the blood pumping. The army ranger captain felt that he could not be more ready.

"Thanks for the warning, but I'm not leaving."

"You won't have a chance against them. They are going to kill you. You have got to believe me."

"Angela it's not a question of my not believing you because I do. But I came here because of my brother Andy, and I'm not leaving until things have been made right."

"If you think that gun you hid in the shower drain is going to keep you from being killed, you had better think again. Because it won't. That's another thing Turk told me about. He said Bo and Cash Wiley searched your motel room this morning and they found the Beretta. Cash did something to the firing pin so that the gun won't be operable. If you don't believe me go check for yourself."

Book felt as though he had been punched in the stomach and trounced underfoot by a dozen men's boots. Angela's revelation left him weak in the knees, feeling sick inside. He knew that she was telling the truth. There could have been no other way for her to have known about the gun.

"No, I believe you. I just wish that I didn't," Book said looking at her. There was real concern in the girl's face. Her green eyes were opened wide. Book stared into them appreciating their warmth.

"Why are you involved with the likes of Bo and Cash Wiley? And rubbing elbows with those Thompson twins? You're not like them. Angela, what are you doing in a town like this?"

"I grew up here," she said to him. "I belong here and you don't. Now let's go. I'll drive you out of here and that will be the end of it. They won't be able to touch you."

"And how will you explain it to Bo Wiley? Taking me out of town when he wants me dead."

"I'll tell him that you made me do it. You forced me to drive you."

"And you think Wiley will believe that? No, Angela, it wouldn't work. Besides I came to Gator's Pond to do a job. To find out why my brother Andy was murdered and to make sure those responsible for killing him were held accountable. Nothing's changed in regards to that. If they're waiting tonight for me at the Gator's Pond Bar, then I won't disappoint them."

"Frank, you're crazy. They'll kill you."

"They'll try," Book said crushing the empty paper cup inside his right hand. "But trying is one thing, doing is another."

CHAPTER TWENTY-TWO

BOOK WALKED THROUGH a rainy drizzle toward the lights of the Gator's Pond Bar. He recognized right off the bugle song being played on the bar's jukebox. It was the Mexican '*El Deguello*—The Slitting of the Throat.' It was the same song General Santa Anna had played for the men at the Alamo prior to his killing them. So Bo Wiley has a sense of humor, the army ranger captain thought as he walked toward the music. Book approached the front door of the Gator's Pond Bar. He opened it and stepped inside.

If there had been any talking going on, it ended the moment Book walked in. Someone quickly pulled the plug on the jukebox. The place went quiet. They were all waiting for him. Bo and Cash Wiley were seated next to one another at the long table in the corner. Turk and Tank Thompson occupied the same table. Both uniformed deputies turned their chairs around to face Book. He was standing just inside the front door. The Thompson twins had identical grins plastered on their faces. While the Wiley brothers sat stone-faced staring at a man they knew would be dead in a few minutes.

Gus, who ran the marina, and Cornelius, the drunk who worked the desk at the Gator's Pond Inn, sat at a round table close to the bar. The two men stared down at their drinks. Neither wanted to witness what was about to happen. But each knew it was too late to get up and leave.

There were a dozen or so Seminoles from Indian Town including Panther and his two cousins sitting around a pair of crowded tables. The Indians occupied a corner of the bar opposite the Wileys. They had been playing poker, but their game no longer seemed important. Cards had been quickly tossed onto the table surfaces. While the sound of chairs scraping the wooden floor became audible as the men turned to face the center of the room. A more interesting game was about to unfold. The Seminoles did not want to miss it.

Oil Can and Deek were sitting on two bar stools at the far end of the bar. Both men displayed wolfish grins. Deek gave an elbow to Oil Can's right side. Then leaning over, he said something into the big man's ear. Oil Can showed a mouthful of crooked white teeth inside a coal-black face. Nodding his wooly head, Oil Can picked up a full beer mug. He emptied the mug in one gulp before slamming it down onto the bar. Glass went everywhere. Deek laughed out loud. Reaching around, the skinny man patted Oil Can's huge back.

Appreciating the moment, Book walked over to the bar. He ordered a whiskey straight up. Maria Carrera stared at him with her dark brown eyes and tantalizing look. She placed both her hands on the bar. While leaning forward, she whispered to Book, "You have got to be the craziest gringo in all the world to walk in here tonight."

Book said to her, "It must be the brown eyes. I know it's not the ham and eggs. And it's definitely not the company you keep. No, it must be those brown eyes of yours that keeps bringing me back."

"You know Oil Can wants to kill you and you came back anyway. You are a fool. A brave one but still a fool."

"You're the one who told me that we all have to die from something. So why not be a good girl and bring me my drink."

Maria Carrera poured a large glass of whiskey. She put it down on the bar in front of Book. The Mexican woman gazed into his dark blue eyes. She observed the cocky half-smile and devil-take-care look on his manly face. There was something about this gringo that got to her. And Maria Carrera disliked herself for it. Ever since she was a young girl Maria had been attracted to brave men. She thought most men to be cowards. Few had courage. Bernardo had it. And that was why she loved him. But this man. This one they called Book. He had courage, too. Maria Carrera turned and walked away.

****

Bo Wiley sat at the corner table holding a whiskey and water in his two hands. He caught each one of Deek's head movements in his direction. Deek was looking for the okay to unleash Oil Can on Book. Wiley ignored him. Nothing would be done until Angela Valadez showed up. What could be keeping her? Wiley wanted the female deputy to witness the fight. And then later submit the proper police report. It would be better with her handling everything than to have one of the Thompson twins getting involved. Turk and Tank had too much baggage already. They did not need to be the center of yet another FBI investigation.

No sooner had Bo Wiley taken a sip of his drink and put it down than Angela Valadez entered the back door of the Gator's Pond Bar. The deputy was wearing her police uniform. She took a standing position directly behind Deek at the end of the bar. Bo felt his brother Cash's heavy stare. Turning, he caught the widening smile, the nodding head. Bo Wiley sat up in his chair and looked around the barroom. Everything was going according to plan. It was time to take the leash off Oil Can. Let the crazed monster rip Book limb from limb. Bo raised his right hand. Deek saw him do it. He turned to whisper into Oil Can's right ear.

Oil Can came off his bar stool in a hurry. He let loose with a loud yell. Book looked down the bar at him. The standing goliath was wearing a blue t-shirt and black short pants along with dirty white tennis shoes and no socks. And he was moving in Book's direction. The man has probably never lost a fight in his life, Book quickly assessed. He's big and strong and hard to hurt. I'll have to hurt him right off. He has to know that I can do it. Otherwise, he'll go right through me.

Oil Can resembled an oversized armored tank rolling across the barroom floor. He looked impregnable to say the least. Two tree-trunk-size arms were outstretched. While thick-muscled shoulders, arched and massive, moved from side to side. The army ranger captain took a swig from his whiskey glass. He dropped the empty glass onto the floor just as Oil Can came within a few feet of him. The man's black face appeared all twisted and menacing. His two huge hands reached out to wrench Book's head from his body. Oil Can's bloodshot eyes stared with a craziness deep inside. Book spat a mouthful of whiskey into them.

The big man stepped back. Instinctively, he brought both hands up to his burning eyes. Book delivered three hard, straight punches to Oil Can's well-muscled chest. The army ranger captain followed with a crisp right kick to his opponent's left knee. Then he quickly moved away. Oil Can took a couple of deep breaths to get air back into his lungs. He blinked the tears out of his eyes.

The spitted whiskey had served to enrage him all the more. Seeing a crouched over Book, Oil Can rushed after him swinging his arms club-like. He delivered hard, punishing blows that the smaller man attempted to block but at a terrible price. They left a stinging hurt to Book's forearms. Some of the heavy punches got through, slamming into the army ranger captain's face. Book backpedaled, zigzagging across the barroom floor in attempt to avoid the onslaught coming straight at him. A wild right hand from Oil Can connected to the left side of Book's head. Knees buckling, Book nearly dropped. Momentum from the thrown punch sent Oil Can spinning onto an empty table. The table collapsed under his weight. Getting up, the big man started toward Book again.

Bo Wiley patted Cash's right arm resting on the table next to him. It would not be long now. Smiles lit up both men's faces. Turk and Tank Thompson cheered, stomping their feet. They yelled for Oil Can to finish Book off. Behind the bar, Maria Carrera watched, her face showing nothing. While deep inside she had hoped Book would beat the big black. But it now appeared that there was no hope. And at the end of bar, Angela Valadez stood staring, asking herself if there was anything that she could do to save Book's life.

A looping right hand sent Book reeling backward. Oil Can rushed in swinging, long sweeping punches. Book ducked under one and sent a hard right to Oil Can's chest. He delivered another vicious kick to the big man's left knee. Faking a right hand, Book doubled up two left hooks to the side of Oil Can's face. He kicked him again in the left knee. Book saw the grimace of pain register on his opponent's face. Oil Can stepped backward favoring his left leg. Book jumped in with two more sharp punches to the man's chest. Breathing deeply, Oil Can started moving forward again. But he found Book no longer in front of him. The army ranger captain had skirted to the right. Oil Can turned looking for Book. He was stunned by a right hand punch to the heart. The big man staggered in the middle of the room. Book kicked him twice more to the left knee. Oil Can went down. He tried to get up. That was when Book directed a hard kick to the left side of the man's wooly head. Oil Can did not move. He lay unconscious on the barroom floor.

****

With Book's back turned, Deek reached down into his right boot for the stiletto. He had it halfway out when the barrel end of Angela Valadez's Glock 9mm. became pressed against the back of his head. It left Deek motionless, afraid to move.

"Deek don't take it out of the boot, or it'll be the last thing you ever do."

"Bo won't like this, Angie," Deek said before letting the stiletto fall back into his boot.

"If you're dead Deek, Bo's likes and dislikes won't matter a whole hell of lot to you anymore, now will they?" Angela pushed the gun barrel harder into the back of Deek's head. "Now walk out that back door and I better not see you in here again tonight trying to stick someone in the back." Deek hurried out the back door without turning around.

"Everybody out of here. And I mean everybody."

Bo Wiley along with Cash and the Thompson twins walked over to Book. They stood in the middle of the floor looking down at an unconscious Oil Can. The Seminoles, after hearing Bo Wiley's order, scurried out the front door. Gus and Cornelius took the shorter route out the back. Maria Carrera watched from behind the bar displaying an amused grin. The gringo Book had upset Bo Wiley's plans for the night. Nothing could have made the Mexican woman happier.

"Take him," Bo Wiley said to Turk and Tank Thompson.

"Which one are you?" Book asked the first of the twins to reach him. The army ranger captain was still breathing hard.

"Turk, why?"

"So next time I'll know who you are by your broken nose," Book said before driving a hard right fist into Turk Thompson's long narrow nose breaking it. Book turned to confront Tank but caught a full-fisted punch to the face. Tank's second punch hit Book in the stomach. Cash Wiley came up behind him. The chief struck Book in the back of the head with a lead sap. The cracking sound filled the bar. The army ranger captain collapsed beside Oil Can on the floor. The back of his head oozed blood.

Bo Wiley said to his brother Cash. "You might have saved us the trouble of killing him."

"No, he's still alive," Tank said after bending down to check on Book.

"Then let me finish him." Turk moved toward Book holding one hand over his bleeding nose. His other hand held the butt end of a gun.

"Bo, wait a minute," Angela yelled hurrying across the barroom floor to Bo Wiley.

"Wait for what? And what the hell were you doing pulling a gun on Deek? He was supposed to be backing up Oil Can. You knew that."

Angela said to him. "Kill Book now and you won't get the flash drive. I stopped by his motel room earlier, and he told me that he knows where Father Andy hid the flash drive. With a little persuasion, I think I can get him to tell me where it's at."

"Bo, you can't let him go," Turk said.

"We can kill him anytime. But if that flash drive ends up in the wrong hands then we will all be in the penitentiary. Bo, let me take Book to my place and fix up his head and get him talking. After he tells me where the flash drive is I'll tell you, and then you can kill him."

Bo Wiley looked to the door leading to the back room. He observed Bernardo standing in the open doorway. Bo walked over to the Mexican. The two men talked briefly before Wiley came back into the bar.

"Angie, we'll give it a try. The minute Book tells you where the flash drive is hidden let us know. We'll get it and take care of him afterwards. Turk and Tank will help you get him into your car."

"Okay, Bo," Angela said. "And as soon as I know where the flash drive is, you'll know too."

CHAPTER TWENTY-THREE

BERNARDO LOOKED OVER at Maria Carrera. She was lying in bed facing him. A flood of moonlight entered via the bedroom window. It cast a bluish glow onto the Mexican woman's face. While her steady nasal sound indicated deep sleep. The two were occupying Bernardo's bed at the church rectory. Carrera had been spending nights at the rectory ever since Father Andrew's murder. Moving closer, Bernardo ran the back of his right hand across the woman's dark brown hair. He had always appreciated the softness of Maria Carrera's hair. And the beauty of her smooth, tan face. And knowing that she was his to do with as he pleased.

Maria Carrera had proven to be most useful in carrying out his plan. She had set up the real Father Miguel in Mexico City. Through Bo Wiley, Bernardo had learned that Father Miguel Santiago was leaving the next day for Gator's Pond. The priest had received word that his new assignment was to be St. Anne of God's parish in Gator's Pond, Florida. A Spanish-speaking priest was needed and his bishop was sending him. The night before Father Miguel was to leave Maria Carrera coaxed the unsuspecting priest to an abandoned tenement. She told him that her father was dying and wanted to see a priest. Bernardo was there waiting for him. He strangled Father

Miguel to death. He then took his victim's identification. Using the dead priest's name and identity, Bernardo came to Gator's Pond.

Bernardo had first encountered Maria Carrera in Mexico City shortly after his arrival from Bogota, Columbia. Carrera was a high-priced prostitute servicing the most influential government officials in Mexico. He cultivated a relationship with her, initially by using the millions of U.S. dollars Bernardo had brought with him from Columbia. And then by getting her to fall in love with him. Maria Carrera possessed both the beauty and intelligence he was looking for in a woman. Bernardo saw in her the feminine wiles and skills that he could use to acquire the political connections necessary to operate a cartel in Mexico. Bribery and blackmail were the weapons Bernardo employed in addition to kidnapping and murder. *Las Arañas Negras cartel,* The Black Spiders, soon became a powerful force. It became numbered among the most feared cartels in all of Mexico. Nuevo Laredo was its home territory. The location enabled The Black Spiders to possess a gateway into the United States. And then Bo Wiley came along giving Bernardo what he had wanted from the very beginning—a land base of operation that could function from deep within the United States.

The plan Bernardo had formulated in his mind so many years ago was mere days away from becoming a reality. It only awaited his final go ahead. Anything that could have possibly hindered its execution had been eliminated. Even the power and might behind the U.S. government had not been able to alter Bernardo's plan. He had the inside track, which kept him ahead of any federal investigation.

Bernardo smiled. His gaze centered on Maria Carrera who was fast asleep. But the smile did not remain long. It rapidly faded from his face. The thought of Book came to him. It caused Bernardo to get out of the bed. The cartel leader had not planned on Book's coming to Gator's Pond. It was bothersome to have to deal with such a man. Bernardo went over to the bedroom's west window to look out at the dark night. Lightning flashed across the sky.

The man was dangerous. Bernardo had watched from the back room of the Gator Pond's Bar. He observed what Book had done to Oil Can in the fight Bo Wiley staged. Such a man could not be underestimated. Too much was at stake for someone like Book to come along and destroy all of Bernardo's plans. Bo Wiley had gone to Bernardo in the bar. He informed him as to what Angela Valadez had said about Book knowing where the flash drive was hidden. Bernardo told Wiley to let Book live so that the flash drive could be found. But had he made a mistake in allowing a man like Book to live? Even for a day?

The leader of The Black Spiders cartel questioned his decision. Leaving the window, Bernardo went back to the bed. He lay down next to Maria Carrera knowing that he would not sleep. Closing his eyes, the man posing as a Catholic priest listened to the rain striking the outside window pane. Yes, Bernardo told himself. When it came to this man Book, he could very well have made a mistake.

CHAPTER TWENTY-FOUR

"LOOKS LIKE WE'RE goin' to be gettin' some rain," Cash Wiley said coming away from the window. He took a seat on the couch opposite his brother Bo in the Wiley mansion living room.

Bo Wiley looked at Cash. He did not attempt to conceal his displeasure. "They expect Hurricane Ruth to hit the Florida Keys the day after tomorrow, which means we'll probably get hit by it sometime right after that. Have the boys board up all the windows here and in town. Tell Gus to shut the marina down tight and then do the same for the bar. Of all times for a hurricane to hit us with everything that we've got going on. Cash, that damn Oil Can quit on me tonight. And did you see the smile on Maria Carrera's face? That greaser bitch wanted me to see it more than she did anyone else. I know she did."

"Bo, Oil Can did the best he could. He just ran up against Book and we didn't figure on the soldier boy being that good. If you want to blame somebody, blame me. I should have checked out Book more than I did. Before coming over here I got a hold of a guy I know at Fort Benning, and he gave me the skinny on Book. He's a Silver Star winner and a war hero. He's also a hand-to-hand combat expert and behind-enemy-lines specialist. They send this guy in behind enemy lines to kill the opposing army's soldiers. We should have killed him when we had the chance. While he was knocked out on the barroom floor."

"I wanted to, but Bernardo said no."

"Who's the boss around here, you or Bernardo?"

"Cash, I don't need to hear that kind of bullshit from you. In a few days Bernardo and that Carrera bitch will be gone and that'll be the end of it. Things can get back to normal then, the way they were before those two came. You wait and see, I know what I'm talking about."

"You're foolin' yourself if you think Bernardo is going to give up the sweetheart deal he has here. He ain't goin' nowhere."

"If he doesn't leave, I'll kill him. One way or another we'll be rid of him."

"And where will you get your dope if he doesn't give it to you? He brings the women in from Mexico and then flies them out. The heroin comes back after the women are sold. We get a half-million a month just for making sure it all runs smooth and a bonus on top of that after he sells the dope. Where else can we make money like that? You need him and he needs you. So you better get used to the idea because nothing is going to change after July fourth. Bernardo is not going to leave Gator's Pond."

"And what about the heat that'll be coming down after he follows through with that plan of his? The whole country will be in an uproar. The Feds will be going crazy trying to trace it back to its base of operation. If they trace it back here, how do we explain Bernardo playing Father Miguel over at the church? We're already under suspicion after that DEA agent turned up missing. The Feds just don't forget about stuff like that. They have to be watching us."

"Let them watch us. They haven't come up with anything so far, and they won't find anything. I trust my people. And Deek and Oil Can have everything to lose if they have to go back to Georgia to face murder charges on killing that guard. We're fine as long as we don't do something stupid."

"Like letting a guy live when it could easily come back to kick us in the ass?"

"Exactly."

"All right then. If Angie can't get the whereabouts of the flash drive out of Book by tomorrow night we kill him. How does that sound?"

"Fine with me. But aren't you goin' to run it by Bernardo first?"

"No, I'm the boss. And I say we kill him."

"That's what I wanted to hear. Now you sound like my big brother Bo."

CHAPTER TWENTY-FIVE

"*BADGER ONE. THIS is Papa Bear, how do you read me?*"

"*Papa Bear. This is Badger One. I read you loud and clear.*"

"*Badger One. Is there any change relating to the priest's flash drive? Has the disc been recovered?*"

"*Papa Bear. Negative. The disc has not been located. But the priest's brother, Captain Book, apparently knows where it can be found. I am monitoring the situation and if the opportunity should present itself I will secure the flash drive.*"

"*Badger One. I take it then that Bo Wiley and Bernardo haven't killed Book. He is still alive.*"

"*Papa Bear. That is affirmative. They tried but failed to kill him. Book showed remarkable skill in beating the man they sent up against him. I witnessed the fight. It was an exceptional one. However, I feel Book's lease on life is temporary. Bo Wiley and Bernardo have delayed his killing in the hope of finding the flash drive. Once they get their hands on the flash drive, Book will assuredly be killed.*"

"*Badger One. Disregard all previous instructions concerning Book. Assist Book if it will enable you to secure the flash drive but you are not to compromise yourself in any way. Do you read me?*"

"*Papa Bear. Yes, I do. I understand perfectly. If the opportunity should present itself, I will do what I can for Book. But time now is of the essence. Does* the DEA realize Operation Silverback and Operation Rescue are one and the same?"

"Badger One. I would suspect that they do. Jim Garrison is nobody's fool. The cartel's panel truck should be entering the state of Florida sometime today and Garrison will undoubtedly be aware of it. The problem I see for the DEA is that they have a female agent secreted among the abducted Mexican women, and she is in an extremely precarious position. If the cartel's truck is allowed to reach the Everglades, it could become difficult if not impossible to extricate her."

"Papa Bear. Should I assist the female DEA agent and the abducted women if it becomes possible for me to do so?"

"Badger One. Negative. Your sole responsibility is to locate the flash drive and that is all. The female DEA agent working undercover in Operation Rescue is Jim Garrison's responsibility, and right now I wouldn't want to be him or her. Is there anything else Badger One?"

"Papa Bear. There is nothing more."

"Badger One. Until our next communication stay safe."

"Papa Bear. I plan to, thank you. Over and out."

CHAPTER TWENTY-SIX

THE EVENING SUN started to disappear in the western sky. Its exiting allowed night shadows to creep over Florida's lush green landscape. Soon the sun would be completely down bringing total darkness. Caesar Gomez had taken the first of the Tallahassee exits. He knew that this overnight stop would be their last. The last three days had seen him and Jose taking turns driving. They would stop at night to drink tequila and do whatever they pleased to the drugged-out women. It had been an ongoing party that the two of them had enjoyed immensely. But by late afternoon tomorrow it would all end. They would have by then reached the Everglades. The cargo would be unloaded and they would get paid. Then there would be the long trip back to Mexico.

Gomez drove the truck down what appeared to be a little used back road. After sighting a grove of tall sand pine trees, he maneuvered the truck around the grove's low hanging branches and protruding tree stumps. He did not stop until confident that the truck would not be seen by anyone from the road. Switching off the truck's ignition, Gomez turned to his traveling companion. He observed Jose Herrera sound asleep in the passenger seat. Gomez took hold of his friend's left shoulder, shaking it.

"*Hay mujeres esperando. Cómo se puede dormir?*—There are women waiting. How can you sleep?"

"*Yo tenía suficientes mujeres. Necesito dormir.*—I had enough women. I need sleep."

"*Bueno mi amigo. Más para mí.*—Good my friend. More for me."

Gomez reached down underneath the truck's front seat to retrieve an open bottle of tequila. He took a long swig from the bottle. He then wiped his mouth on the sleeve of his well-stained shirt. Letting loose with a loud belch, Gomez took another drink. He wiped his mouth again. The thought of women lying almost naked in the back of the truck came to him. A widening smile sprang up on his unshaven face. The fifteen women confined to the back of the hot, suffocating truck were getting rancid after three days. They smelled of urine and feces and body stench that would have made most men turn away. But not Caesar Gomez. The smell did not bother him. He smelled nearly as bad himself. And what was a little bit of stench when it came to a woman. A man having his way with her. Doing whatever he wanted to her.

Gomez took another drink of tequila. One of the women's faces came to his mind. It was a face he had seen somewhere before. But he could not place where he had seen it. For the past three days he had been thinking about that face. Gomez decided on having her tonight. She would be the woman that he would rape. Maybe then he would be able to remember her. And recall how it was that he knew her face. Gomez raised the bottle to his lips. He took another long drink of tequila before letting loose with another loud belch. The truck driver from Nuevo Laredo smiled. Yes, he thought to himself. She will be the one I take tonight.

****

Gabriella Lopez had felt the bounce and roll of the truck after its leaving the back road. The truck's tires drove over uneven ground before coming to a stop. She knew that meant the truck would not be moving anytime soon. It was probably parked for the night. On previous occasions, the truck remained parked until the sun rose in the morning.

The truck's stopping for the night brought back to Gabriella the unrelenting fear. It never really left her but now it was even more so. Because each time the truck had stopped for the night men with flashlights came to unlock the truck's overhead door. They would flash their bright lights inside. And then two of the women would be taken outside and raped for hours on end. While lying in the darkness, Gabriella had listened to the men's ceaseless drunken laughter. And she had heard the women's incessant cries for help until she could not listen anymore. She would then cover both her ears and pray to God that somehow he would make it all go away. But he never did. It never went away. And now the truck had stopped again for the night. That meant the men would be coming soon.

A hot consuming fear infused Gabriella's body. It brought sharp needles that probed and poked. Incessantly, they attacked. Her stomach churned. She felt like vomiting. Gabriella fought to keep her nerves steady, but nothing that she tried seemed to help. The men with the bright lights would be coming at any moment. And she knew that they would take two more women out to be raped. Try and stay calm, she told herself. Think. Don't let the fear of being raped take you over. But she could not help herself. Would it be her turn this time? Would they choose her to drag out of the truck?

Gabriella started to crawl. She wanted to be farther from the door. Hurry. Get away from the door. Climbing over sleeping women, she conjured up images of corpses not yet buried. Rape them not me, she thought. Take the ones closest to the door. Not me. The pang of guilt hit Gabriella hard. She hated herself for thinking it. But what if they took her? What could she do? She would have to let them rape her. If not, they would know she had evaded being drugged. That would place her under suspicion. Most probably get her killed. But the thought of the men's dirty hands and mouths touching and kissing her along with the actual rape itself left Gabriella feeling weak. Aleena. She must do it for her sister Aleena. The unlocking of the truck's back door reverberated, sounding loudly inside the enclosed space. The hard sound shook Gabriella to her core. Any thought of helping Aleena quickly left her.

CHAPTER TWENTY-SEVEN

"*MALDITA SEA*—DAMN it."

They were having trouble with the lock on the truck door. Gabriella could hear them banging on the metal bolt trying to loosen it. Then there was the metallic clang of the bolt sliding free. The back door opened immediately after. Gabriella saw only one bright light shining into the truck. She kept her head down and eyes partially closed. She flattened her body hoping it would not be seen.

A man stepped into the truck. He began shining his flashlight down at the women lying on the truck floor. Taking hold of one woman's head, he raised it. The man shined the light into the woman's face before letting her head drop. He moved on to another woman. He did the same. The man was working his way back into the truck checking women's faces and letting their heads fall onto the metal floor. He is searching for someone. There is one particular woman that he is looking for. Gabriella was certain of it. It has to be me, she told herself. I have to be the one he is looking for. A wave of panic swept through her. He must be the truck driver. The one I wrote the citation to, and he's searching for me. I can't let him see my face. I must hide my face.

Gabriella felt the tug at her hair. The raising of her head. The bright light was blinding. He said something to her but she could not understand it. Suddenly Gabriella's entire body was lifted off the floor. She was being slung over the man's right shoulder. He carried her out the truck's back door.

Gomez dropped Gabriella like a sack of flour. The oxygen immediately left the young woman's lungs. Panic set in. She could not breathe. Turning onto her left side, she gasped for air. Gomez rolled her onto her back. He moved on top of her. Taking hold of Gabriella's pajama top, he raised it up. Two naked breasts fell under the flashlight's beam. Gomez reached for them. Gabriella could feel his hand on her left breast. Then his mouth fastened onto her mouth. His wet tongue penetrated deep inside. She tasted the tequila on his tongue.

He pulled his mouth away. The Mexican moved it down to Gabriella's left breast. Immediately she felt the hurt of his teeth. The tug at her nipple. Her body instinctively shifted beneath him. His right hand struck hard. Gabriella's head fell to one side. Don't move, she told herself. You have to remain still. But when his hand reached down between her legs it caused her body to rise up. He said something to her. There was another slap. Gabriella opened her eyes. The flashlight beam was bright, blinding. It was in her face. Then it came to her. She did not have to pretend any longer. He knew.

"La policía—The police," she heard him say.

Gomez started to choke her while pressing down with both arms. The weight of his upper body added pressure to Gabriella's throat. She attempted to fight back, scratching at his eyes. He cursed while sitting on top of her and pressing down with all his strength. Gabriella could see the flashlight lying there in the sandy grass. She reached for it with her right hand. Taking hold of the flashlight, she slammed the butt end into the left side of Gomez's head. Gabriella struck him a second time. The Mexican removed his right hand from around her throat, punching her in the face. It was a close-fisted punch. Gabriella turned her head in time to avoid the full impact of the blow. But the punch left her dazed, feeling hurt. Gomez had both hands around her throat again. Gabriella felt the life being squeezed out of her. She tried hitting him again with the flashlight. The strength to fight was not there anymore. The flashlight fell from her hand. Gabriella looked up into the dark face hovering over her. She knew that it would be the last thing she would ever see. But there was something. Gabriella saw something more.

Two large arms enclosed Gomez's head lifting the squat Mexican's body high into the air. Gasping for breath, Gabriella stared at the kicking legs and squirming body. One hand was covering Gomez's mouth, while the other hand was pressed against the back of the man's neck. There was no mistaking the loud snapping sound that followed. It resembled a dry tree branch being broken underfoot. But Gabriella knew that it was not a tree branch that she had heard. It was Gomez's neck. She watched the Mexican drop to the ground.

Shadow. Gabriella made out the tall, lean body and shape of his head. She rushed to him. The young woman tripped over Gomez's dead body falling into Shadow's arms. He held her while she pressed against him. She rested her head against his chest. Gabriella heard herself saying over and over again, "Thank God, thank God ..." Tears came. They flowed like water over a breaking dam. Gabriella's body shook as Shadow brought her closer to him. The DEA agent felt the pent up anguish draining out of Gabriella Lopez.

"I can't believe that I'm still alive," Gabriella said not taking her head off his chest. "I wrote him a traffic citation about a month ago and he recognized me. I knew him right off back at Nuevo Laredo, but he didn't know me until now. Shadow, it's been terrible. The women inside the truck have been through hell. They're all drugged out. And I don't even know what day it is or where I am."

"It's Friday. And you're just outside Tallahassee, Florida. Listen Gabriella, it's over. First off, I'm going to take care of that guy sleeping in the truck, and then I'm going to call in the swat team units to help with the women. This whole thing was a mistake. It could have gotten you and the women in the truck killed."

"You mean you're going to end it?"

"That's exactly what I'm going to do."

"You can't. What about my sister?" Gabriella said, pulling away from him. "And those women transported along with her? And all the other women who will be abducted if you don't get the men behind the abductions? You can't end it. There's too many lives at stake."

"This guy's dead. There's no getting around the fact. The other guy sleeping in the truck will definitely become suspicious once he discovers that his partner has been killed. We can't change it. There's nothing left for us to do but to get the women out of here. At least we rescued them and they're safe."

"No. There has to be some way to make it work."

Gabriella picked up the flashlight from the ground. She directed the flashlight's beam toward Gomez's dead body lying at her feet. The Mexican's face bore scratch marks on both cheeks, while traces of blood showed on the front of his white shirt. Gabriella bent down over him.

"I scratched him pretty good. But he was drunk and could have come by those scratches after walking into low hanging tree branches. It could have happened that way."

"And the blood on his shirt? Scratches from tree branches wouldn't have caused that much blood."

Gabriella unbuttoned the front of Gomez's shirt. Lifting one arm at a time, she removed the shirt leaving the dead man's upper body bare-chested. She looked up at Shadow.

"He took the shirt off and dropped it somewhere. He was drunk, walking around and just got rid of his shirt. And when the sun comes up in the morning, his friend in the truck will find his body sitting up against the back wheel of the truck holding a tequila bottle in one hand and the flashlight in the other. It'll look like he was drinking and had a heart attack. Too many women. The guy's ticker just gave out. Shadow, I know it will work."

"Maybe," Shadow said staring down at the flashlight beam lighting up Gomez's impassive face.

"It will," Gabriella insisted. "The guy in the truck won't get paid if he doesn't take the women to where he's supposed to drop them off. That'll make him want to believe a heart attack. And he'll find the truck's back door locked, because you'll have bolt locked it behind me after I've gotten back in. Nobody will think anything of this scumbag dropping dead in the middle of the night."

"Alright, I agree. It's worth a try. We're in Florida and running out of real estate so the abductor's headquarters can't be too far from here. And I'll stay as close to the truck as I can. But right now give me a hand. Grab this guy's legs so we don't leave any drag marks in the sand."

"More than happy to," Gabriella said picking up Gomez's legs and helping Shadow carry the dead body over to the truck.

CHAPTER TWENTY-EIGHT

ANGELA VALADEZ LOOKED down at Frank Book's unconscious body stretched out across her living room sofa. Turk and Tank Thompson had carried Book from the police squad car into Angela's house and then unceremoniously tossed the army ranger captain's body onto the living room sofa. The Thompson twins had been none too gentle in carrying Book. Turk could not pass up the opportunity to place several well placed knee thrusts into Book's vulnerable back. While Tank rammed the man's dangling head into every obstacle that presented itself. Angela had no trouble in determining which brother did what to Book. The Thompsons were no longer identical in appearance. Turk was easily recognizable by his disfigured, broken nose. Angela stood by as Turk brought a right hand up to his bloody nose to only then wipe the blood onto his pants. It left Turk Thompson's right uniform pants leg showing smeared, darkish stains. While the stains on the front of his gray uniform shirt appeared bright red.

"I can't believe this son of a bitch isn't dead already and dumped in the swamp," Turk said after flinging Book onto the sofa.

Angela responded, "He will be as soon as he tells me where the flash drive is. And Turk, I'll help you kill him if you want. What he did to your nose is just awful. It really damages your looks."

"I guess it will leave me the only good-looking one now," Tank laughed while appreciating the concerned look on his twin brother's face. "There's nothing wrong with my nose."

"If you don't keep your fool mouth shut there will be," Turk said before turning around and walking out the front door of Angela Valadez's house. A still laughing Tank Thompson followed his brother out the door while Angela hurried to lock it.

It took twenty-seven stitches to close the gash on the back of Book's head. Cash Wiley's lead sap had left a gaping wound. Angela first took a straight razor to shave the area around the wound before going to work with a needle and thread to suture the nasty gash. Moon Woman had taught her adopted granddaughter well. Angela often assisted the Seminole medicine woman in patching up the residents of Indian Town. The indigent residents had no other place to go after becoming injured. She only wished that Moon Woman was here with her now so the old woman could take a look at Book. The army ranger captain had been unconscious for more than three hours. Angela was getting worried. There could be hemorrhaging on the brain or some other serious malady that she was not aware of. He should be in the hospital under a doctor's care and having his head x-rayed. But that was not going to happen with Bo Wiley running things in Gator's Pond. Book was lucky to be alive, even if it was for only one more day.

Angela was on her way back from the kitchen with more ice for the back of Book's head when she observed him stirring on the sofa. A series of low moans came out of him. His eyes opened and then closed again. Angela put down the ice tray. She took hold of Book's right hand and held it between her two hands. She gently squeezed it.

"Frank wake up. Try to open your eyes and keep them open."

"What?" Book opened his eyes and stared blankly up at Angela who was sitting on the edge of the sofa holding his hand. He tried to rise, but she gently held him down. "Don't try getting up just yet, stay down. You got a nasty whack on the back of your head, and I'm not sure how much damage was done."

"Where am I?" Book asked looking past Angela to the colorful floral paintings on the beige-colored wall. His gaze then quickly shifted to the ceiling fan rotating around and around overhead.

"You're at my house in Indian Town. Frank, you're safe for now so don't worry, just rest for a while and let your head clear before you start trying to move around."

"I don't have time to rest," he said rising up and coming to a sitting position. A wave of dizziness hit him. Book buried his face inside his two hands. "Who hit me and with what?"

"Cash Wiley came up behind you and hit you with a sap."

"I owe him for that one. What else happened? It feels like somebody took a baseball bat to my back."

"Turk Thompson kneed you quite a few times in the back when he and Tank carried you in here. Some of those knots on your head are courtesy of Tank."

"Two sweethearts those two are. Angela what am I doing here? Why didn't Bo Wiley have me killed?"

"I told him that you knew where Father Andy's flash drive was at and if given the chance I could get you to tell me where it was. So he let me bring you here. He's only giving me until tomorrow night to find out, after that they're going to kill you. Frank, do you know where the flash drive is?"

Book stared into Angela's green eyes trying to make sense out of everything that happened. He remembered the fight with Oil Can and his punching Turk Thompson in the nose but nothing much afterward. And now his head was aching, while his lower body felt like one big hurt. And he had this pretty, young woman sitting close asking him about Andy's flash drive. Book could not keep the smile from creeping onto his aching face.

"Is this some kind of bedside manner interrogation that they teach at the police academy? Bring the banged up guy home with you, and he'll tell you everything. Angela, I might have been hit over the head, but I wasn't knocked senseless. Tell Bo and his brother Cash that if they want to ask me something come over and ask it themselves. Don't send a fresh-faced kid with beautiful green eyes to do it for them."

"So that's what you think? I save your life and you throw it right back in my face."

"You just told me that you saved my life in order to get the flash drive. Am I supposed to be grateful for that? Yeah, here's the flash drive baby, now bring back the Thompson twins so they can put a bullet in the back of my head. Lady, you got to be crazy asking me to tell you where the flash drive is. Right now, it looks like that flash drive is the only thing keeping me alive."

"But not for long," Angela said before getting up to walk across the living room's wooden floor to the huge fireplace on the other side of the room. A stack of dried-cut logs rested on the fireplace's brick bottom. While a large black, iron kettle hung suspended above the logs. Angela ducked down inside the fireplace before reaching up with her right hand. Book observed the young woman remove something prior to her walking back to the sofa. She handed him a black leather holder.

"It's my Drug Enforcement Administration identification card along with my photo designating me as a DEA agent. You'll also find a letter stating my date of appointment to the DEA. Look closely and you'll see that it is signed by Jim Garrison who heads the DEA's Special Operations. He recruited me more than a year-and-a-half ago just prior to my graduating from the University of Miami. Bo and Cash wanted a female deputy for the Gator's Pond Police Department hoping that it might help to soften the department's image, especially with everything that has been going on. Garrison knew that the Wiley's wouldn't take an outsider, so he approached me.

"And it didn't take much convincing on his part to get me to take the job. I've despised Bo and Cash Wiley my whole life. I've seen what they've done to people in Indian Town and to anybody else they felt like hurting. If it means anything, your brother Andy is the only other person in Gator's Pond who has seen that identification card. And another thing that you should know. Father Andy broke into Father Miguel's computer and downloaded everything that was on it because I had asked him to do it. I suppose then if you wanted to, you could blame me for getting your brother murdered."

Book stared at the photo identification card while holding it in his right hand. The photograph of a somber looking Angela Valadez was depicted on the card. The title—*Drug Enforcement Agent*—was emblazoned in gold lettering underneath the photograph. It definitely appeared official, but was it? Or was it just some ruse concocted by Bo Wiley to get him to turn over the flash drive? Book tried to get his aching head to work. He had to figure this thing out. The girl appeared genuine. She was standing looking down at him with an expectant expression on her face. Book knew that he would have to say something.

"How do I know this is real? It wouldn't take any time at all to have had this made, and you could've been just waiting for an opportunity like right now to show it to me."

"Now who's the crazy one?" Angela took the black leather holder containing the identification card back from him. "You've only been in Gator's Pond for two days. What did I do run down to the corner Office Max and have someone make it for me? Oh, there is no Office Max in Gator's Pond. Well, maybe then someone at Willie's Bait Shop made it for me. Or Tank Thompson put it together all by himself at the police station. Frank, you looked at it and know damn well that it's official. You had better shake the cobwebs loose and start thinking rationally. We don't have much time."

"All right, I believe you. You told me before about the gun that I had hidden in the shower drain and Bo Wiley finding it. I know him and Cash wouldn't have wanted me to know about that gun being tampered with. So you are a DEA agent. I'm sorry Angela for doubting you. And I want to thank you for saving my neck back there at the Gator's Pond Bar. It's going to take a little while for me to get myself back on track. Right now I feel like there's a freight train running through my head, and it's hard to think straight. What I really need is a stiff drink. Do you have anything?"

"Is Jack Daniels stiff enough?"

"Please," Book said before moving a right hand to the back of his throbbing head. He felt the tight stitches Angela had sewn to close up the wound. The spot was swollen and sore. Book stayed watching her as she walked from the living room into the kitchen. He saw her take a bottle down from an upper cabinet and start pouring him a drink. His gaze took in Angela's short, light brown hair and pretty face along with the green eyes that seemed to grab a hold of whoever gazed too long and hard into them. She was wearing a bright yellow blouse and cropped white pants. The short pants showed off two beautiful, olive-skin legs while accentuating a slender waist and trim figure. Angela caught him looking at her. A smile quickly appeared on the young woman's face. She came back holding a half-filled glass in one hand and a bottle of Jack Daniels in the other. Book took both from her. He drank the half glass of whiskey in one gulp.

"You don't look half bad out of uniform," he said pouring himself another drink from the bottle.

"I'll take that as a compliment."

"It was meant that way. And thanks for the Jack Daniels. I don't remember needing a drink more." She took a chair from across the room and dragged it over to the sofa where she sat down next to him. There was no mistaking the determined look on Angela's face.

"So you want to know about the flash drive?"

She nodded. "Frank, it is imperative that the flash drive gets into the right hands. Where is it?"

"I wish that I could tell you, but I don't know." Book went on to explain how he had come back from Afghanistan to learn that his brother Andy had been murdered, and that Andy had mailed him a letter dated the day before the murder expressing concerns over a certain Father Miguel, an impostor priest. Andy indicated in his letter that the man had a sinister plan that could have devastating consequences for the United States of America. The evidence was all on a flash drive that Andy had downloaded from the phony priest's computer. Book told Angela about Andy's leaving a clue as to where he had hidden the flash drive, and that it concerned the Blessed Mother. The location of the flash drive had something to do with her.

"Is that why you were checking out the statues in the church?"

"So you saw me. Yes, I looked over the Marian statues for some kind of compartment or hidden space that might contain the flash drive, but there was nothing."

"What could Father Andy have done with it? Frank, Father Miguel's real name is Bernardo Arellano and he's the leader of a Mexican cartel called the Black Spiders. Bo and Cash Wiley give him and the cartel sanctuary here in Gator's Pond. Abducted women are brought in from Mexico and then flown out of the country where they are sold on the black market. Middle Eastern heroin is then brought back into the United States, and the cartel sells it for millions of dollars. It has been going on for more than two years. Bo and Cash had a DEA agent murdered after they had discovered he was passing himself off as an indigent field hand hanging out in Indian Town. They killed him and threw his body somewhere in the swamp."

"Who killed Andy?"

"Bernardo did after first torturing him for hours in trying to find out what your brother had done with the flash drive containing the information downloaded from Bernardo's computer. Whatever was on it has something to do with the July fourth date. That's all Bernardo and Bo Wiley talk about. Frank, we have to find that flash drive."

"Angela, why doesn't the DEA just come in and arrest Bo Wiley and his brother Cash and take Bernardo in for killing my brother? I don't understand the delay."

"The DEA doesn't know where the abducted women are being held before they're taken out of the country. That is what I've been trying to find out. It has to be some place deep in the swamp. If we could produce the women, Bo and Cash Wiley wouldn't have a leg to stand on in court. Right now there is only my testimony without anything concrete to back it up. But the flash drive could change things. It could be rock solid evidence tying the Wiley brothers in with the Black Spiders cartel and the murder of Father Andy."

"And along with the man Turk and Tank hanged with the guy's own belt in the jail cell."

"Yes, Charlie Steed's murder too."

"And what about phoning out of Gator's Pond on a cellphone?" Book asked her. "I keep getting no signal every time I try calling out."

"The signal has been jammed for quite some time now. Bo Wiley doesn't want anyone phoning in or out of Gator's Pond. The only land-based phone still operable is at the police station, and Cash has complete control over its use. The church rectory lines were cut the night before Father Andy was murdered, so right now we have no way of reaching the outside. I haven't been able to talk to Jim Garrison for several days. I haven't been able to inform him that Bernardo is the leader of the Black Spiders cartel. That means the

DEA is unaware that a Mexican cartel is in full operation here in Gator's Pond. Frankly, I don't know what to do next."

"Well, I do," Book said pouring himself another drink and easing his hurting body back onto the sofa. "We finish off this bottle of Jack Daniels and call it a night."

CHAPTER TWENTY-NINE

CASEY BLURMEISTER SHOOK his head, a big smile coming to his face. He and Vince Dewitt were presently engaged in a competitive eighteen rounds of golf with two excellent players at a prestigious country club just outside of Washington D.C. One thousand dollars rested on which pair turned in the lower score. They were on the eighteenth hole. DeWitt had just driven his tee shot into a hazard area rendering the chance of finding his ball highly unlikely.

"Found it, guys," Dewitt yelled to the other team after having slipped a ball out of his pants pocket to drop onto a flat piece of ground. Casey had all to do to keep himself from laughing out loud. Leave it to Vince, he thought. Losing was never an option, not for his lifetime chum. Even when they were kids back in Boston, and Vince was going for high school class president. Bobby Dickerson was giving him stiff competition but even then losing never came into play. A false rumor of Bobby being gay suddenly sprang up. It spread like wild fire throughout the entire school. Vince ended up winning the class presidency in a landslide, while Bobby didn't even get a date to the senior prom.

"Vince, nice shot," Casey Blurmeister heard himself say after seeing DeWitt put the ball within three feet of the hole on his next swing of the club. "Partner, it looks like we win again." Still smiling, Casey added, "Nice game fellas. I guess we were just lucky today."

After the golf game the two friends stopped for a late morning beer at the club lounge. They took the two bar stools at the very end of the bar. DeWitt handed five one-hundred-dollar bills to Blurmeister who put the money in his front pants pocket. Satisfied grins were spread across both men's faces.

"Easiest five hundred I ever made," Casey said before taking a swig of beer. "Vince, I can't stay for another one, I got a hot date."

"Wait a minute buddy boy, whose this one now?" Dewitt asked laughing. "Is it that brunette you met the other night at Kelly's pub? She looked about nineteen and not a day older."

"Lisa is twenty-three and a legal secretary for some lobbyist. No, this dolly is the one I met a couple of years ago at the bar next to my place. She's from out of town and comes here on business a few times a year. Whenever she does we get together for a quick afternoon romp, and that's it. I like it that way. There's no wining and dining bullshit like you have to do with most of these broads. I think she's married, so it works out nice for her, too."

"I don't want to get in the way of your love life, but what's going on with the Operation Silverback brief that you were supposed to have given me no later than yesterday?"

"It's at my place. I finished it last night. It'll be on your desk first thing in the morning. How's that?"

"Fine, just make sure that it is because I will be hand-carrying that brief over to the Senate Committee on Homeland Security right after I have read it over. Now get going. I don't want to stand between you and your hot date."

"Thanks Vince, I'll see you tomorrow."

"Just make sure that I also see that brief along with you," the smiling U.S. Attorney for the Southern District of Florida said as he watched his chief investigator and best friend hurry out of the club lounge door.

****

Casey Blurmeister took a deep breath. And he took another in an attempt to get his breathing under control. The afternoon romp had proven to be a wild one indeed. He looked over at the blond-haired, blue-eyed woman lying naked on the bed next to him. The rising and lowering of her round, dark-nipple breasts captivated him. She too breathed heavily. She was looking at Blurmeister through two large blue eyes. The woman's facial expression resembled that of a wounded animal waiting to be attacked all over again.

"It's a good thing you only get to town a few times a year otherwise you'd be the death of me," Blurmeister said getting out of the bed.

"You should workout more," she said to him smiling.

Casey shook his head. The chief investigator let loose with an amused chuckle. Never before had he encountered a woman like her. She was absolutely gorgeous lying there naked on the bed. Enticing, challenging, everything he could want. She was now daring him to mount her again. If he was man enough. *Come and take me if you are man enough,* she seemed to be saying. But he knew that he would not. There was nothing left in him. Casey turned his back on her. He walked naked into the bathroom. Soon the sound of a running shower could be heard. The woman quickly got out of the bed.

Casey Blurmeister had one foot inside the bathroom shower when the thought struck him. He would ask her to join him. And see then if he had anything more left. Grinning like a kid sneaking cookies, Casey went into the bedroom. And to his surprise found the bed empty. Where could she have gone? The door to his office was partially open. He moved toward it, pushing on the wooden frame. The door opened. Casey saw her.

She was sitting naked, cross-legged in his desk chair reading the Operation Silverback brief. Showing a deadpan expression, she looked up at him as though he had caught her reading some monthly periodical or yesterday's newspaper. He froze not quite comprehending at first. But then the realization came to him. Everything appeared so clear. Garrison and the leak and his haphazardly meeting her two years ago in the bar next to his residence. And then of course the missing agent presumed dead at Gator's Pond.

"Who are you?" he finally was able to get out while moving toward her.

"Why your lover, of course," she said springing out of the chair. She drove the ball point pen deep into the left side of Casey Blurmeister's neck. He screamed, grasping at his neck. She drove the pen deeper. Blood gushed out over both their naked bodies. He fell to the floor. She grabbed the brief and hurried to the bedroom. Ripping the top sheet off the bed, the woman wiped away the blood covering her breasts and stomach. She dressed quickly. The blood-stained brief was on the floor. Reaching down, she picked it up. While not bothering to look back, the blond-haired woman ran out the apartment's front door.

Casey squirmed through the thick puddles of his own blood. He pulled the desktop phone down onto the floor. A quivering finger punched the numbers 9-1-1 into the phone. The sound of ringing followed. Then there was the emergency operator's voice, "You have reached 9-1-1, what is your emergency?" But Blurmeister did not respond. He never heard the ringing of the phone. Nor had he heard the emergency operator's voice. He was dead.

CHAPTER THIRTY

DEA'S SPECIAL OPERATIONS Head Jim Garrison had received the phone call less than thirty minutes ago. Already his black Lincoln was through the CIA security gate and pulling up to the Langley headquarters building. Two uniform guards displaying automatic pistols on their belts stood attentively on either side of the main entrance doors. The meeting was to take place in the most secure room at CIA headquarters. It was nicknamed the *vault*. And it was so named for a good reason. The 25 by 30 foot room consisted of several feet of reinforced steel—ceiling, walls, and floor—all quite impregnable. Standard operating procedure called for the enclosed area to be debugged or checked for listening devices on the half-hour. The room had been constructed to secure all meetings relative to top secret planning and CIA terrorist counter offensives. Garrison had been invited to the *vault* on only one other occasion. That was immediately following the September 11, 2001 terrorist attacks on New York City and Washington D.C. So the DEA Special Operations Head knew that the upcoming meeting with the CIA's Director of National Clandestine Service (NCS) had to be of extreme importance. Something inside Garrison's gut warned him that this was not going to be a pleasant meeting.

"Jim good to see you again. I just wish it was under better circumstances."

"Jack, it's that bad? I knew it would be," Garrison said while looking at fifty-three-year-old Jack Ross. The man appeared thin as a rail with hair once shiny black now almost entirely gray and receding in the front. Ross's left hand rested at his hip. His pale-blue eyes stared hard at Garrison from the other side of the long gray metal table which separated them. The two men were alone in the *vault*. Just being there had Garrison's stomach tied up in knots. He knew that it partially had to do with his being in the same room with a legend like Jack Ross. It took a lot for Jim Garrison to respect a man. He barely tolerated most men. But he had respect and then some when it came to Ross. The armless right sleeve on Ross's white shirt told it all as far as Garrison was concerned.

In 1992, then CIA field operative Jack Ross was in southern Lebanon working closely with Israel's intelligence agency, Mossad, in combating the terrorist group Hezbollah. Four years earlier Hezbollah members had captured, tortured, and murdered U.S. Lieutenant Colonel William Higgins. Higgins had been in Lebanon on a United Nations' peacekeeping mission when he was killed. Israel's Mossad uncovered information linking Abbas al-Musawi, Hezbollah's secretary general to the lieutenant colonel's abduction and murder. The Israelis were also able to connect al-Musawi to the bombing attack earlier that year on the Israeli embassy in Buenos Aires, Argentina, where twenty-nine people were killed. Mossad acted quickly. While driving on a dirt road in southern Lebanon, Abbas al-Musawi's car exploded after being struck by a fired missile. The Hezbollah Secretary General died instantly. Two days later Hezbollah security forces caught up to Jack Ross. The CIA field operative was attempting to leave the country under a travel visa identifying him as a professor of geology from the University of Chicago.

Hezbollah tortured Ross for two weeks in an underground bunker outside the town of Hasbaya in southern Lebanon. They used a chain saw on his fingers. One finger at a time was cut off. A hot metal poker was used to stop the bleeding. Ross would pass out from the pain only to be quickly revived. The methodical cutting would then begin again. Eventually, Ross's entire right arm had been cut away inch by inch. The CIA agent refused to tell his torturers anything. They had wanted an admission connecting the CIA and Mossad to the assassination of Abbas al-Musawi. But Ross would not come off his cover story of being a professor of geology from the University of Chicago. Two years after his capture Jack Ross was released in a prisoner exchange deal between Israel and Lebanon.

Thereafter, Ross rose through ranks of the CIA. He gained a reputation as being a no-nonsense, hard-nosed, uncompromising task master who would defend the United States of American no matter what the cost to himself or to anyone else. He became both loved and hated within the clandestine community. Jim Garrison sided with the former.

"Jim, we got one hell of a mess on our hands, and I'm using the word 'we' because it is going to take both the DEA and CIA working together to get this country out of the trouble that it is in. Otherwise there is going to more pain in store for the United States than it has ever experienced before on the home front. I'm talking about losing thousands of innocent lives, not to mention an economy wrecked so badly that it might not ever recover. That's why I wanted to talk to you face to face without a bunch of candy-ass bureaucrats getting in the way. That also means the FBI. I didn't want them getting involved with their prima donna-everybody else-can-go-to-hell-attitude. Besides they'd just mess things up anyway."

Ross motioned for Garrison to take a seat at the table across from him. The CIA director then turned on a tabletop computer and began banging away at the keyboard. Something quickly flashed up on the computer screen. Satisfied, Ross turned the screen so Garrison could get a better view.

"This photograph was taken just under four hours ago by a CIA surveillance team that has been watching Casey Blurmeister's Maryland apartment. I know that you are familiar with Blurmeister and DeWitt so let me get on with this. The woman with the blond hair is leaving Blurmeister's apartment building by way of the front door entrance. Take a good look at her, especially as to what she is wearing. Later on you will know why I am asking you to do it. Just so you know, immediately after the surveillance team took this photograph, our woman got into a leased auto parked down the street from Blurmeister's apartment and drove off. The car checked out to a Patti M. Smith of Miami, Florida. She happened to be the same Patti M. Smith who was on a flight to Miami, Florida out of Dulles International Airport a little more than an hour after this photograph was taken."

"Who is she to Casey Blurmeister?" Garrison asked while staring at the computer screen. He observed the blond-haired woman dressed in a yellow blouse and white slacks holding a brown folder in her left hand. The black strap of the woman's handbag rested across her right shoulder.

"She's the person who killed Blurmeister, probably minutes before this photograph was taken."

Garrison almost fell out of his chair. The somber look on Ross's face sent chills through the DEA's Head of Special Operations. Garrison looked once more to the woman in the photo before returning again to Ross. It was difficult for him to get the words out.

"You're saying she killed Casey Blurmeister no more than four hours ago? How?"

"She stabbed him in the neck with a ball point pen. He bled to death. Blurmeister was able to phone 911 before he died and that's how my people were able to get on it rather quickly. Less than thirty minutes ago I had a talk with Vince DeWitt. He told me that Blurmeister had met the woman a couple of years ago in the bar next to his apartment building, and that he's been seeing her off and on for afternoon sex. We've been watching Blurmeister for some time now ever since your agent came up missing in Gator's Pond. Like you, we also suspected a leak. I should come clean with you, Jim. The CIA knows all about Operation Silverback and Operation Rescue and has known about both operations since their inceptions. Our two agencies have similar interests when it comes to Bo Wiley and Gator's Pond. And like you, we also have an agent on the ground."

Garrison sat back in his chair. He ran a right hand across his face. It took a lot to get him shook up but Ross had done so. Garrison tried to reflect on how this new turn in events could affect Operations Silverback and Rescue. He also wondered about what possible interest the CIA could have in his cases. Garrison looked across the table at Ross's craggy, sunken face. The man's light blue eyes seemed penetrating, having a hard glint to them. Garrison felt as though they were probing his mind with their hardness.

"What's the CIA's interest in Bo Wiley and Gator's Pond?" Garrison asked.

Ross typed something into the computer keyboard. Instantly the head and shoulder photograph of a man wearing a military uniform appeared on the screen. The man had thick black hair and a dark brown complexion with bushy eyebrows hanging down over two black marble-sized eyes. The eyes seemed dead. They appeared empty like the expression on the man's face. Garrison thought the person in the photo looked to be in his mid-forties while the gold braids on his uniform seemed consistent with someone having a military ranking.

"You're looking at Colonel Arash Hosseini who heads Iran's foreign intelligence unit within The Ministry of Intelligence and Security, better known to those on the inside as MOIS. He is a Shiite, and the absolute best the Iranians have when it comes to subterfuge and acts of terror. We became acquainted twenty years ago when he was a young Iranian intelligence officer on loan to Hezbollah. Jim take a good look at him. And don't ever forget his face. We've been tracking Colonel Hosseini, who also goes by the code name Black Spider, across the better part of the globe for the past three years. He's been setting up networks of Iranian agents in various locales, sleeper agents I call them. They become a part of whatever country they are in for the sole purpose of later committing a terrorist act whenever called upon to do so. Colonel Hosseini is presently doing his dirty work in Gator's Pond. You may know him by the name of Father Miguel Santiago or perhaps Bernardo Arellano."

"In Gator's Pond? You mean this Colonel Hosseini has something to do with Bo and Cash Wiley, and the narcotics set-up and the women sold into slavery? Are you telling me the Iranian government is involved in Operations Silverback and Rescue?"

"Yes. And a great deal more. The worst fear our government has always entertained was for some enemy foreign power to align itself with a Mexican cartel and gain a foothold within the borders of the United States. That has now happened. Colonel Hosseini has been successful in setting up his own Mexican cartel, calling it the *Arañas Negras,* and using Iranian money to buy off the Los Zetas down in Nuevo Laredo, Mexico. That has enabled him to create a land base within striking distance of the U.S. He has been smuggling hundreds of Iranian agents, disguised as undocumented Mexicans, across the border into Texas and then dispersing them throughout the United States. Cities like New York, Chicago, Los Angeles and many others have welcomed them with open arms refusing to check their legal status because it might offend the Mexican community. Now those cities have a big problem."

"Does this have anything to do with the priest's flash drive and the July fourth date? The last correspondence I had with my agent in Gator's Pond, and before Bo Wiley began jamming the cell phones, was that the priest's missing flash drive contained some kind of plan that concerned the fourth of July."

"That's right. And that's why we want that flash drive so badly. Jim, I am going to tell you something that can't leave this room. There are fifty Iranian suicide bombers presently outside of Havana, Cuba waiting to board a plane so they can be flown into Gator's Pond. From there they will be transported to Miami and given documentation along with airline and bus tickets to take them to various locations throughout the United States. Colonel Hosseini plans for them to activate bombs in designated crowded places simultaneously on July fourth. Thousands of Americans will be killed, not to mention the thousands who will be left maimed and injured."

Garrison's face turned ashen. Both of his hands tightly gripped the tabletop. He had been concerned about Operation Silverback and Operation Rescue prior to this meeting with Jack Ross. But now a far greater concern consumed the DEA Head of Special Operations. The safe-keeping of his country was at stake. He knew that such a strike by Iran at the underbelly of the U.S. would have a devastating effect on the country as a whole. It would leave its people paralyzed with fear.

Garrison said, "You're not going to let suicide bombers into the country. You can't. There has to be some way to stop them."

"The plane will never get off the ground. The fifty Iranian suicide bombers are as good as dead. They are not our concern. It's Colonel Hosseini's Plan B that we have to worry about. He must have one. Once Hosseini has received word that his suicide bombers have been killed he will most certainly activate Plan B, which could mean Iranian agents shooting and killing people in shopping malls, schools, supermarkets, you name it. We have to know who and where his agents are. If not, once the suicide bombers are taken out we could end up with a bloodbath in this country."

"Jack, why are you telling me all this? What possible help could the DEA give you? There is nothing we can do to help. If there is something I'm missing just tell me and I'll do whatever I can."

"Abort Operation Silverback and Operation Rescue. That's why I set up this meeting. I want the DEA out of the picture without any interference. I don't want Colonel Hosseini getting spooked by your people where it might cause him to jump the gun and go right to Plan B. Jim, I need time right now. I'm asking you to abort both your missions."

CHAPTER THIRTY-ONE

GARRISON TURNED HIS head to the side. He tried to think. He had to evaluate, to frame out what the ramifications Jack Ross's proposal would have on Operations Silverback and Rescue. Especially after the many months of planning that he and the others had put forth to ensure both plans successful outcomes. He also had to take into consideration the DEA agents on the ground. How would they be affected by both missions suddenly being aborted? Garrison thought of Agent Roy Peterson who gave his life in Operation Silverback. Would he be betraying Peterson's memory and every other hardworking DEA agent if he just cancelled everything and pulled his people out?

"What about Bo Wiley?" Garrison asked before returning to Jack Ross's unrelenting gaze. "Do he and his brother Cash just skate on all that they've done? They killed one of my people along with a Catholic priest and who knows how many others. Not to mention all the innocent women they've helped your Colonel Hosseini sell into a lifetime of slavery. If I abort, what happens to those two sons-of-bitches?"

"Once Colonel Hosseini and his Iranians have been dealt with the Wiley brothers will be all yours. You're welcome to them. They have made it possible for Hosseini to establish his base inside the

U.S. all because of their greed, accumulating a lot of money over the past two years. But Jim, if you agree to abort Operations Silverback and Rescue, it has to be done now and stopped completely. That means pulling your swat teams off the panel truck that is nearing Gator's Pond as we speak. The women in the truck will have to be left on their own, and that includes the female Laredo police officer working undercover inside the truck. There's a high probability that she and the other women will be flown out of the country and never be heard from again. But we have no other choice. Any hint of federal agents descending on Gator's Pond right now could very well cause Colonel Hosseini to push the button and start Plan B. That would be catastrophic. I'm sorry, but that is the way it has to be."

"How about my agent on the ground in Gator's Pond? You said earlier that you have someone there. Could you help me get her out before everything blows up?"

Ross shook his head. The CIA director could feel Garrison's anguish. He had been there in similar situations. It never gets any easier when it comes down to making the tough choices.

"Again Jim, I'm sorry. Angela Valadez and Captain Frank Book are most probably dead now anyway. And even if they are not, I couldn't take a chance on having my agent compromised at this time. It would be too dangerous."

Garrison asked him. "What makes you believe they are dead?"

The CIA director went once more to the computer keyboard. A new picture showed on the monitor screen. The black-and-white photo still appeared grainy, nowhere near the high quality of the earlier-shown color photographs. This photo depicted the same blond-haired woman who had been seen earlier leaving Casey's Blurmeister's apartment building after he had been killed.

"A Miami airport security camera took this photograph sometime after Patti M. Smith's Washington D.C. flight landed in Miami. You can see it's the same woman. Remember I asked you to pay attention to what she was wearing. I know you can't tell colors from this photo, but it's the same blouse and slacks, and there's the handbag carried over her right shoulder, and the folder in her left hand. You can also see that she's entering an airport women's restroom. Do you agree with me that it is the same woman seen in the earlier photograph?"

"Yes, I do. It's the same woman."

"All right then, I'm going to fast forward about fifteen minutes to about here. See her. She's coming out of the women's restroom wearing the same clothes and carrying the same handbag and folder, but look at her hair."

"It's no longer blond. Her hair is a dark color now and her face looks different somehow."

"It's her eyes. She had blue contacts in before and took them out. Now her eyes are dark brown, their natural color. She rinsed the blond coloring out of her hair in the women's restroom and took out the blue eye contacts. Her name is Maria Carrera. She's Colonel Hosseini's Mexican lover and called upon murderess whenever he wants her to fulfill that role. She's a treacherous bitch if there ever was one. She's the reason why I feel your agent Angela Valadez and Captain Book are now dead."

"How so? What does this Carrera woman have to do with Agent Valadez?"

"The brown folder she's carrying in the photograph was stolen from Casey Blurmeister's apartment. It contains the entire file pertaining to Operation Silverback. Agent Valadez has been compromised. By now Bo Wiley and Colonel Hosseini know that she is a DEA agent. Jim, those are the facts, and I hate to be the one that has to show them to you."

"How do you know it's the Silverback file?" Garrison asked coming out his chair. There was a twisted look to the DEA man's face. Ross felt as though he were seeing a pit bull whose heavy metal chain had been removed. It was now poised and ready to attack.

"Dewitt told me in our phone conversation that he had instructed Blurmeister to put together a brief regarding Operation Silverback so that he, DeWitt, could bring it before the Senate Committee on Homeland Security. He asked me if it was in Blurmeister's apartment, and after I told him that it was not, we both knew then that Carrera must have taken it."

"The dirty bastard. He was to keep that file under lock and key. Right now I could have another dead agent in Gator's Pond. Jack, I'm sorry, but I've got to go."

Garrison started toward the door but stopped prior to reaching it. Turning around, he faced Jack Ross once again. There was no concealing the pain in Garrison's face.

"We'll do it your way. As of right now both Operation Silverback and Operation Rescue are being aborted." Without saying anything more, Garrison walked out the door.

CHAPTER THIRTY-TWO

JOE TORRES, CODE name Shadow, drove the black sedan southbound on I-75. He realized that soon the white panel truck would reach the outskirts of the Florida Everglades. That was the truck's destination. Torres was almost certain of it. He ignored the call for him on the portable transmitter radio. He chose instead to stare straight ahead. Intermittently, he would glance down at the steady blink coming from the tracking monitor on the passenger seat next to him. He told himself Gabriella Lopez was close, no more than three miles ahead. She was still locked inside the back of the truck with the other abducted women.

Earlier that day just after sunrise, Jose Herrera had awakened to find Caesar Gomez's shirtless, dead body resting against the truck's rear wheel. Gomez was holding a bottle of tequila in one hand and a flashlight in the other. Herrera tried shaking his friend but soon came to realize that Gomez was dead. The Mexican mule for the Arañas Negras cartel immediately unlocked the back of the truck to check on the women inside. He counted them all using a pointed finger. Torres watched from behind a clump of bushes. He appreciated the man's predicament while at the same time hoping that the Mexican did not look too closely at Gomez. Torres did not want Herrera to discover that his partner's neck had been broken. The DEA agent observed

Herrera shut and lock the truck's back door before looking around to see if anyone might be in the area watching. It was as Gabriella had said it would be. The man wanted his money. And the only way he could get it was if the women were delivered. Herrera got in the driver's side of the truck, started it up, and drove off. He left Caesar's Gomez's dead body lying in the sandy grass under a stand of tall pine trees.

"Agent Torres, do you read me? Operation Rescue has been aborted. The swat teams have been recalled and you are to stand down. All personnel assigned to Operation Rescue are ordered to stand down. Do you read Agent Torres?"

Torres ignored the command like he had been doing for the past two hours. He did not acknowledge the order from his district supervisor. Instead he continued to stare down the road in front of him. What could they possibly be thinking? Abort Operation Rescue. What about the women in the white truck who were no more than three miles ahead? What about Gabriella Lopez? Torres looked to the tracking monitor. The light was still blinking. She was still there. The flashing light told him so. Perspiration wet his forehead. Torres started to feel clammy all over. Then Anna's smiling face came to him. Torres saw the flashy brown eyes. He heard the carefree laugh.

"No Anna, not at this time," Torres had told her. "We have enough incriminating evidence on the Los Zetas to put some of their top people away for a long time. Besides that they must be getting suspicious after the DEA hit both their major suppliers only last week."

"Joe, they don't suspect me. If I thought they did I wouldn't go back to the restaurant and put myself in that kind of danger. I just have to be there when they go over their plans for the next shipment. It will be the largest one ever. It could be more than all of the others combined."

Torres's gut told him no. Don't let her go. It was too dangerous. Besides the operation was already a success so why push things? He had everything he had hoped for and then some. He even had all of DEA headquarters in Washington D.C. buzzing over what he had sent them. Word through the grapevine had it that a big promotion was in the works for him because of his role in spearheading the operation. Torres wanted to tell Anna no. But a shipment of Mexican heroin as large as what she was describing rarely came on the DEA's radar. And if it was seized coming into the U.S., it would receive a tremendous amount of attention in Washington D.C. And so would the agent in charge who supervised the seizure. Torres told Anna yes.

Early the next morning Torres received word from Anna. It came in the usual manner. He casually entered the small plaza in Nuevo Laredo at the intersection of Monterrey and Anahuac streets. Lifting up the plaza flower pot, he retrieved her note. The DEA agent in charge immediately recognized Anna's handwriting. The note instructed him to come to the Colosio Boulevard Bridge without delay. Torres was familiar with the location because he and Anna had met on a number of occasions under the Colosio Boulevard Bridge. He knew that whatever she wanted to see him about had to be extremely important. Anna would not have told him to meet her there otherwise.

A bright morning sun shone down making it difficult to see. Joe Torres had to shade his eyes using his right hand. He walked closer to get a better look. Something was hanging down from the bridge overpass. The DEA agent in charge could not make out what it was until he was almost directly underneath it. It was then that Torres recognized Anna's battered face. He saw her protruding tongue. And the rope wrapped around her neck. A piece of cardboard attached to Anna's ripped white blouse had something written on it. "Dead Americano agent," it read. Joe Torres stood underneath Anna's body for two hours. It took that long before someone could come to help him take her down.

"Agent Torres, do you read this transmission? Operation Rescue has been cancelled and aborted. You are hereby ordered to stand down. Acknowledge this transmission. Agent Torres, do you read me?"

Joe Torres reached over and turned off the transmitter radio. He had tried everything but the guilty feeling never seemed to leave him. Anna's tortured face always came back. There was no escape from what he had done. Using the palm of his right hand, the DEA agent in charge wiped the tears out of his eyes.

CHAPTER THIRTY-THREE

THE SOFT BREEZE coming through the screened-in lanai felt good to Book. Especially after the early afternoon heat had made his entire body feel clammy, wet all over. Book shifted in the wicker chair and reached for the glass of water on the table next to him. Angela's 9mm. Glock rested on his lap. The gun budged slightly with the movement of his body. He put his left hand over it. The army ranger captain knew Bo Wiley would be arriving at any time with his small army of mercenaries. And then the battle would begin. Angela did her best in trying to get him to leave.

"It won't just be Turk and Tank Thompson coming for you," she had said to him. A hint of concern accompanied by an edge of nervousness permeated her smooth, olive-skin face. "Bo will send ten or fifteen armed men with orders to shoot you and dump your dead body in the swamp so no one will ever find it. Frank, you still have time to get away. I can take you to Miami in the police car before they come here to kill you. Or you can just take it yourself. I will tell them you overpowered me and got the keys from me. It's the only chance you have."

"Angela, we went over this before and I said no then and I'm saying no now. I'm not running from the likes of Bo Wiley and that slime ball Bernardo. They killed my brother, and they're going to pay for it. And as long as I have this gun and two full ammo clips, I am more than happy to take on whatever Bo Wiley might want to throw at me."

The conversation had taken place after he had awakened feeling sore and stiff all over. His head still ached but not nearly as bad as the night before. He had spent the night on the living room sofa tossing and turning, trying to find a comfortable position. Angela woke him shortly before sunrise to a cooked breakfast—eggs over with ham and diced potatoes, the potatoes fried hard the way he liked them, along with buttered rye toast and plenty of hot black coffee. The coffee was strong tasting like he preferred it. So strong it shook loose the cobwebs inside his head and opened half-closed eyelids. It enabled him to see clearly Angela's smiling face and bright green eyes.

She had on a light blue top and cream-colored long pants. The pants legs touched dark brown sandals opened at the toe. She wore no socks. Book smiled back at her. He immediately experienced the ache to his bruised face. And along with it something more. He felt the urge to reach up and take Angela into his arms, to kiss her and bring her down onto the sofa with him. It was the greenness of her eyes that brought on the urge, he told himself. There was also the smooth delicateness of her face. And the fact that he had spent the last two years fighting the Taliban in the remote mountains of Afghanistan where he could only dream of a woman as beautiful as her. That is what Book was thinking, but he knew there was more. There was something else about this woman that got to him. And it had nothing to do with her pretty smile and attractive body. He chalked it up to the intangible that one person detects in another. The hidden something that is not seen but only felt. And no matter how hard he tried Book could not figure out what it was about Angela Valadez that drew him to her.

"So what am I to do? Just stand by and watch them kill you?" Angela asked after seeing him get up from the sofa and come to a standing position. "I won't do it. I'm going to bring the police car around to the front of the house and you are going to get in it. Frank, I am speaking as a DEA agent now. I am ordering you to leave Gator's Pond immediately. There will be no further discussion, you are going."

He looked at her and said nothing. Angela's face showed her anger. She moved in the direction of the back door. It did not take long before Book heard the back door slamming shut behind her. The army ranger captain sat down again settling his still hurting body onto the sofa. He questioned his decision about staying to face Bo Wiley's men. Book wondered if it was nothing more than foolish pride on his part. Or if it truly was the right thing for him to do. He did not have time to come up with an answer. An out of breath Angela suddenly came back into the house. She had a panicked look on her face.

"They cut the battery cables on the squad car. It had to have been done sometime late last night when we were both asleep. Frank, there is no way out now. They'll be coming for you."

"Let them come. I'll make sure some of them wish they hadn't."

"But they'll kill you, too. If there was only some other way. We could try the swamp but without a boat they would be on us in no time."

"Forget the 'we' part. You get out of here and stay away until it's over. Angela, don't get yourself involved in my trouble. Tell Bo Wiley you tried, but I wouldn't give up the flash drive. You can even tell him that you played up to me, and I fell head over heels for you. That I spent the night with you and I told you that I loved you. Tell him whatever you want."

Angela's face lit up. Any trace of panic was gone. She stood, staring into Book's dark blue eyes, steeling herself so as not to give into the moment. His words had stoked embers deep within her. Did he mean any of it? Was there something behind the words he had just spoken? *"That I spent the night with you, and I told you that I loved you."* Angela peered into his upturned face. She wished to know the mind of the man now looking so intently at her.

"Do you really want me to say that? To tell Bo Wiley you said that you loved me?"

"Yes."

"Well, I won't tell Bo Wiley anything because I am not leaving you. I'll give you my gun and the two ammo clips. I can be of some help when they come because none of them will suspect me. They will still believe that I am on their side so I might be able to get close. Close enough to get one of their guns."

"Angela, you'll end up getting yourself killed. Leave now and let me handle this thing. It's what I have been trained for. It's what I'm good at. You'd only be in my way, probably getting me killed right along with you. So get out of here before it's too late."

Angela walked away without saying anything. Book knew that she was not going to leave. There was a stubborn streak in her and he could do nothing to change it. Strangely enough he found himself attracted to her all the more.

****

Book took another drink from the water glass. His gaze remained fixed on the dirt road leading up to the front of the house. It had rained overnight. The road was puddled over. The overnight rain would make it easy for him to spot them. Their cars would come splashing through the water and no dust would be raised to obstruct his line of fire. He would also be able to hear them well before they came into view. That would give him plenty of warning. He would have more than enough time to go out and meet them. Book settled back in the wicker chair, relaxing his sore muscles. The army ranger captain readied his mind for what was soon to come.

The thought of his brother Andy came to him. Book reached into his front pants pocket for the photo that he had found in Andy's bedroom. It was the photograph taken back in Detroit when they were both kids. Their mother had taken it. Andy's rosary beads came out with the photo.

Book held the beads in his right hand. He thought about the countless times Andy must have held the same beads while praying the rosary. Even while growing up, Andy was always a good one for praying the rosary, he remembered. His younger brother harbored a strong devotion to the Blessed Mother. He would pray the rosary daily. Book opened his hand to look down at the beads. They were rounded, brown in color with a brown wooden crucifix depicting the figure of the crucified Christ. The army ranger captain looked closely at the Christ figure, touching the wooden crucifix with his fingertips. There was something odd about it. Not that Book was any expert on crucifixes. Unlike Andy, he had not prayed the rosary nearly as much. Using the edge of his right forefinger, Book ran it along the sides of the cross. He stopped only after feeling the protruding metal. That was when he knew. It was unambiguous in its clarity. As though Andy had whispered it to him leaving no room for doubt. That the crucifix he was holding in his right hand contained Andy's flash drive. Book had in his possession the reason behind his brother's murder.

CHAPTER THIRTY-FOUR

"FRANK THIS CHANGES everything," Angela said after she had heard him yell for her to come out to the lanai. "We have to get this flash drive to Jim Garrison in Washington D.C. With it the DEA can bring down Bo and Cash Wiley and their whole rotten operation. There also must be something very important on it involving Bernardo and whatever he has planned for July fourth, because he wants it terribly."

"But how? I can't walk from here to Miami to catch a plane to Washington D. C. There has to be some way of getting a car."

Angela told him. "You could hide along the side of the road and when they come into the house I could stall them. It would give you enough time to take one of their cars. That is if they leave the keys behind in the car."

"That's a big 'if.' If there is no ignition key then we're right back where we started."

"We have to do something because they will be here soon. I actually thought they would have been here by now. Frank, what else can we do?"

The knock at the back door brought Book out of the wicker chair and standing with the Glock in his right hand. He motioned for Angela to get into the bedroom off the lanai. She shook her head no.

"Turk and Tank Thompson wouldn't knock. Besides we would have seen them driving up to the front of the house. It has to be someone else. I have no idea who it could be other than perhaps someone from Indian Town. People come by here from time to time looking for a handout. I'll go and see who it is."

Angela returned in less than a minute with her right arm draped around Yellow Flower, Bo Wiley's mistress. Book observed closely the thinly-built, young woman. She sported fresh bruises on both sides of her face. Her dark eyes darted from Angela to Book back to Angela again. Yellow Flower appeared nervous. She displayed every indication of not wanting to be there. She was dressed in a plain green blouse, faded-brown shorts, and no shoes while her long black hair fell back in a shoulder-length ponytail. The ponytail was held together by a single yellow ribbon.

"What is she doing here?" Book asked before glancing once more at the road leading up to front of the house.

Angela said, "Yellow Flower can tell you herself. Go ahead sweetie, tell him."

"They will be coming for you in one hour. I heard Bo Wiley tell the Thompsons to get some men together and for them to come here and kill you. He also told them to kill Angela because the Carrera woman told him that Angela works for the DEA. I brought a canoe and left it in the swamp down by the big cypress tree. If you leave now you will have enough time to get away from them. But Bo Wiley will send someone after you."

"Who will he send?" Book asked while looking at Yellow Flower's battered face and her blazing dark eyes. He could not help but witness the presence of fear in the young woman.

"Bo Wiley will send Panther and his two cousins. He always sends them when he wants someone killed, to never leave the swamp ever again."

"I know this man, Panther, the one you are talking about. He has the eyes of a hunter. And the eyes of a killer as well. Do you know him?"

"He is my brother," Yellow Flower answered. "And if you do not kill him, he will certainly kill you. You must hurry. The canoe is waiting for you down by the water, and if you go now it will give you a head start. But remember, Panther will eventually catch up with you. He always does."

CHAPTER THIRTY-FIVE

MEN'S VOICES OUTSIDE the truck woke Gabriella Lopez from a fitful sleep. She was curled up on the panel truck's metal floor in a tight fetal position. The heat and humidity was all consuming. It caused a nagging dryness to dominate Gabriella's mouth. She craved madly for a drink of water. The young woman could not remember the last time anyone inside the truck had been given water. Or allowed to leave the truck to relieve themselves. The rancid smell of urine mixed with fecal matter abounded. It was heavy and pressing all around her. It left Gabriella's eyes blurred with tears.

The opening sound of the truck's overhead door shook loose her lethargy. It must have shaken the other women inside the truck as well because their bodies began to stir. It had been many hours since the last hypodermic injection and the lingering effects of the drug had virtually disappeared. Gabriella closed her eyes to the bright sunlight. It shone abundantly through the panel truck's opened door. She blinked away its brightness to focus on the group of men standing outside. The men's heavy glares fell upon the filthy-looking, pajama-clad women strewn about the truck.

"They smell like swine covered in their own piss and shit," Bo Wiley said bringing a white handkerchief up to cover his nose. "Have 'em remove those dirty pajamas they're wearing before hosing them down. Then give them some clean clothes and put 'em in the storage building with the other women. Right now I wouldn't give you ten bucks for the whole lot."

"There won't hardly be enough room in the storage building for these fifteen along with the twelve already in there now," Cash Wiley interjected before backing away from the truck. The heavy stench emitting from inside had gotten to him. "When is that damn plane coming to haul them out of here?"

"In a couple of days, right after the big storm blows through," brother Bo answered. "In the meantime squeeze these in with the rest. Deek, you and Oil Can hose 'em down and get 'em some clean clothes. Then give 'em some water and food. I don't want any of 'em dying on us before we get paid."

"You got it, Bo," Deek said before motioning for Oil Can to get the hose from the water truck parked under the shady sycamore tree no more than twenty feet away.

It was not long before fifteen disoriented Mexican women dressed in clean blue-colored workman clothes were led by Deek and Oil Can through the grassy compound in the direction of a weather-battered concrete building. Gabriella walked grim-faced. She kept her attention focused on the thickly-forested line of trees on either side while also appreciating the protruding swamp encompassing one part of the compound. It was in the direction of the swamp that she and the other women were heading. Escape, Gabriella thought. But where to? In what direction? The young woman had no idea as to where she and the other women had been taken. It was a secluded location apparently a good distance from any populated area. And Gabriella had heard the men talking about a plane coming to take the women someplace else. Most probably out of the country, she reasoned. If not, the truck would have driven straight through to the ultimate destination. There would have been no reason for them to have first stopped at this isolated spot. Gabriella quickly thought of

Shadow, wondering how far away he was at this moment. Did he have the two swat teams already in place? Were they about to descend upon the compound to rescue her and the other women? And what about Aleena? Would Aleena be one of the twelve women she had heard the men by the truck talking about?

The concrete building was no more than fifty yards ahead. Gabriella concentrated on the area around the building noting the sloping ground down to the water and the high weeds along both sides. There were two wooden boats pulled up on the shore close by. But were there any oars for the boats? She did not see any oars. Gabriella caught sight of two men gripping long leather leashes. The men were walking Doberman pinchers on the opposite end of the compound. And there was another man. He was dressed in green camouflage fatigues and wearing dark sunglasses. The man was sitting in a chair near the compound entrance holding an automatic rifle. Gabriella tried to remember every detail of the compound, calculating distance as best she could. It was while taking in the swampy water and estimating the distance from the shore to the trees that she felt a hand grip her right wrist. It pulled her toward the bushes alongside the concrete building. Gabriella screamed. It was then that another hand immediately covered her mouth.

CHAPTER THIRTY-SIX

"YOU DUMBASS NIGGER, what're you doing? How many times do you have to be told to keep your hands off the women?"

"Deek, I told you that I don't like being called dumb," Oil Can responded while letting go of Gabriella's right wrist and removing his other hand from her mouth. Oil Can had taken a special interest in Gabriella. He first noticed her at the hosing down when all the newly arrived Mexican women had been ordered to remove their dirty, soiled pajamas. That was before Deek and Oil Can went about spraying their nude bodies with fresh water from the truck. After watching Gabriella standing wet and naked outside the truck, Oil Can found it nearly impossible to suppress the desire building within him. He wanted Gabriella in the worst way.

Deek said to him, "Oil Can, you are dumb and stupid. You know you are. Bo already warned you that the next time he caught you sampling the merchandise he was going to castrate you like he would a German shepherd. Now is that bitch worth you losing your balls over?"

"No, she ain't," Oil Can conceded while instinctively both huge hands immediately dropped down to his groin. The hot urge inside the big black man rapidly diminished until it was no longer there. Perhaps he was not very bright, but Oil Can did possess enough savvy to know that Bo Wiley would not hesitate to follow through with his threat.

"Then maybe you're not as dumb as I thought you were. Come on, let's get these women in the storage room before Bo sees us. He's been in a terrible mood ever since finding out about Angie's working undercover for the DEA."

Deek slid back the steel bolt before opening the concrete building's large metal door. There was a loud creaking sound that came from the door's rusted hinges. Prior to its housing abducted women, the building had been used for storing tractors and farming equipment and not much else. It had two glass windows draped in barbed wire high up the walls on either side. While four air vents were sectioned out of its cement roof. Deek motioned for the Mexican women to enter. He stood off to one side, waving his right hand for them to go through the opened door, much like a gatekeeper at a sporting event would do in wanting the spectators to hurry inside. Gabriella was the last of the women to enter.

It took a couple of minutes for Gabriella's eyes to adjust to the room's dark interior. Then she picked up the rays of sunlight pouring through the room's windows. Filtered shafts of dust-filled light dispersed limited amounts of brightness onto the crowded space. The newly-arrived women came face to face with the women who had been confined to the storage room for many days. A flurry of excited female voices erupted. Hurried questions in Spanish were uttered by both groups. Gabriella searched out Aleena's face from among the many faces all around her. She moved through the crowd of female bodies. The women were all clothed in the same type of blue-flannel work clothes. It became difficult to distinguish one woman from another. Gabriella thought for a brief moment that she had seen Aleena only to discover upon closer inspection that she had been mistaken. The young face was not that of her sister. It was the face of some other girl who had met the same fate as Aleena.

Could she possibly not be here? Gabriella asked herself. Or perhaps there was another location that the women had been brought to? A feeling of dread, hot and heavy filled her. Panic started to consume, to nibble at her self-control. Could she be dead? Raped and murdered by the men who had transported her from Mexico? Hurrying through the crowded room, Gabriella made her way to the rear. She observed a lone figure huddled in a corner. The person's back was to Gabriella. She ran to it.

"Aleena," Gabriella said after taking the young woman's hands away from her face. A blank look stared back at Gabriella. It showed no recognition. Life was absent from the brown eyes and drawn out face. Gabriella took her sister into her arms. She brought Aleena closer to her. She kissed the top of Aleena's head. Tears filled Gabriella's eyes. The tears were warm in their wetness. They ran down both sides of her face.

"What have they done to you, little sister?" Gabriella cried while clutching Aleena. "God, what have they done to hurt her so?"

****

Agent Torres figured that it would be about a mile walk down the dirt road before he reached Gabriella's location. Joe Torres, code name Shadow, kept to the road's edge so that he could easily jump into the heavy foliage running alongside if he should hear a car coming or observe someone walking in his direction. The DEA agent earlier had driven the new sedan into a swampy area. He had covered it with green saw palmetto leaves, which he hoped would keep it hidden from anyone passing by on the road. But before stashing the car, Torres had removed from the trunk a knapsack containing two 6-volt battery lanterns, an adequate five day supply of food and water, and seven yards of nylon netting to keep out the insects that would surely be attacking him once it got dark. Torres was confident that the car would not be discovered any time soon. And with a little luck the same for him, as well. Gabriella's tracking device hung from his pants belt. Torres had fastened the device to the belt before looping it around his neck. The light continued to flash indicating that Gabriella was stationary. She and the truck had not moved for the past hour.

It was late afternoon and the hot sun beat down hard. The ungodly humidity sapped him, leaving him sweating profusely from every pore. Torres wiped his face with what was once a clean handkerchief. He tried to clear his blurred vision. It was a good thing that he had because the sight of an armed man dressed in camouflage greens and wearing dark sunglasses suddenly appeared before him. Torres quickly ducked into the heavy weeds off the road. He did not stop until he was well away from both the road and the man holding an automatic rifle. The DEA agent had a fully-loaded Beretta 9mm. in his shoulder holster. There was an extra ammo clip for the gun inside his left pants pocket. That was all the firepower he had at his disposal. Torres knew it would not be nearly enough against a man with an automatic rifle.

He stayed low traveling through the thick underbrush and high saw palmetto plants. Slowly he made his way forward while trying not to cause too much attention. There could be more than one lookout ahead. Through the weeds Torres saw the clearing and with his right hand he carefully pushed aside the large green leaves in front of him. He observed the white panel truck and the naked women standing near it. Two men, one huge and black, the other skinny and white, were spraying the women with a large hose that was connected to a water truck. The men were laughing and enjoying the women's obvious distress. Torres finally located Gabriella in the group. He was glad to see that she had survived the ordeal so far. Joe Torres felt the tension slowly drain out of him. The feeling of dread, a feeling that had been gripping him ever since he was told to abort the mission, instantly went away. He watched the women being escorted across the grassy area in the direction of what appeared to be a white concrete storage building.

Something caught his attention. Without hesitating, Torres flattened his body out onto the ground. He had sighted two men walking Doberman pinchers near the edge of the compound. One of the dogs was coming his way. It would be on top of him in a matter of minutes. Quickly, Torres slid backwards deeper into the underbrush. He did not stop moving until he came to a stand of cypress and hammock trees. Secreting himself in the trees' thickest section, Torres dropped into a set of bushes. He took two deep breaths to get his breathing under control. The DEA agent felt it would be too dangerous to try and get any closer to the compound. Especially if there were dogs and their handlers patrolling the outer edges. He would have to content himself with spending a night in the bushes. There was nothing much more that he could do. He would have to wait it out, and hopefully, if all went well, find a way to contact Gabriella in the morning.

CHAPTER THIRTY-SEVEN

ANGELA AND BOOK loaded the canoe with whatever nonperishable food Angela could put together in a hurry. There was also a metal cooking pot, nylon netting, two sharp knives, two flashlights, and a three-pronged fishing spear that Angela hoped to use in the procurement of fresh food. She also packed rain gear for each of them. A storm of hurricane proportions was reportedly heading toward the Everglades. It would undoubtedly dump plenty of rainwater in its wake. Before leaving, Angela went back up to the house to say goodbye to Yellow Flower. And while doing so, she handed the young Indian woman a piece of paper.

"You've done so much for me already I hate to ask you to do this, but it is terribly important," Angela said grasping Yellow Flower's right wrist in an attempt to emphasize the importance of what she was about to ask the girl to do. "Jim Garrison's name and phone number are on this piece of paper. He has to be told that Book and I have in our possession Father Andy's flash drive, and that there is probably enough evidence on it to send Bo and Cash Wiley away to prison for the rest of their lives.

"Yellow Flower, you'll have to find a way to get into Bo's study because that's where he keeps his private phone. Call the phone number on this paper and tell Garrison that we are taking the flash drive to the park ranger station at Armadillo Flats. There will be a ranger on duty there and we should be able to send everything that's on the flash drive to Garrison's office computer in Washington D.C. Do you understand what I am asking you to do?"

"Yes, I will make the call. Bo keeps the phone locked up in the bottom drawer of his desk, but one night after he got drunk I saw him put the key to the desk drawer in a black book on the top shelf of his bookcase. I'll get it and make the telephone call to Garrison for you. Angela, you are smart going to the ranger station. Bo and Cash will have the highway watched in case you double back, and taking the canoe on the sea of grass, where there is so much open water, would be a mistake. They will have airboats patrolling and catch you easily."

Angela told her, "That's the way I see it, too. So that leaves only the ranger station at Armadillo Flats or to try for Everglades City. Everglades City would be shorter once we reached the Barron River, but I think Panther would expect us to take that route. Armadillo Flats is farther away and the swamp harder to get through, so he shouldn't figure us to take that route. Hopefully, we'll be able to reach the ranger station before Panther finds out that we fooled him."

Angela hugged Yellow Flower before hurrying down to the water. She found Book waiting for her. After she got into the canoe, Book used the canoe's only paddle to shove off from the shoreline. He pointed the front of the canoe in the direction of the heavily forested swamp. Cypress, pop ash, red maple, and hammock trees awaited them, while the marshy surface water abounded in green duckweed sprinkled with sprouting reeds and cattails. Long stem flowers loomed above the water showing an array of whites and pinks. A red-shouldered hawk shrieked displeasure at the sight of the slow-moving canoe invading its territory. It swooped across the tree line in a display of indignation.

"Stay to the right," Angela instructed while squatting in the tip of the canoe. She directed right or left with the motion of her hand. "It'll be hard going for a good while before it starts to thin out a bit. I figure we're in about three to four feet of water depending on how the bottom slopes. If this weren't rainy season, it wouldn't be half as much."

The air was hot and humid leaving both of them sweating profusely. The light-fitting clothes each was wearing soon became wet and tight, sticking to their backsides like layers of newly-formed skin. Book took deliberate dips with the paddle. He slowly propelled the canoe forward through the brackish water and the vast assortment of greenery that seemed to endlessly dot the water's surface. He could not help but notice that the canoe was nothing more than a hollowed-out cypress log crudely fashioned. It had probably been made in the same manner as those constructed by the Seminole Indians years ago. The thought of it took the army ranger captain back to a different time, causing the sounds of the swamp around him to become intermingled with those of days gone by. For the moment he found life to be as simple as a man and a woman in a hollowed-out cypress log gliding upon the water.

The sun was going down. The swamp began to reflect the oncoming twilight. Shadows crept where it was once bright. And low-hanging trees hovered hauntingly. Their slumping branches appeared like knotted fingers groping for whatever might be upon the water. Angela pointed up ahead indicating the direction that she wanted Book to maneuver the canoe. She leaned forward to search the darkened surface for any protruding tree stumps. He stopped paddling after seeing Angela raise up her right hand.

"This is Pine Cone Island and the highest ground we'll find anywhere around here. We'll stay on the island tonight and get an early start in the morning."

"Doesn't look like much of an island to me," Book said taking his paddle out of the water. He took in the healthy stand of pine trees and the abundant undergrowth that covered what appeared to be nothing more than a muddy section of earth in the midst of the swamp. Book watched Angela jump from the front of the canoe and pull the nose up onto solid ground. He followed after her stepping out onto the muddy embankment.

"It'll do us for tonight," Angela said before taking the three-pronged fishing spear out of the canoe. She then reached into the knapsack for the metal cooking pot. "I'm going to try and get us some supper but there's plenty of pine cones around and dry wood if you want to get a fire going. We can have the luxury of a campfire tonight because Panther and his two cousins won't be coming after us until morning. But tomorrow night we'll have to sit it out in the dark."

Book watched with a half-smile as Angela pranced off along the water's edge. She was holding the three-pronged fishing spear in her right hand and the metal cooking pot in her left. The young woman looked perfectly at home in the middle of the swamp with the sun going down and the night creatures of the Everglades starting to stir from their long daytime slumber. Alligators, big cats, poisonous snakes abounded. And here she was prancing off like some school girl going to a Saturday night dance.

Book pulled the canoe farther up onto the embankment. He then went about adjusting the Glock 9mm. in his pants belt so that it could find a more comfortable position. Book had done his army ranger training in the Everglades and knew the danger that awaited anyone who took the swamp lightly. It could be both beautiful and treacherous at the same time. But to someone like Angela who had been virtually raised inside the Everglades the danger had become a part of life. It was like someone who had been raised in the city. They had to deal with cars speeding every which way but when the time came to cross a busy street there was no apprehension. It became second nature for the person to cross and not let the danger be felt. The same held true for Angela. She was at home in the middle of the Everglades. And she was not in the least fearful. Most women, especially with night descending, would have been petrified beyond belief.

It did not take long before Book had a blazing fire going. The pine cones were dry and immediately caught flame. While the pine knots and other dry wood only added to the burning fire. It was now almost completely dark and the crickets and frogs were coming alive with their cacophony. Audible stirrings in the water told Book there were alligators moving about. He knew as long as the fire burned brightly it would keep them and the pesky mosquitoes away. Not to mention the nits and countless other blood-sucking insects that could suck a man dry before he even knew it. Book caught sight of Angela walking up to the fire. She had a smile on her face. Seeing him, she held up the metal cooking pot as though it were some kind of trophy she had won.

"It's full of crawfish and frog legs. We'll be eating like royalty tonight. And here I was thinking how you would have the white linen cloth all spread out along with the gold-plated candle holders and the candles lit, and maybe even a little Wagner or Chopin playing in the background. What's wrong with you, Frank? Don't you know how to wine and dine a girl?"

Book could not help but laugh. Angela had smudges of mud on both cheeks as well as on the tip of her nose, while her green eyes were ablaze reflecting off the firelight at her feet. The light blue-colored top and shorts she wore had smudges of mud on them as did her knees. Book surmised the young woman had knelt down on the muddy shoreline to collect the crawfish. But it was the carefree smile on Angela's pretty face and the total ease about her that captivated Book. He found the pent-up tension that had been consuming him these past few days slowly dissipate, leaving him more relaxed than he had felt in quite some time.

Book said to her, "I could easily take off this dirty shirt I'm wearing and lay it down for you, and maybe even light up a few of those pine cones for candles, and just to get the right mood, I might then treat you to my rendition of Cole Porter's *Begin the Beguine*, hummed of course. Now think about it. How many girls could say after spending a night in the Everglades with a man that they were wined and dined like royalty?"

"Not too many that's for sure," Angela said laughing.

"That's what I thought you would say," Book answered before allowing a smile to take over his face. "And after hearing my rendition of *Begin the Beguine*, most would probably never come back."

The two of them laughed together.

Book took the metal pot from her and set it down on the fire. Angela went about washing off the mud from her face and arms. Book watched her squatting at the shoreline splashing handfuls of water onto her face and arms then doing the same to her legs. The army ranger captain found it stimulating to say the least. The young woman was not only attractive but enticing as well. Book took out one of the knives from the knapsack. After kneeling down beside the fire, he began to stir the contents of the pot. He did his best at keeping his mind centered on the task at hand. Not on Angela who was now standing, peering down at him.

"Frank, we should reach the ranger station the day after tomorrow if all goes well. I am fairly certain in the morning Panther and his two cousins will take the route that leads to Everglades City, but we still have to be careful. Panther knows these swamps better than anyone and Bo Wiley will be offering him, along with Acorn and Raindrop, a lot of money to kills us. Besides that, he and Bernardo must suspect that you have Father Andy's flash drive. That will make them want to catch us even more."

Book looked up at Angela while continuing to stir the pot with the knife. The water in the pot was starting to simmer and the sweet smell of the cooking crayfish and frog legs permeated the air. Book attempted to keep the look of concern from showing on his face.

"Panther won't be taking the route to Everglades City. He'll be taking the route to the ranger station because that's the way we're going."

"How can you be so sure?" Angela asked while taken back by Book's apparent certainty. The hint of fear instantly surfaced in the young woman's face.

"Because that's what I would do. And I have looked into his eyes and saw a lot of me in him. Angela, Panther's a hunter and killer the same as I am. We might be coming from different perspectives but both of us have hunted men and killed them. I can't explain it any better than that. Trust me when I tell you that Panther and his two cousins will be after us tomorrow. And you can help right now by telling me what kind of guns they have?"

"Bolt action deer rifles. I don't know if they carry handguns. I wouldn't be surprised if they did."

"And all three are probably excellent shots," Book surmised.

"Yes, they've been hunting these swamps since they were young boys. Frank, if they catch us there isn't much we can do against the three of them. We only have my Glock handgun and up against three hunting rifles what chance does that leave us?"

Book came to his feet. He took hold of both Angela's arms holding them firm. Having her become panic stricken was the last thing Book needed. They would both have to keep their wits about them if they ever hoped to survive the next couple of days.

"We are going to have to even out the odds somehow. I think that I know Panther well enough, tell me something about his cousins. You called them Acorn and Raindrop. What are they like? And how did they ever come by those names?"

"They've always followed their cousin Panther and did whatever he told them to do. They've been that way since they were kids. Acorn and Raindrop would have a difficult time making it on their own. They're not very bright, but with Panther they make a living hunting and poaching alligators along with whatever dirty work Bo Wiley pays them for doing. You asked about their names."

A smile came to Angela's face. "Moon Woman told me that at the time Acorn was born his father and his father's brothers were sitting outside the chickee hut smoking and drinking when an acorn fell from a tree overhead. It fell to the ground at the exact moment that the baby cried for the first time. So the father named his firstborn son Acorn. And when Raindrop's time came, his father felt a drop of rain right after hearing the baby cry for the first time, so he named his second son Raindrop. Moon Woman said that it was the old way of doing things, but it doesn't happen that way much anymore."

Book's face took on a hard look. He said to Angela, "It's too bad Moon Woman hadn't drowned both of them at birth so that their father could have named them Dead and Deader, because some time tomorrow we are going to have to deal with them along with Panther. I figure by late afternoon they should have caught up to us."

"Frank, I hope you're wrong."

"I won't be, but let's worry about it tomorrow. These crawfish and frog legs are about cooked and I remember before leaving the house you stashing a bottle of merlot in the knapsack along with two tin cups. That wine should go rather nicely with the crawfish and frog legs. I don't know about you, but I'm hungry."

"That makes two of us," Angela said smiling while all the anguish and trepidation concerning what they might be facing on the morrow quickly left her. She removed the bottle of merlot from the knapsack along with the two tin cups. Book dumped the full pot of crawfish and frog legs onto an already laid out mat of multi-layered maple leaves. Angela handed him the wine bottle and he used his knife to pop the cork off. She held up two tin cups for him to fill.

"Have you ever dined in a better restaurant in your entire life?" Book asked her while pouring the merlot into the cups.

Angela laughed with delight. "Frank, I must admit that earlier I was entirely wrong about you. You most certainly do know how to wine and dine a girl. And who needs candles when we have the stars? Look how bright they are shining up there. And as far as music, who cares if we don't have music. We have the crickets and frogs singing to their hearts' content. This reminds me of those times when I was a little girl and my father would take me overnight in the swamp and we would look up at the stars in the dark sky and see the moon glowing down on the water like it is right now. And we would hear this sound, the sound of the Everglades in beautiful song, singing for us alone. Frank, I just love it."

Book stared into Angela's face seeing it come alive, taking on a glow all its own. He wanted to reach out and bring her to him. Instead he put down the bottle of wine and held out his hand.

"Are you going to keep talking all night or are you going to hand me the cup?"

"Sorry," she said handing the cup of wine over to him. "It's just that sometimes I get carried away when I'm out here at night. But you're right, enough talk. Let's eat, I'm starvin'."

****

The wine he had consumed along with the heavy load of crawfish and frog legs not to mention the trying day, on top of the last couple of trying days, had left Book drained. He was more than ready for sleep. The warm feel of the burning fire did not help either. It was not long before the army ranger captain's eyes began to close. Angela watched him curl up on a bed of maple leaves next to the fire.

"Wake me when breakfast is ready," he said to her. And before drifting off to sleep he added, "Don't forget to throw some more wood on the fire before you go to sleep. I don't want to end up being someone else's breakfast in the morning."

"I won't forget," she said while looking over at him. His eyes were closed. The sound of his steady breathing soon came to her. Angela took in his unshaven two-day-old beard and squared-off jaw along with his resting blond head. She caught herself thinking about how she would prefer his hair a bit longer. And if he was her man she would tell him so. Then the thought came to her. What would it be like to have his two-day-old beard rubbing against her face and his strong arms wrapped around her? She pictured his mouth covering her mouth. And both their hands moving slowly up and down each other's body ... Stop it, Angela told herself. What are you doing? You don't even know him. He's a killer. He even said so himself. Besides what would he want with someone like you? You were born and raised in Indian Town. He even had to shut you up after you went on and on about all the times you and your father spent nights alone in the swamp together.

Angela immediately grasped the gold bracelet on her left wrist. She squeezed it knowing that it was the only thing she had left to remember her parents by. The tears began to flow. She allowed them to run freely down her face while the popping sound from the heated pine cones in the fire came to her. Wiping at the tears, Angela looked out at the moon glowing upon the water. She also saw the shining, red-blinking of the alligators' eyes as the silent creatures moved about in the moon's hazy glow. The accented hoot of a Barred Owl overhead, *oo-aw*, brought the young woman back to the moment.

Picking up two large pieces of dry tree limb, Angela dropped them into the blaze at her feet. She observed sparks flying upward, sending burning embers high into the night sky. She watched the burning embers rising higher and higher until they faded away into nothing. They disappeared in the dark of the night. Something that had once existed would never exist again. Much like people, Angela thought. We are here. Then we are gone.

Finding a dry piece of ground, Angela sat down allowing her head to fall back against the knapsack. The sound of Book's steady breathing came to her once again. It adjoined the other night sounds. Angela edged closer to the fire. She permitted herself to listen while wondering what life would be like married to Book. Could such a man come to love her in the way that she had always wanted to be loved? Would a man like Book even want a wife? Let alone have children. And if so would he be there for them? Angela pondered the possibilities long into the night. They did not leave her until sleep came to take them away.

CHAPTER THIRTY-EIGHT

A RED-FACED BO Wiley paced back and forth on the front porch of the Wiley mansion. He resembled a caged tiger wanting desperately to kill anything that happened to be gawking at him. His brother Cash sat smoking a cigar while sprawled out in a padded chair at one end of the porch. Panther and his two Indian cousins stood on the sandy ground in front of the house. They were looking up at Bo Wiley. Panther's face remained expressionless. It showed nothing. While Acorn and his brother, Raindrop, wore worried looks. Both men fidgeted nervously.

"How do you know they got into a canoe?" A wild-eyed Bo spat out at Panther who had gone to Angela Valadez's house along with ten other men to kill Book and Angela.

"By their footprints leading from the house down to the water, and the mark in the sand left by the paddle when they pushed the canoe away from the shore. They are maybe two, three hours into the swamp, no more. It is dark now so they will try and find dry ground until daylight tomorrow."

"Are you sure they're in the swamp?"

"Yes, I'm sure."

"Where do you think they'll go?"

"Armadillo Flats. There is a park ranger station there."

"Why not Everglades City? It's closer and not as hard going through the swamp. That's what I would do if I wanted to get away and notify the authorities. I think you're wrong."

"You're the one who is wrong. Angela will want you to think that she and Book are going to Everglades City, that's why they will go to Armadillo Flats."

Bo Wiley rarely second-guessed himself. But this was one of those times. There was no one better than Panther when it came to hunting someone down in the swamp, and if he said Armadillo Flats only a fool would dismiss it. And Bo Wiley was nobody's fool.

"You could be right," Wiley conceded. "But I'm still going to have Turk and Tank watch the highway in case they double back; and I'll have men in airboats out in the open water in case they try for Miami. And no matter what you say, I'll have people on the Barron River should they happen to decide on Everglades City."

Panther shrugged his shoulders. "Do what makes you feel good, but they are going to Armadillo Flats and we will get them."

"And when you do, I want you to kill 'em and bring me back their ears like you done to those Mexicans I sent you after. Do you hear me?"

Panther said to him. "It will cost you more money this time. Five hundred for Angela and one thousand for Book."

"Are you crazy?" Cash Wiley exclaimed, coming erect in his chair. Cash quickly removed the cigar from his mouth. "You got fifty dollars for each one of those Mexicans who ran out on us. Where do you get off wantin' fifteen hundred for these two?"

"These two won't be as easy as the Mexican farm workers. Angela knows the swamp and this man Book, I've looked into his eyes. He won't be easy to kill."

"Are you afraid of Book?" Bo taunted displaying a scornful look. Wiley stepped down off the porch to get closer to Panther. The two men stood face to face.

"The only thing I'm afraid of is having no money," Panther said while looking Bo Wiley squarely in the eyes. "I'll kill Book for you, but you'll have to pay me what I want for doing it."

"Well you better kill him and her, too. And search their bodies for that flash drive. There's an extra five hundred in it for you if you come back with the flash drive. Now get out of here. Bring me back their ears and I'll have the money waiting for you."

"Bo, what do you think?" Cash asked after Panther and his two cousins had gone. "Do you think they can handle Book? I keep remembering what Book did to Oil Can. We were sure then too, but he surprised us."

Bo Wiley said to his brother. "There'll be no surprises this time. Panther and his two cousins are more than able to take care of Book. You can count on it."

"But Bo, there is a back road leading to that ranger station. It wouldn't take long for our people to get there and be waiting for Angela and Book to come out of the swamp. We could kill 'em both and then check their bodies for the flash drive. It'd be easy."

"Did you forget about the park ranger who is stationed there? I don't want that kind of trouble along with everything else that has been going on. Besides Panther will catch up to them before they even get close to the ranger station. And to show you how certain I am, I'm going in the house right now to find me a bigger jar because the one that I've been using doesn't have enough room for two more sets of ears."

CHAPTER THIRTY-NINE

MARIA CARRERA WAITED until dark before gathering up her two suitcases. She quickly walked out the back door of the Gator's Pond Bar. Carrera wanted no one to see her driving out of Gator's Pond on her way to Nuevo Laredo, Mexico. She was going there to get things ready for Bernardo who would be joining her sometime after the American cities had been bombed. Carrera's job in Gator's Pond was finished. She had completed everything Bernardo had instructed her to do. She had obtained the DEA file from Casey Blurmeister. It meant killing the federal investigator in order to get it but that had been fine with Carrera. She hated everything about the man. And after she had returned to Gator's Pond from Washington D.C., Carrera handed the file over to Bernardo. He in turn gave it to Bo Wiley.

"So this is how you protect me and my cartel," Bernardo had said earlier that day to a sober-looking Wiley who was sitting down in his own dining room staring in disbelief at the document set before him. It revealed that Angela Valadez was in fact a DEA agent. "We would all be in federal custody if it were not for my lack of trust in you and your imbecile brother who runs your police department. I want both Valadez and Book dead before the sun goes down today. Do understand me?" A stunned Bo Wiley could only nod his head.

Maria Carrera smiled. The look on Bo Wiley's face was something that she would never forget. Now hurrying to her car, Carrera used the key to open the trunk before putting both suitcases inside. It was after walking around to the driver's side of the car that she saw him. He was leaning against the car door smoking a cigarette. The man looked at her. Carrera observed the gun in his right hand. It rested along his flank. A black silencer was connected to the barrel.

"What are you doing here?" she asked him while having difficulty associating the man with the gun.

"Sending you to hell," he said before shooting Maria Carrera between both eyes. The woman's dead body collapsed in a heap. The man picked it up along with the set of keys that she had dropped. Wasting no time, he opened the trunk and tossed Carrera's lifeless body inside. He then closed the trunk.

The man drove the car onto the dirt road toward Indian Town. Not long out of Gator's Pond, he pulled over to a spot that he had previously checked out. It had a steep grade leading down to the canal. Leaving the engine running and still in gear, the driver exited the compact. He stepped to one side and watched the car roll down toward the water. The man remained vigilant until the compact's top dipped beneath the water's surface. It was only then did Badger One start walking back toward Gator's Pond.

CHAPTER FORTY

A STEADY NIGHT rain fell on the streets of Miami's *Little Havana*. The time was well after midnight. The solitary figure traversed the puddled sidewalk along Calle Ocho on his way to a place where he knew men would be waiting for him. The man also knew that he had to hurry because he was more than an hour late. Wearing a black rain slicker and hood, he walked briskly keeping his head down and his face concealed. His dark form moved past closed storefronts and lighted night spots. There were lounges where men and women laughed loudly and the high-pitched sound of Cuban music reverberated through the night air.

This man was not one to take chances. Deftly, he ducked into an enclosed doorway of a closed flower shop. Remaining hidden, he waited. No sound of footsteps could be heard. No figure suddenly appeared on the empty street. Satisfied, the man proceeded to cross Calle Ocho stopping in front of an older building. The building had a sign on its front door which read, *Used Furniture Store Opening Soon*. It was only after he had looked into the surveillance camera on the wall did Colonel Hosseini, also known as Bernardo, knock on the furniture store door. The front door opened immediately. A man in his early thirties with a dark look about him stepped forward.

"Baradar—Brother," Lieutenant Farad Madani of Iran's Foreign Intelligence Unit said in an Iranian Persian dialect. The lieutenant attempted to embrace Hosseini. He found himself being pushed away.

"How many times do I have to tell you to speak English and not Iranian? One time is all it will take for someone to know that you and your men are not Cuban refugees. Then everything that we have worked for will be gone. Yes, Farid, I love you like a brother too, but I would rather see you dead than lose this opportunity to grievously harm the Great Satan, the United States, with what we've got planned."

"Colonel, I am sorry," Lieutenant Madani answered while his face showed the pain of humiliation. There was no more loyal member of the Iranian Intelligence Unit than Farid Madani. No one held Colonel Hosseini in higher esteem. "You are right, of course. It will not happen again. It is just that I am so happy to see you. The men and I have been worried about you. We expected you more than an hour ago."

"It could not be helped. I drove from Gator's Pond and had to be careful that I wasn't being followed, while I thought it best to park the car several blocks from here in case it aroused someone's attention. We cannot be too careful at this stage. There is too much at stake. In the meantime, I hope all is ready and in place for the fifty suicide bombers who should be arriving here by truck the day after tomorrow. Are all their identifications complete, driver's licenses, student IDs, everything that they will need to get on the planes and buses that will be taking them to their assigned cities? Farid, I want no mistakes."

Lieutenant Madani beamed proudly. He placed his right hand on Colonel Hosseini's left shoulder before directing his superior officer into another room just off the main entrance. The two men stepped into a spacious room lined with tables. On the tables were placards indicating the names of American cities located throughout the United States. Photo identification cards along with transportation tickets and a full set of clothes were set in front of each placard. Colonel Hosseini walked alongside the tables taking note of the named cities.

"New York City will have its Yankee Stadium bombed at the same time a baseball game is being played," he said brushing the New York City placard. "And Chicago's Sears Tower will be reduced to nothing but dust, while Boston's John Hancock Tower will topple and Denver's Republic Plaza will become a burning inferno. All of those American cities, look at them Farid," Colonel Hosseini said pointing. "They will feel Allah's wrath and we shall be the ones to carry it out."

Hosseini stopped walking. He turned to look at his friend and subordinate. A spreading smile took over the colonel's dark face. It brought a similar response to the face of Lieutenant Madani.

"Yes, Colonel. We will be Allah's messengers of death. It is an honor for me to serve both him and you."

Hosseini nodded his head in appreciation. Everything was going according to plan. He could not be happier. The Iranian colonel looked over to the concrete wall on the other side of the tables. There he observed the stacked wooden crates of C4 explosives, M16 rifles, rocket launchers, and hand grenades. It was a small arsenal that would be used following the July fourth bombing of the American cities. Colonel Hosseini had plans to destroy as many of the U.S. military locations throughout the country as possible.

"Farid, I could not be more joyous," Colonel Hosseini said turning once again to Lieutenant Madani. "Where are the men? I must say something to them before I leave."

The lieutenant left the room and returned within minutes with six dark-skinned men. They wore shabby work clothes, lending the appearance of tradesmen. The men stood at attention with their eyes fixed on the man they knew to be their supreme leader. In their minds Colonel Hosseini was above all other men. One word from him and anyone of the six would gladly give up his life.

"Allah be praised," Hosseini said, "That such men as you have been given to me so that I may strike at the very heart of the United States of America. I thank you in his name. Stay strong my brothers for we shall be victorious. I must go now and prepare the way for those brothers who shall be coming the day after tomorrow."

Colonel Hosseini bowed graciously to his men before motioning for Lieutenant Madani to follow him to the front door. The colonel and lieutenant stood near the door looking intently at one another. Both knew that they would not be seeing each other again until sometime after the July fourth bombings.

"Farid, has there been anything that could have thrown suspicion on us here? Anything at all?"

"Colonel, nothing. People in the neighborhood think we are just Cuban workers renovating an old building that will one day be a furniture store. We don't leave except to get food from the small grocery store down on the corner and then only sandwiches. I do all the ordering and speak only English with a Cuban accent. You taught me the accent and you know how good I am at it. No one suspects anything."

"Good. That is what I wanted to hear."

Colonel Hosseini had no way of knowing that Lieutenant Farid Madani had intentionally lied to him. And that just the week before while standing in front of the store counter waiting for Isabel Fernandez to make up his men's ordered ground beef sandwiches, Madani had inadvertently said something in Iranian to one of his men. Isabel Fernandez had overheard him. And Lieutenant Madani was fully aware that she had.

Unbeknownst to Madani, Isabel Fernandez was a paid CIA informant and had been one for several years. She also happened to be involved in an on-going sexual relationship with a certain CIA agent by the name of Payo Valdes. Agent Valdes's primary interest, other than scoring with Fernandez, centered on Castro agents sneaking across the ninety-plus mile stretch of water from Cuba into *Little Havana*. While one night in bed after having had better than the usual sex with Isabel Fernandez, the CIA agent's interest became peaked.

"So you never heard this type of language before, and you don't think he is really Cuban?"

"I always was wondering about him and the others in that old building working all the time and not seeing them bringing in any kind of building material. How can you fix up a building without any paint or lumber? And his accent is not right for someone who just came from Cuba. Something is not right about those men."

Payo Valdes recalled a recent CIA memo initiated by the Director of the National Clandestine Service (NCS) requesting that any suspicious activity involving foreigners in or around the city of Miami be reported immediately to him. The next morning Valdes did just that. He dispatched a brief memo to Director Jack Ross detailing what Isabel Fernandez had told him.

Two days later a CIA surveillance team arrived in *Little Havana*. One hour after the team's arrival an observation point had been set up. It was situated on the second floor of a building directly across the street from the old furniture store. And it so happened that twenty-four hours later, a one-arm CIA agent using highly sensitive night-seeing equipment came to observe Colonel Hosseini exit the front door of the old furniture store.

"Bingo," Jack Ross said before handing over his binoculars to the CIA agent standing next to him. "We hit the mother lode."

CHAPTER FORTY-ONE

JOE TORRES STARTED untangling the nylon netting. He had been wrapped in it since the previous evening. And like everything else the netting was wet from the early morning dew. It had been an uncomfortable night for the DEA agent. He had hidden himself in the thickest section of bushes and paid a price for it. Buzzing mosquitoes had somehow found a way through the netting's nylon mesh and feasted on what seemed like every part of him. Sharp branches poked and scratched every time he had shifted body positions through the night. Torres reached behind him to remove the pointed branch that had been sticking in his back for the past hour or more. He told himself that it would feel good to get out of these bushes. The sun was starting to come up. That meant he would be leaving soon. He would wait for the sun before attempting to contact Gabriella.

Torres observed the blinking light on Gabriella's tracking device. It would no longer be needed. He already knew Gabriella's whereabouts. What he really needed was a way of getting her and the other women out of the compound and free of their captors. Torres removed the device from his belt, letting it drop to the ground. He then placed the leather belt back around his waist. The DEA agent knew that the Beretta in its shoulder holster would prove cumbersome while he crawled along the ground trying to get closer to the compound. Torres took the gun out and stuck it inside his pants belt. He then reached into the knapsack for a bottle of water and a package of saltine crackers. Breakfast. The water and crackers would have to carry him through most of the day. He could not take the knapsack with him. It would slow him down too much. And the knapsack's bulkiness would make it that much easier for him to be seen crawling through the foliage. The sound of a man's voice suddenly came to him. It seemed to be coming from the direction of the compound. Torres could not make out what the man was shouting. He was yelling to someone. The DEA agent decided to move in the direction of the voice. He clambered out of the bushes and headed toward the compound.

"Keep 'em walking and don't let any of 'em go near the trees. If any of 'em run let the dogs loose. The rest won't even think about runnin' after they see what the dogs do to whoever runs."

Torres had reached the edge of the compound. He could go no further. If he did, they would surely spot him. There was a maze of saw palmetto plants lining the exterior of the compound. The DEA agent took up a position in the thickest section. He counted five armed men. Two of the men held Dobermans on leashes. They were stationary in the middle of an open grassy area, while the other three men were walking with the Mexican women along the outer edges of the compound. Early morning exercise, Torres guessed. Keep them in shape before you sell them. The man doing the yelling was apparently in charge. He was a scrawny, unkempt-looking fellow. Torres recognized him immediately as being the one who, along with the big, black man, had hosed down Gabriella and the other women. He was the closest to Torres. In his right hand the man held a large caliber pistol. Not very far away from him was Gabriella. She was holding onto a young woman and walking slowly. It must be Aleena, the DEA agent surmised. *If only I had my two swat teams. We could* take these guys out in the blink of an eye. Torres kept his attention focused on Gabriella.

The sun was nearly up. A strong southerly breeze started blowing. Torres knew a big storm was coming. For the past week, the radio stations had been forecasting warnings of Hurricane Ruth's approach to southern Florida. He would have to do something soon or find a way of riding out the storm. But Gabriella had to be contacted first. She had to know that he was here. Otherwise, she and her sister might attempt an escape on their own. It would end up being disastrous. Torres could not let that happen. He would have to somehow make contact with Gabriella.

She and her sister were walking slowly in his direction. But the man with the gun was walking in the same direction. Torres reached into his front shirt pocket. He removed the notepad and pen. Quickly, he scribbled a few lines onto a piece of paper before tearing the paper from the notepad. Now how to get it to her. She was nearly in front of him. In a moment she and her sister would walk past. Reaching into his front pants pocket, Torres removed a bullet from the metal ammo clip. He folded the piece of paper around the bullet until it was tightly wrapped. Gabriella. He could almost reach out and touch her. Torres flung the wrapped bullet into the air. It struck the right side of Gabriella's face. Instinctively, the young woman brought her right hand up to her face. She looked in his direction. He could tell that she did not see him. Gabriella's gaze dropped to the ground before glancing back at the man with the gun. Torres watched as Gabriella bent down to pick up the wrapped bullet. She and her sister walked past him.

****

Gabriella knew Shadow had to have been only a few yards away from her. He must have been somewhere in the high saw palmetto plants.

Gabriella tried to make eye contact. She had looked into the dense foliage but was unable to see him. Then her eyes spotted the wrapped piece of paper lying at her feet. The young woman's heart had nearly leaped out of her chest. But where was the man with the gun? He had been only a short distance behind her. Gabriella did look back. She saw that the man's attention had been diverted elsewhere. Quickly, she had bent down and picked up the wadded piece of paper. But it was not until after the women had been returned to the concrete building that Gabriella was able to examine it.

She left Aleena at the entrance door before hurrying to the farthest corner. Gabriella could not wait to read what was on the paper. Shadow had come at last. All the women inside the storage building would soon be rescued. She hurriedly unwrapped the piece of paper. The bullet dropped down onto her lap. The scribbled writing on the paper was difficult to decipher. It also took Gabriella's eyes time to adjust to the bunker's dim light. Eventually, she was able to read it.

Gabriella: Both you and Aleena must stay. Do not try to escape. My swat teams have been recalled and I am alone. But I will find a way to rescue you and the rest of the women.
   Shadow

Gabriella stared at the piece of paper. The young woman experienced a sinking, hollowed-out feeling deep in the pit of her stomach. The joy she had been feeling regarding her and the other women's imminent rescue was no longer there. It had left her. Emptiness pervaded now. And anger. Where were the swat teams? Why had they been recalled? Gabriella felt betrayed. Shadow. The face that had been occupying nearly every moment of her time in captivity appeared once again in Gabriella's mind. You promised. There were supposed to be two swat teams. They were going to rescue us. I found my sister and the other women. I did what I was supposed to do. But you did not live up to your promise.

Tears came to Gabriella's eyes. Her experience as a police officer told her there was little hope that she and the other women would be rescued. Shadow was one man against five, heavily-armed men. And soon a plane would be coming to take her and the other women out of the country. The thought sent shivers up and down Gabriella. The young woman settled back against the concrete wall of the bunker. Shadow's piece of paper fell from her hand. Aleena was walking over to her. Gabriella saw the hopeful look on her sister's face. She opened her arms to her. Aleena fell into them.

CHAPTER FORTY-TWO

"BADGER ONE. THIS is Papa Bear how do you read?"

"Papa Bear. I read you loud and clear."

"Good Badger One. Has the cause for our Washington D.C. problem been eliminated?"

"Yes, Papa Bear. The problem has been eliminated. Her body was disposed of and will not be found. She was leaving for Mexico so her absence from Gator's Pond should not raise any suspicion. Are there any further orders for me other than locating the flash drive?"

"Badger One. We have a location on the flash drive. Bo Wiley's mistress has phoned Jim Garrison on behalf of Agent Valadez. The woman had been instructed by Agent Valadez to inform Garrison that Agent Valadez and Book have the priest's flash drive and are taking it to the park ranger station at Armadillo Flats. The two are going by way of canoe through the swamp. Badger One, can you be of any assistance?"

"Papa Bear. I cannot see how I can be of any assistance. I am not familiar with the swamp and would not be able find my why through it in order to help them. And I know that presently both Agent Valadez and Book are being pursued by three of Bo Wiley's Indians. These Indians are excellent hunters as well as hired killers. Bo Wiley has used them before in hunting down people that he wanted killed. Agent Valadez and Book will have to deal with the Indians on their own. There is no way I can be of any assistance."

"*Badger One. It is understood. Your orders then are to monitor the situation. If the flash drive should somehow come into Bo Wiley's possession, you are to retrieve it. Obtaining the flash drive is paramount. Do you understand your orders Badger One?*"

"*Papa Bear. The orders are understood. I will contact you as soon as I learn more.*"

"*Badger One. Very good. If there should be any word on Agent Valadez and Book please let me know.*"

"*Papa Bear. Will do. Over and out.*"

CHAPTER FORTY-THREE

BOOK OPENED HIS eyes and raised his head. He looked around to see Angela only a few feet from him. She was asleep with her head resting on the knapsack. It was already dawn. The hint of a rising sun appeared on the eastern horizon. A heavy, misty fog had settled upon the water. The gray mist rose up high into the pine trees, hovering amongst the branches like a gray-colored veil. Book could barely make out the trees in the dim light. An eerie quiet pervaded. The overnight sounds had gone. New sounds would soon be coming. The morning sun would bring them to the Everglades.

Book had awakened twice during the night to throw more wood onto the camp fire. And each time alligators with glowing red eyes had glared back at him from the water. It did not make for a good night's rest. He had hardly slept at all. And now the fire was nearly burnt out. Nothing remained except for some smoldering embers. Book caught movement out of Angela. He saw the young woman working her way into a sitting position. He watched her stretch both arms above her head. The army ranger captain quickly came to his feet.

"Is breakfast ready?" Angela asked him while showing an exaggerated yawn.

"I thought that was going to be my line," Book said back to her before kicking the fire's smoldering embers toward the water.

Angela looked up smiling. "I thought breakfast came with the overnight lodging. I must speak with the hotel manager about this."

"The hotel manager says you had better skip breakfast and get the rest of you up and moving. Because he doesn't think Panther and his two cousins are sitting around having breakfast right about now."

"The hotel manager is probably right," Angela said before hurrying to her feet. The smile had left her. "They will be in the swamp by now. Frank, if you're right about them coming after us we can't outrun them. They will be in two canoes and each of them will have a deer rifle. Is there anything we can do to stop them from killing us?"

"Yes, kill them first."

"But how can we? You have the Glock and that's all we have. What can one handgun do up against three deer rifles?"

Book walked over to her. He could see the fear in Angela's eyes. She was looking to him for answers. But he did not have any to give her. The odds were that both of them would not live out the day. Book knew that he could not tell her that. He would have to somehow change the odds. But how? The Indians knew the swamp and they were excellent riflemen. Think, he told himself. How can you make the odds so that you and Angela have a fighting chance?

"You said yesterday that Acorn and Raindrop weren't too bright. And that Panther does the thinking for the two of them."

"Yes. Neither one of them could make it without Panther. He handles the money they get for any poached animal skins that they take out of the swamp along with whatever Bo Wiley pays them to do a job. He's their cousin but more like a big brother to them. They do whatever he tells them to do."

Book kicked more of the hot embers from the fire into the water. He then went over and picked up the knapsack and tossed it into the front of the canoe. The army ranger captain's mind was racing. He knew that in a gunfight against three deer rifles there was not a chance in the world for him and Angela to come out alive. And ambushing three Indians who knew every inch of the swamp was also out of the question. No, he had to take one or two of them out without a confrontation. He had to lay a trap for them. Something they would not expect. It would have to appear natural. And there would have to be some kind of bait that they could not pass up. But Panther was the question mark. He was the one who worried Book the most. For any kind of a trap to succeed it would have to get by Panther. Somehow Panther would have to be distracted.

"Let's go," Book said to her. "We have to put some distance between them and us. I've come up with an idea that might work. We'd have to be lucky, and everything would have to fall into place. But it could happen if we worked together. Angela, both of us would have to part with something that neither one of us wants to give up. Now get in the canoe. I'll tell you about it later after I get it all sorted out."

****

Book and Angela looked like two ghosts floating upon the surface of the water. Their wooden canoe passed through the heavy mist of morning fog. Angela was in the canoe's front watching for any sign of protruding tree stumps or jagged limestone. Book paddled while not at all happy with the snail's pace Angela had forced upon him. The slowness of travel irritated Book. He wanted to put distance between him and Angela and the three Seminoles. But Angela had warned against going too fast in the thick fog. Acquiescing, Book went along by intermittently dipping his paddle into the water while following Angela's direction about which way to steer the canoe.

"I can't see Panther and his two cousins going this slow. At the rate we're going, they'll be bumping into us in this fog. And another thing, if we are to be setting the trap that I have in mind for them we will need time. Traveling at this speed, I don't see us having that time."

"It'll clear soon enough," Angela responded without looking back at him. "The sun has already started to shine through. And the wind is picking up. It shouldn't be too much longer and we'll be able to go faster. And as far as Panther is concerned, he can't move his canoe any faster than we can move ours. He knows what a tree stump or rock can do to the underbelly of a canoe. And besides that, it's easy to make a mistake in this fog. Taking the wrong waterway means we don't end up at Armadillo Flats."

Book said to her, "I hope you're right about him not going any faster than us. Because if you're not they'll soon be on top of us and we'll be shooting it out with them."

"Forget about the fog and tell me about your plan. I want to hear everything. But I must admit that I already don't like the part about me giving up something that I care a lot about."

"All right, I guess this is as good a time as any to tell you," Book said while wondering how receptive Angela was going to be. "Back in Afghanistan we used to lay booby traps for the Taliban. After a skirmish, we would take their dead guys' weapons and put doctored rounds into the gun magazines. We would then leave them there for the Taliban who would return after we left. Each of the rifles was rigged to explode whenever fired again. It would either kill or maim the one who fired it. That's pretty much what I've got in mind for Panther and his two cousins."

"We only have one gun. You can't be planning on leaving the Glock behind for them. That would leave us completely defenseless."

"No, not a gun. This is going to be a different kind of booby trap. We're going to use a cottonmouth for our booby trap. I must have seen two dozen or more cottonmouths in the water since yesterday. In the water they're easy to grab. You take them from behind the head and hold 'em tight. We'll need a big one for what I got in mind."

"Frank, I don't understand your plan. How are you going to use a cottonmouth as a booby trap?"

"I'm counting on the assessment you gave me of Raindrop and Acorn as being two guys who are none too bright. And their greed of course. Because after I catch our cottonmouth, I'm going to drive a knife into his tail and stake him out in a patch of bushes. He should eventually settle down and wrap himself around the knife. I'm then going to bait the trap with something that Raindrop and Acorn can't pass up. It'll be in the open where they will have no trouble seeing it. And when either one of them goes to pick it up—WHAM—our cottonmouth comes out of the bushes and bites him. It should take both Raindrop and Acorn out of commission. The one who is bitten will need the other one to take him back to Gator's Pond for a shot of anti-venom serum. That will leave us just Panther. We will have a chance then. Not much of one but still a chance."

Angela turned back around and held up her right hand. Book stopped paddling. He caught the wide-open green eyes and the strands of brown hair that fell aimlessly across her forehead. Angela had a lopsided grin on her face. It said that she thought he was crazy. Book found her looking even more attractive in the early morning fog. In the middle of a swamp covered over in dirt and sweat, Angela still looked good to him. He found himself smiling back at her.

"Something tells me that you don't think much of my plan," Book said still smiling.

Angela told him. "Frank, if that's all you got for a plan we may as well just sit here and wait for them. Because we don't a have a prayer. What in the world could ever make either Raindrop or Acorn put their hand anywhere near a bush so a snake could bite it?"

"Your gold bracelet. I told you that we would both have to give up something that means a lot to us."

"My bracelet?" The grin quickly vanished from Angela's face. It was replaced by a look of indignation. "I would rather die than give it up. It means everything in the world to me. And you of all people know that. Frank, I told you what this bracelet means to me. And what about you? You said that both of us would have to give up something. What do you have that could possibly compare to my mother's bracelet?"

Book took the photograph of him and Andy out of his front pants pocket. He showed it to Angela.

"This is all I have left of my family," he said to her. "I plan on sticking it to a tree where Panther can find it, somewhere up ahead of the place where we leave the bracelet. I told you before that Panther was the question mark. He has to be distracted for this booby trap to work. If he's left wondering why I stuck this photo to a tree, it could give Raindrop and Acorn the opportunity to see your bracelet shining in the sun. Hopefully, their curiosity and greed will override their caution. They'll want your gold bracelet bad enough to go reaching for it where they shouldn't. Angela, I know it doesn't have much of a chance of working, but it's the only chance we have. And it might work. If it doesn't, we're dead anyway."

Angela turned her back to him while kneeling down in the front of the canoe. Her gaze was directed toward the water. Motioning with a right hand, she ordered Book to commence paddling. He observed the young woman's right hand drop down to take hold of the gold bracelet on her left wrist.

"Frank, are you sure there is no other way?"

"Yes, I'm sure," Book said while wishing that there was something else he could use for bait. Dipping the canoe's paddle into the water, the army ranger captain could not see Angela's face. But he knew there had to be tears filling up both her eyes. Book saw the tears when she came back around to face him.

"All right, you can have it." He watched Angela quickly remove the gold bracelet. She set it down on the knapsack in front of him. While looking directly at Book, she said to him, "I only hope that the man who ends up with my mother's bracelet gets a cottonmouth's bite along with it."

"Me too," Book told her before picking up the bracelet and putting it inside his front pants pocket along with the photograph of him and Andy.

CHAPTER FORTY-FOUR

THE SUN HAD burnt away most of the early morning fog by the time Panther and his two cousins pulled their canoes up onto the muddy embankment of Pine Cone Island. White ash from Book and Angela's overnight fire was evident on the ground where Book had kicked the smoldering embers into the water. Acorn bent down and took a handful of ash.

"Not warm," he said to Panther who had his back to him. Panther did not respond. Standing by the water's edge, the Seminole stared out into the swamp. He gazed upon the waterway that he knew Book and Angela had taken through the sycamore trees. The Seminole's black eyes squinted against the bright morning sunlight while his thoughts stayed on the quarry that he knew was no more than two hours ahead. The two had spent the night on Pine Cone Island eating frog legs and crawfish. And before the sun had risen, they took their canoe through the heavy fog, going slow to avoid protruding tree stumps and rocks. They would not have taken a chance on traveling through the fog unless they had felt Panther and his two cousins were coming after them. Book. He had to be the one pushing them. It had to be him, Panther reasoned. Angela would have felt safe. She would have thought that he and the cousins had taken the route to Everglades City. No, it was Book. Panther had been right about the army ranger. He had seen it in the man's eyes that day at the marina when they exchanged looks. Panther recognized the eyes of a hunter in Book. And that Book had killed men before. The Seminole felt a sudden surge of adrenalin pass through him. He and his two cousins should reach Book and Angela by late afternoon. Then they would kill them and cut off their ears. And bring the ears back to Bo Wiley so they could get their money. It would be a good hunt. It would be one that Panther would always remember.

"Let's go," he said not bothering to look over at Acorn and Raindrop. The Seminole shoved his canoe into the water and jumped into it. "But be careful," he added before briefly turning back to look at them. "This man we are hunting is not like anyone we have ever hunted before."

****

The afternoon sun was hot while a steady wind blew out of the south. Panther knew a big storm was coming and would soon be descending upon the Everglades. He and his two cousins had been paddling at a back-breaking pace for more than four hours. While Book and Angela could not be more than an hour, maybe even less ahead of them. Panther wanted to end the hunt so that he and his cousins could return to Gator's Pond before the storm's arrival. He glanced over his left shoulder to look at Acorn and Raindrop. The two brothers were in the canoe behind him. Both men's faces showed the strain after hours of heavy paddling. Panther knew that they needed rest. He should have called for a stop long ago. They would all have to be at their best when the time came to confront Book and Angela. Book was armed with a Glock semi-automatic handgun. And he would be adept at using it. Should they stop or keep up the hard pace? What to do? It was a question filling

Panther's mind as he rounded the stand of Sycamore trees where he observed a photograph hanging from a tree branch.

"What is it?" Acorn asked him after seeing Panther reach up and take down the photo.

"I don't know for sure," Panther replied while he stared intently at the photograph of two young boys with their arms around each other. Both were smiling. The eyes of one of the boys drew him. Panther focused on the boy's eyes. But why, he thought. Why would he leave this old photo of himself for me to find? He had to have a reason. Panther could not divert his gaze from the young face in the photograph. Puzzled, he looked up wanting to show Acorn and Raindrop the photo. His two cousins were no longer there.

The bright sunlight reflected off the shiny gold bracelet. The outcropping of muddy ground had a cluster of bushes along with a small section of open ground. The gold bracelet lay shining on the section of open ground. Acorn and Raindrop's canoe had nearly reached the extension when Panther yelled for them to stop. The two brothers either did not hear him or had chosen to ignore his warning. Because Acorn came out the front of the canoe and Raindrop was right behind him. Both men saw the gold bracelet. And both men wanted it. Raindrop grabbed Acorn. He threw his brother down onto the ground and dove for the gold bracelet. Laughing, he held it up for Acorn to see. The black snake struck. It came out of the bushes fastening onto Raindrop's right wrist. The cottonmouth's fangs sunk deep. Raindrop screamed. He dropped the bracelet. A rifle shot sounded loudly in the swamp. The snake's black head became separated from the rest of its body. Panther had shot it off from more than fifty yards away.

****

Book stopped paddling the canoe. Angela turned around in the front of the canoe to look at him. They both had heard the rifle shot. By the sound, it was not too far away. It would have been in the area of where they had left the bracelet and the snake. That meant Panther was less than an hour behind them.

"We don't know if it worked or not," Book said to Angela before once again dipping his paddle into the water. "But we do know that they're close."

Angela said to him, "We should be reaching dry land fairly soon. Maybe then we can find somewhere to ride out the storm that's coming. Frank, I hope to God it worked. Otherwise, we'll be dealing with all three of them before the day is over."

"But even if it did work we still have to get a better lead," Book told her. The army ranger captain commenced to swiping harder at the water with his paddle driving it deep.

CHAPTER FORTY-FIVE

DEA HEAD OF Special Operations Jim Garrison sought the seclusion of his war room while attempting to come to grips with his decision on aborting Operation Silverback and Operation Rescue. He had agreed with Jack Ross. Nothing should jeopardize the CIA's neutralizing of Colonel Hosseini and the Iranian agents who had come into the United States from Mexico. The CIA Director had informed Garrison that recent data revealed that more than two-hundred-thousand people of Lebanese and Syrian descent presently live in Mexico. It was anyone's guess as to the number of foreign agents amongst them. The threat to the United States of America was real. Garrison could appreciate it. But he still had Angela Valadez to think about. She was his responsibility and his alone.

Garrison remembered the day he had first met Angela at the University of Miami. Their meeting took place in the office of the president of the university. The young woman could not understand why she had been called to the university president's office. She took a chair opposite Garrison who went on to explain the DEA's desperate need for her services. The mere mention of Bo Wiley's name brought out the reaction from Angela Valadez that Garrison was hoping for.

"I was born and raised in Indian Town so there is nothing you can tell me about Bo Wiley and his brother Cash," Angela had volunteered. "They are both evil and everything about them turns evil as well."

"How would you like to put a stop to that evil?" Garrison had asked the university senior who was preparing to graduate in another month from the University of Miami. He told Angela about the job opening for police officer at Gator's Pond. And that her being both female and from Indian Town undoubtedly would land her the job. "You would be a trained DEA agent prior to your taking the police officer's job at Gator's Pond. Your DEA assignment would be to work undercover and gather enough evidence for federal indictments to be obtained against Bo and Cash Wiley. Angela, you would report to me and to me alone. But I must inform you that the last undercover DEA agent assigned to Gator's Pond was discovered. And Bo Wiley had him murdered. His body has not been recovered and it probably never will be."

Garrison told Angela Valadez that he would give her a week to decide on whether she would take the assignment. He received her phone call the following day saying that she would. Angela's young pretty face now appeared in Garrison's mind. Was she already dead? Would her body also not be recovered?

Yellow Flower had telephoned Garrison on Angela's behalf. Bo Wiley's mistress told the DEA Head of Special Operations that Angela and Book had possession of the priest's flash drive and were taking it to the park ranger station at Armadillo Flats. They were traveling by canoe through the swamp. While Bo Wiley had sent three Seminole Indians after them with orders to kill both Angela and Book. The Indians were good hunters and being well paid by Wiley.

Garrison slammed his closed fist down on the table in front of him. His own agent, the one he had personally recruited, was fleeing for her life, while he was sitting safely hidden away in his war room basement. A hard grimace took over Garrison's face. The DEA Head of Special Operations had given his word to Jack Ross that he would not interfere. That both Operation Silverback and Operation Rescue would be aborted. But he could not just sit and do nothing. Ross was in Miami keeping surveillance on one of Colonel Hosseini's terrorist cells. He had invited Garrison to join him. And Miami was a lot closer to Armadillo Flats than Washington D.C. Garrison immediately took out his cell phone. His personal secretary answered on the first ring. The CIA Head told her that he wanted to be on the first flight to Miami. Any seat would do as long as he was on the first flight out. Yes, coach seating would be fine. Absolutely not. Nobody was to be told where he was going or who he was seeing. His whereabouts were to be kept strictly confidential. And no, Garrison had no idea when he was coming back.

CHAPTER FORTY-SIX

DEA AGENT JOE Torres remained hidden in the heavy foliage throughout most of the day. He had stayed low to circle the edge of the compound checking out whatever security the women's captors had put in place. Two large canvas tents were set up at one end of the compound. Torres assumed that the tents served as some sort of rest area, probably the men's overnight sleeping quarters. A green-colored, sheet-metal shed was situated close to the tents. While a red-colored pick-up truck was parked nearby. Torres did not see any other vehicles inside the compound.

Keeping well hidden, Torres watched the four men sitting underneath a tent flap located not too far from the concrete building. The men had been sitting for hours smoking cigarettes and drinking cans of beer. Their loud voices, interspersed with coarse laughter never seemed to wane. All were armed with handguns prominently displayed at their sides. While close by, Torres spotted a stack of rifles leaning against a large metal drum. Two Dobermans were lying on the ground next to the rifles. The large black dogs had chains around their necks with leashes fastened to two wooden stakes protruding out of the ground.

And there was a fifth man. Torres recognized him as the sentry he had spotted the day before. The man was wearing the same green fatigues and sunglasses. And he was sitting in a chair by the compound entrance with an automatic rifle on his lap. Like the men by the tent, Torres had watched him all afternoon. The man would finish a can of beer, toss the empty can into the weeds, and then take a fresh beer out of the cooler that he had resting on the ground next to him. Torres counted twelve beers in a little more than five hours.

The sky overhead was growing darker, while a southerly wind had turned gusty. Torres noticed that the men were getting nervous. Apparently, the ominous change in the weather had proven bothersome to them. They took turns coming out from under the tent flap to look up at the black clouds rolling in. A scatter of rain began to fall. Lightning streaked the sky further to the west. The wind was increasing, growing stronger. Torres observed the surrounding tall pine trees bending in the wind. Thunder crashed overhead. The sentry at the compound entrance leaped out of his chair. Clutching his rifle, the man ran across the grassy area to be with the others. The four men were already packing up. Hurriedly, they started throwing their belongings into the back of the pick-up truck. Two of the men began taking down the tents. One man placed the Dobermans in the back of the truck. He then got into the truck's cab. It was raining harder. Torres wished that he had a rain coat, something to keep the pelting rain off him. He saw the big black man run over to the concrete building where the women were being held. The man was doing something to the door. Padlock. The man had padlocked the concrete building door. Torres watched Oil Can as he ran back to join the other men. But they were already inside the truck. It was pulling away. Oil Can jumped into the back of the moving truck sharing space with the two Dobermans. Through a torrent of falling rain, Torres had difficulty making out the moving vehicle as it drove out of the compound.

After he came to his feet, a gust of wind nearly knocked Joe Torres over. The DEA agent knew that he did not have much time.

Hurricane force winds would soon make it impossible for him to move about. He would then have to seek cover. Torres ran through the heavy undergrowth to where he had left his knapsack. Reaching the bushes, he quickly grabbed the bag before heading back toward the compound. Heavy sheets of rain whipped at his face. Torres attempted to block the stinging wetness by holding up the knapsack. The DEA agent knew that he had to hurry. The wind and rain were growing more intense; but he knew that the concrete building would afford him safety.

The storage building's metal door was on the north side of the structure. Torres headed for it. He fought the driving wind and slashing rain. The roar of the wind sounded in his ears. He nearly slipped twice on the rain-soaked ground. Reaching the building's door, Torres fell against it. It gave the DEA agent momentary respite from the driving wind and rain. At the same time he discovered that the door's sliding bolt lock was fortified by a heavy metal padlock. The men had left the compound to escape the hurricane. But before leaving they had made sure that the women were securely locked down. He would have to somehow remove the padlock. But how? He had no sledge hammer or axe. It was a heavy padlock. Torres knew that a rock would never crack its hard metal. No, he needed a sledge hammer. The green-metal shed. It could be used to store tools. Holding up the knapsack, Torres ran towards the shed.

Broken off tree branches and debris filled the air. They pelted him on his way to the metal shed. Torres kept the knapsack raised to protect his face but no matter how hard he tried some of the debris got through. Getting closer, he observed that the shed had lost several strips of siding. It had a cannibalized look. Its metal frame shook violently. Torres knew it would not stand much longer. He kicked the shed door open and went inside. Large canisters of gasoline were everywhere. Torres waded through the metal containers until reaching the back of the shed. Shovels lined a wall but no sledge hammers. He took hold of the closest spade to him. Torres was holding the shovel in his right hand when he spotted the metal axe. It was resting upright in a corner of the shed piled high with cords of wood. Torres let loose of the shovel and quickly grabbed the axe. He then hurried toward the door. Aluminum strips were blowing off the roof overhead. The metal shed was giving way all around him. Torres was halfway back to the concrete building when the shed collapsed.

****

Gabriella held onto Aleena with both arms. The raging storm outside had made the blackness of the storage room even more frightening. There was no longer any light coming from the overhead windows. Just darkness. Women were crying all around her; Aleena's trembling body only added to the anguish. Was there any hope left for them? Were they all to die in this awful place? Then the terrible pounding started. The building's metal door was being struck over and over again. Frightened women crawled along the dirt floor to the rear of the storage room. The women wanted to get as far away as possible from the entrance door. Who was outside trying to get in?

And then the pounding stopped. In its place was the sound of the storage building's door being opened. Gabriella placed Aleena behind her and stood up. She would face the impending danger alone. A rush of adrenalin took over. Gabriella could feel it surging through her. All the earlier fear was gone. She would be brave. She would stand up to whoever came through the door. Then a light appeared in the darkness. Gabriella saw it. Holding up both hands, she covered her eyes. The light was so bright that it hurt. And she heard a voice behind the light. At first Gabriella did not recognize the voice. Then she did. It was loud and forceful and so good to hear.

"Gabriella, it's me, Shadow. Where are you? Everything is going to be alright. I've come to take you and the women home."

"Here Shadow," Gabriella shouted while walking toward the light. "I'm here. I knew that you would come. I knew that you would never leave me."

Gabriella hurried toward the light.

CHAPTER FORTY-SEVEN

THE BULLET SLAMMED into the cypress tree only inches away from Book's head. He heard the bullet whiz by his right ear. The hunting rifle's loud report quickly followed. Its cracking sound caused a large flock of White Ibis to take flight. And for Book to grab the back of Angela's head to pull her down into the canoe. The army ranger captain took a quick glance back. He did not care for what he saw. Panther was standing up in a canoe no more than two hundred yards away. And the Indian was raising his rifle for another shot.

"Stay down," Book told Angela before plunging his paddle deep into the water alongside the canoe. Immediately, the canoe diverted off to the left into a heavy growth of cypress trees. "It's Panther and he's right on top of us. He nearly got me with that shot. I can't believe in this wind he was able to come so close. The trees are thicker up ahead. That should take away any chance of his getting a clear shot, but we'll have to put some distance between him and us."

"What about Acorn and Raindrop?" Angela asked. He watched her rip a dry piece of bark off the trunk of a cypress tree to use as a make-shift paddle. She immediately began paddling.

"I didn't see them. Our booby trap must have worked. If they were still around, they would've been firing their rifles right along with Panther. And, by the way, I like your paddle. We should get a good lead on him with both of us paddling."

Angela smiled back at him. "I started to feel bad after seeing you doing all the heavy work. And besides we're going to need that lead. Pretty soon we will be leaving the water and going the rest of the way to the ranger station on foot. That's when Panther's rifle is going to become a major problem. There's a lot of open ground on the way to Armadillo Flats while not much cover to speak of. And the storm will be hitting us right about then."

Book said to her. "That means we'll have to carry the canoe so we can use it to get under once the storm hits. It's going to be tough hauling this thing but I don't think we have any other choice. And we won't be alone. Panther will have to do the same with his canoe. So he shouldn't end up gaining any distance on us."

Another rifle shot echoed through the swamp.

"Where is he?" Angela exclaimed. "He's shooting at us again. Frank, do you see him? With all these trees, I can't make him out. How can he see us?"

Book touched Angela's back with the tip of his paddle before dipping the paddle back into the water.

"He can't Angela. He's playing mind games by firing his gun in an attempt to make us think that he's shooting at us. The sound bounces off the trees and water leaving one to think that the shooter is closer than he really is. It's an old trick. Keep your quarry on edge and he might make a mistake. You can bet that there'll be more rifle shots before we're out of this swamp."

Book watched Angela drive the piece of tree bark down into the water once again. The canoe spurted forward through the overhanging tree branches and white lily flowers careening out of the dark water. There appeared in Angela a renewed strength of purpose. Book could understand how she felt. He felt the same. Both of them wanted out of the swamp. No one liked to be hunted. And in order to have their role reversed a major change would have to take place. Panther would have to make a mistake. Book was counting heavily on the Indian making it. A mistake on Panther's part was the only chance that he and Angela had to survive. The army ranger captain knew that a game of cat and mouse was being played out. And in the end it was usually the cat that won. Somehow he and Angela would have to take over that role. But how? Certainly not in this swamp. It would have to be where Panther least expected it. Where his guard would be down and he felt safe.

Book looked over at Angela. The young woman was paddling hard with no letup in her. She was giving it everything she had. For her sake, Book hoped it would be different this time. That somehow in the end the mouse came out the winner. Think, he told himself. Figure out a way. Get in his head. Know the man. Then you will know what he will do. Suddenly Book's thoughts were interrupted. He lost all sense of concentration. The sound of another rifle shot echoed across the swamp. The army ranger captain drove his paddle deep into the dark water.

CHAPTER FORTY-EIGHT

YELLOW FLOWER RESTED in bed listening to the wind howling outside her bedroom window. She knew that Bo Wiley would be joining her at any moment. He would be coming through the bedroom door with an angry look on his face. Along with whiskey on his breath and hate in his eyes. Yellow Flower had seen that same look many times through the years while serving as Bo Wiley's mistress. It usually meant another beating. And her being bruised and hurting for days on end. But Yellow Flower knew that this time things would be different. Bo Wiley was not going to be satisfied with just another beating. No, this time he planned on killing her. Yellow Flower had come back early to the Wiley mansion from Indian Town due to the storm. While standing close to the downstairs kitchen door, she had overheard Bo Wiley tell his brother Cash that he was going to kill her.

"Cash, are you sure about this?"

"I'm positive. After you told me about your desk key being in the book on a different page than where you had left it, I contacted the telephone company. Their records show that a call had been made last night from your desk phone to the DEA office in Washington D.C. Bo it had to have been Yellow Flower who made that call. There is no one else. Besides she and Angela were like two hens clucking away whenever they were together. No, Yellow Flower telephoned the DEA for Angela. She must've known that you kept the desk key hidden in one of the books on the shelf. What are you goin' to do about it?"

"What do you think?"

"You got to kill her. She probably knows about that plane with the suicide bombers comin' in tomorrow after the storm passes. And the women at the storage shed who will be takin' the same plane back to Cuba. Big brother, we can't let Yellow Flower be around to testify against us. Either you kill her or I'll do it. It don't matter to me who does it as long as it's done."

"No, I'll do it tonight after she goes to bed. I'd just like to know what she told the DEA."

"Why don't you ask her before you kill her?"

"I plan on doing that."

Yellow Flower heard Bo Wiley's heavy footsteps in the hallway. They stopped outside her bedroom door. The bedroom was dark but after he opened the door the hallway light shone in. She saw his large frame silhouetted in the doorway. It was a figure without a face. Yellow Flower heard Wiley's heavy breathing. Then she observed his large shoulders rise up in an arch. He took a step into the bedroom before turning on the light.

"Before I kill you I want to know what you told the DEA," he said to her. She saw a burning hate in his eyes. It caused Yellow Flower to shudder. She had never before seen such hate in anyone. Not even in Bo Wiley.

"I told them what Angela told me to say."

"Which is what?" he asked while rocking back and forth on unsteady legs. Wiley had been drinking heavily. Yellow Flower could see that he was drunk. She answered him in a steady voice.

"That she and Book have the flash drive that will put you and Cash away for years and years. And that they were taking it to the ranger station at Armadillo Flats."

"You dirty …"

"Don't come any closer, Bo," Yellow Flower said before jumping out of bed and raising up a blue-steel revolver with both hands. The Indian woman was fully clothed and had the gun pointed directly at Wiley.

"Where did you get that?" he asked her while not quite believing what he was seeing.

"Angela gave it to me."

"Did she teach you how to use it?"

"Yes, she did."

"I don't believe you. Give me that gun."

He started towards her.

"Bo, I'm warning you."

"You're warning me?"

Bo Wiley took one more step. It was his last. The Indian woman fired three shots. All three struck Bo Wiley in the center of his chest. The man was dead before his body hit the bedroom floor. Yellow Flower went over to him and looked down.

She said to him, "Bo, I don't feel anything. I don't feel good that you're dead and I don't feel bad. I don't feel anything at all. I guess that's what living with you all these years has done to me. I don't feel anything anymore."

Yellow Flower got back into bed. Prior to pulling up the covers, she put the gun back underneath her pillow.

CHAPTER FORTY-NINE

"*NO TENGAS MIEDO*—Don't be afraid," Joe Torres told the Mexican women who were gathered around him in a tight circle. Two 6-volt battery lanterns, which Torres had removed from his knapsack, illuminated the group. The DEA agent took note of the anxious faces and frightened looks. Gabriella and her sister, Aleena, were the closest to him. They, along with the other women, were sitting on the concrete building's dirt floor. Torres smiled in an attempt to portray confidence while deep inside he was feeling just the opposite. Fear for the women's safety tore at him. Tomorrow all of the women could end up dead. Their bodies discarded somewhere in the swamp. His decision could very well mean either life or death for them. And Torres could think of only one decision. They had to make a run for it.

Immediately after the storm and with enough light to see by, they would attempt their escape. He would have Gabriella escort the women along the outer edge of the swamp as far as the river. Once there, they would follow the river to the main highway. At the bridge overpass, a motorist could then be flagged down and the Everglades City police notified. He would stay behind to fend off the dogs. The two Dobermans would be off their leashes and coming fast. While the armed men would not be far behind the dogs. Torres could see no other way to get the women clear. It was the only chance they had.

In Spanish, Torres told the women what they would have to do. He prefaced it by telling them that he was a U.S. federal agent who had come to take them back home to Mexico. He also made sure that they could see the 9mm. Beretta inside his waistband. He had Gabriella stand up so that she could be introduced as the undercover agent working with him. Torres noted the women's anxious and frightened looks slowly begin to disappear. Some of the faces even produced smiles. The women began talking amongst themselves. They had been rescued and were going home. Torres raised his hand for them to quiet down. Pointing to Gabriella, he told them that tomorrow they were to listen to whatever orders Gabriella gave them. She would be in charge. He would stay behind in case they were being followed. Everything was going to be alright. All of them were safe. They no longer had to be afraid.

"Now tell me the truth," Gabriella said to him after she and Torres had found a secluded corner away from the women. "First of all, what happened to the two swat teams, and secondly, why are you staying behind and not escaping with the rest of us?"

"The operation was aborted and the swat teams were pulled off," Torres said to her while staring hard into Gabriella's dark brown eyes. She was staring back at him equally as hard. "Don't ask me why they were recalled because I don't know," he continued. "And for your second question, someone has to stop the two Dobermans. The dogs have been trained to kill and there's no way we are going to outrun them. I'm the guy with the gun so I stay behind. It's as simple as that."

Gabriella asked him, "If the operation was aborted, why didn't you withdraw. Why didn't you back off like the others had done? Shadow, what made …"

"I didn't, and let's just leave it at that," he said, cutting her off. Torres could see that she was not going to be satisfied with his answer. "I have my reasons," he added. "And it has nothing to do with you. But then maybe it does. Because, after I have given someone my word, I keep it. And I gave it to you that day back in Laredo after you agreed to go undercover and put your life on the line for your sister and the other women. I said that I would always be there for you. Well here I am."

He stopped talking and turned his head to the side. When he came back to her, Gabriella saw the hurt look on his face. "I've made mistakes in the past," Torres said looking at her once again. "Things that I'm plenty sorry for. Things that I wish I could go back and change. But I have never intentionally lied to anyone that I cared about. Gabriella, you've got to believe that."

The glow from the lantern resting on the ground next to them cast a golden light. It illuminated Joe Torres's face. Gabriella looked at the dark stubble along with the dozen or so scratch marks across the forehead and cheeks. She knew that the scratches came from the saw palmetto plants at the edge of the compound. He had received them while trying to get his note to her. It was a beautiful face, she thought. Gabriella felt tears coming. Don't, she told herself. Don't ruin it by crying.

"What's your name?" she finally said to him. "And don't tell me it's Shadow."

"Joe Torres," he quickly answered. Gabriella leaned forward and kissed him. She felt him kiss her back. Then she saw him reach down to turn off the lantern before taking her into his arms.

"Joe Torres," Gabriella whispered to him. "I like that name."

CHAPTER FIFTY

PANTHER CLOSED HIS eyes and listened to the raging storm outside. The Seminole lay beneath his dugout canoe with his deer rifle alongside him. The canoe's concave sides shook from the strong winds, while sheets of rain pelted the wooden frame. Crashing trees fell all around him. An angry god had descended, unceasing in its wrath. The Seminole feared no man, but this wind-god frightened him.

Panther opened his eyes. He stared into the empty darkness of his improvised sanctuary. The Seminole knew that Book and Angela were less than three hundred yards away. They had left the swamp and, like him, were riding out the storm underneath their canoe. It was all a part of the game, Panther thought. And by morning the game would be over. He would put an end to it. After the storm passed, he would begin shooting at the limestone outcroppings Book and Angela were hiding behind. His rifle shots would keep them pinned down enabling him to flank them. Then there would be only the matter of whom to kill first. Panther had decided on Angela. He would save Book for last.

The Seminole's right hand touched the gold bracelet fastened to his left wrist. The bracelet had once belonged to Angela but now it belonged to him. Raindrop had dropped the gold bracelet after being bitten by the cottonmouth. Panther picked it up after Acorn hurriedly whisked his brother away to Gator's Pond in order to obtain the anti-venom serum. The army ranger captain had laid the perfect trap. Anticipating Raindrop and Acorn's foolishness and greed, he had set the gold bracelet down where it could be readily spotted. Then he had carefully placed a captured cottonmouth within striking distance. And the photograph. Book had left the photo pinned to the tree for me to find, Panther deduced. He knew that I would be distracted by it. And it allowed time for Raindrop and Acorn to first see and then go for the gold bracelet.

What kind of man is he? Panther asked himself. He is like no man I have ever met. And he persuaded Angela to give up her mother's bracelet. Panther knew that Angela would rather die than to have parted with it. The Seminole smiled. It suddenly became so clear to him. Angela was in love with Book. Otherwise she would not have surrendered her mother's gold bracelet. But does he love her? If so, there was his weakness. He would want to protect her. Book might have gotten away if he had left Angela. He was good enough to have survived on his own in the swamp. But he did not leave her. Book had made a mistake. He had reasoned with his heart and not his mind.

"That is why in the morning I will kill him," the Seminole said out loud before closing his eyes and going to sleep.

****

Angela moved the piece of lit candle closer. The small flame illuminated Book's face with its soft light. Two dark blue eyes appeared only inches away from her along with the all too familiar half-grin. Angela searched his tired face for something that would give her strength and a feeling of hope. She and Book were confined together underneath the hollowed-out canoe listening to the storm raging all around them.

"Do you have any idea where he is?" Angela asked. "I heard the shots and saw where some of them landed but I never spotted him. But I know he couldn't be too far away."

Book took hold of Angela's two hands. He knew that she was scared and looking for him to take her fear away. Book also knew that the next twelve hours would determine whether they lived or died. Somehow he would have to get that fact through to Angela without causing her more fear. They had one chance to survive. He had to find a way of explaining it to her.

"Panther's about three hundred yards away by a stand of trees. He's under his canoe just like we're under ours waiting out the storm. But once this storm blows through he'll be coming out. It will be daylight by then and easy for him to pick out a target. He'll keep us pinned down and begin circling out of the Glock's gun range. Eventually we'll be flanked. Panther will have a good shot at both of us at that point."

"So what you're saying is there's no hope for us," Angela said looking at him. He could see her green eyes in the candle light. They appeared on fire while Angela was fighting back the tears that were trying to come out. Book gently squeezed her two hands together.

"No, that's not what I'm saying," he said while bringing forth a smile. "Panther won't be flanking us tomorrow because tonight I'm going out and getting behind him. In the morning when he crawls out from underneath his canoe he'll find me there waiting for him. I'll take the three-pronged spear with me and leave you the Glock. If for some reason I don't get him, the gun will at least give you a chance."

She tried to stop him from talking but he would not let her.

"No, listen," Book said. "He's counting on me to not chance it in this storm. That's the one mistake I've been waiting for him to make. He wouldn't go out in a storm like this so he thinks no one else would either. That's the way Panther looks at things. It's always about what he would do. Well this time, he's wrong. And it's going to cost him his life."

Angela told him, "There has to be something else that we could do without you going out in the storm."

"There isn't," Book responded while reaching into his front pants pocket. "Here I want you to hold onto the flash drive just in case this doesn't work out the way I planned it. If I'm not back by the time the sun comes up keep low and head for the ranger station at Armadillo Flats. And if he starts shooting don't stop. Run a zigzag pattern until you're out of rifle range."

Angela took the rosary beads from him. She ran her fingertips across the crucifix containing the flash drive. Book watched her cross herself with the crucifix before placing it to her lips. Then he saw the worried look come to her face.

"Frank, you can't go out there. That wind will kill you. There's trees being blown over and debris flying through the air that if any of it struck you, you'd be killed for sure. Stay here with me. We'll find some other way in the morning to deal with Panther."

"There is no other way. Look at me, Angela. Tell me that you understand that I have to go."

"Alright, I understand, but I still don't want you to go," she said looking at him. The tears that she had been fighting suddenly filled her eyes.

"Don't worry," Book said before leaning forward to kiss her. "I'll survive the storm and be back in the morning."

CHAPTER FIFTY-ONE

CIA AGENT ADOLFO Sardina put down the binoculars and picked up the hand-held transmitter. He saw that the transmitter was showing a green light. That meant the two-way radio was operable. And in a few minutes he would be able to confirm to his superior that the Russian-owned ATR-72 Twin Propeller passenger plane along with its fifty passengers had been destroyed. Sardina's assignment was successfully completed. The fifty suicide bombers headed for the United States mainland were no longer a threat to America. And he, Adolfo Sardina, could now return to Havana and his second floor apartment above the bakery where his lovely wife, Eva, and their two beautiful children Emmy, age 9, and Lolo, age 7, were presently having breakfast.

The Cuban military base was located six miles outside of Havana, overlooking the Atlantic Ocean. The base's single airstrip had 24-hour military protection, which included motion detectors, canine patrols, and electrified fencing that encompassed the entire base. The protection extended for three miles in circumference. Sardina had positioned himself in a rocky enclave four miles from the airstrip. He had been waiting since early morning for the Russian-owned airplane to take on its fifty passengers. Sardina's wait was over. He had watched the last of the suicide bombers board the airplane.

Putting down the hand-held transmitter, Sardina picked up the FIM-92A Stinger. The rocket launcher fired an infrared homing surface-to-air missile (SAM), which locked on to the heat in a plane engine's exhaust. Maximum range: 5 miles. Sardina brought the Stinger up to his right shoulder and put his eye up to the scope. Through the peephole, he observed the pilot begin guiding the plane onto the runway. A man on the ground waved a yellow flag giving the all clear for takeoff. Sardina took a deep breath and let it out slowly. He steadied the Stinger against his shoulder. The plane was moving forward along the runway. It was starting to gain speed. Sardina followed the plane with the Stinger. He could not wait much longer. The Stinger had only a maximum range of five miles. The front of the plane lifted skyward. The Stinger's lock-on signal came to him. Sardina's right forefinger pulled back on the trigger. The missile made a rushing sound coming out of the launch tube. Sardina watched it speeding 1500 miles per hour towards its target. A fiery explosion suddenly lit up the darkish-gray sky. Shattered pieces of plane mingled with bright, red fire. Clouds of thick, black smoke settled over the military base. Sardina dropped the Stinger and immediately picked up the hand-held transmitter. He pushed the black button on its side.

"Mother Goose is cooked," he said before repeating it over again. "Mother Goose is cooked, do you acknowledge?"

"Yes, Mother Goose is cooked," the voice said back to him over the transmitter. "Now get the hell out of there."

****

CIA Director Jack Ross changed the frequency on his hand-held transmitter. The airplane carrying the suicide bombers was no longer a threat. That meant he could go ahead and implement phase two of his plan. He pushed the black button on the transmitter's side.

"Mother Goose is cooked. You can now deliver your package to the big, bad wolf. Proceed with the delivery."

"Yes, sir. The package to the big, bad wolf is on its way," a voice responded back.

Ross turned to the man seated next to him in the CIA undercover van. The two men occupied the back of a Chevy van parked on the same block as the old furniture store undergoing renovation in Miami's *Little Havana*. Jim Garrison, the DEA Head of Special Operations, had an amused smile on his face. The smile was not lost upon Jack Ross.

"You appreciate our nursery book approach to things, don't you, Jim?"

"Yes, I do. Especially when the package consists of Sarin nerve gas siphoned through the air vents of a furniture store roof where a bunch of Iranian terrorists are hiding. But why go and kill them outright? You can't obtain information from a corpse."

"And then again a corpse can't come back to bite you in the ass either," Ross quickly retorted. "Using a non-lethal knockout gas might give one of them a chance to send out an alarm to the rest of the terrorist cells. That could very easily end up causing the wholesale slaughter of thousands of Americans across the country. Sarin nerve gas enters the body through the lungs and skin. It takes the guy out quick without giving him much time to react. Hopefully, that's what will happen inside the furniture store. We won't know for sure until we get in there to look it over. About an hour from now, we'll go in and see."

Ninety minutes later six men wearing white hazmat suits stood outside the old furniture store on Calle Ocho. One of the men began banging on the front door with a sledge hammer while the others stood behind him holding Koch MP5 submachine guns. The furniture store front door gave way with a resounding boom. The six men hurriedly entered the building.

"Jim stay close to me while we go through this place. I want the two of us seeing everything at the same time so we know exactly what we have," Ross said to Garrison through his hazmat face shield.

Garrison nodded his head before following behind Ross. A dead man greeted them in the front hallway. The Iranian was sitting on the floor with his back against the wall and an automatic pistol on his lap. Blood covered the man's nose and mouth. He was shirtless leaving his black-hairy chest red from the blood that had oozed out of his ruptured lungs.

Ross said, looking down at the man, "He has to be their front door sentry. The Sarin must have gotten to him quick. He didn't even have time to seek help before the stuff entered his lungs and killed him. Hopefully, it got to the rest of them as fast as it got to this guy."

"Jack, look at that," Garrison said pointing to the large room off to their right. "On the table, look at the names written on those placards. New York, Chicago, Boston. That's where they had planned on sending the suicide bombers. The Iranian terrorist cells must be working out of those cities."

Ross and Garrison walked into the room. Two more dead bodies lay on the floor at the far end of the table. Like the sentry at the front door, both were covered in their own blood. Ross and Garrison ignored them going to the table. Each took note of the names of the various cities along with the piles of documents set in front of each placard.

An excited Jack Ross could not keep his exhilaration in check. "We can move swat teams into these cities right away. Jim, I'll need every agent the DEA can spare. Between both our agencies and some help from local law enforcement we can take these sons-of-bitches out once we have the flash drive that your Agent Valadez is bringing to the park ranger station. The flash drive should give us the locations of what safe houses the terrorists are using. After that, those terrorists will be getting a dose of Sarin nerve gas just like these rats got here in Miami."

"Jack, we have to bring the FBI in on this," Garrison said moving forward to make eye contact with Ross. "It's there jurisdiction. All hell will break lose if we try to keep them out of it."

"Hell be damned and the FBI along with it. I'm not going to give the FBI the opportunity to blow this and that's exactly what they'd do if we told them about it. Jim, American lives are at stake. We don't need a publicity seeking bureaucracy getting involved in something as important as this. The FBI would have the news media notified and defense lawyers available for each one of the terrorists. Look at those two dead terrorists on the floor over there. They don't need a lawyer. They need a hole in the ground to put them in. And that's the way every one of the bastards who came here to kill Americans are going to end up before this operation is over."

"All right Jack, if that's the way you want it."

"That's exactly the way I want it," Ross said. "Now lets you and me finish what we have to do here so we can find ourselves a restaurant. Garrison, I don't know about you, but I'm getting mighty hungry."

CHAPTER FIFTY-TWO

THEY WERE NO more than an hour away from the concrete building when Joe Torres heard the dogs barking. At first light and with the storm no longer a factor, he and Gabriella had gathered up the women and directed them toward the path bordering the swamp. The once powerful storm had transformed itself into nothing more than a light rain accompanied by a steady southerly breeze. Most of the women were showing weakness from the lack of food and terrible living conditions. Vomiting and diarrhea among them had become a problem. It made hurrying the pace that much more difficult. Torres observed Gabriella turn back to look at him. He could tell by the expression on the young woman's face that she too had heard the dogs. The fear showing in her brown eyes spoke volumes. It told the DEA agent that Gabriella knew as well as he that the unleashed Dobermans would soon be upon them.

"Joe, the women are too weak. They can't move any faster," Gabriella said to him after she had dropped back to join Torres. "The dogs are getting closer and it won't be long before they reach us. We are not going to be able to get away from them."

"I know," Torres responded while looking at Gabriella and seeing how tired and exhausted she was. He had watched her helping those in need of help, going from one stumbling, falling down woman to another, smiling, giving encouragement, always being there for anyone who needed her. Torres put his right arm around Gabriella's waist and brought her close to him. She in turn rested her head against his shoulder. The two walked together trailing the line of women who were moving slowly up ahead.

"I'm going to stop here," Torres said after they had reached a rise in the muddy path. He removed his arm from around Gabriella's waist. "Stay with the women and keep them moving as best you can. After you come to the river follow it until the highway overpass. You and the women should be safe at that point. Gabriella, I just wanted to …"

"What goodbye? Is that what you just wanted to say? No, the women can make it to the highway overpass on their own. I'm staying here with you."

"No, you're not," Torres said pushing her forward with both hands. "There's only one gun and I got it. There's nothing you can do by staying except for maybe getting yourself killed. And that wouldn't help you or your sister or anyone else. Thanks for everything that you've done. Now get out of here before those dogs show up."

"You won't be able to stop two charging Dobermans without help."

"I'll kill them and catch up with you afterward. Now get out of here before I forget you're a woman."

"They'll be charging you at full speed once they see that you're alone. I could distract them by waving my shirt. It would give you a chance to shoot them running by, not having them charging you head on. You know as well as I do that it's going to take more than one bullet to stop a Doberman that size. They're big and mean and hard to kill. Joe please let me stay. Let me help you."

"Gabriella, I don't need your help, but those women do. That includes Aleena. If for some reason they became disoriented and head into the swamp that would be the end of them. You know that. Now get going and finish the job that you signed on for. I'll meet you at the highway overpass. I promise."

"No, you won't," she said shaking her head and backing away from him. "But I'll go because that's the way you want it. I'll get the women to the overpass and if by some miracle you survive all this I'll be waiting for you."

"Goodbye, Gabriella," Torres said to her. He watched her turn and run down the path to catch up to the women. The chorus of barking dogs caused him to come back around to face what he knew was coming. Torres placed his left knee down onto the muddy ground. He then steadied his gun arm by setting right elbow onto right knee. The dogs' barking told him that they were close. It would only be a matter of a few minutes more. They would come side by side directly at him. Gabriella had been right. It would take at least two or three well-placed shots to bring down each Doberman. Torres would have to make sure that he killed one outright before shifting his aim to the other dog. Otherwise he would never survive an attack by both. Torres saw them coming through the trees. The Dobermans were running abreast taking long strides with their heads carried low. They must have spotted him as well, he thought, because both had stopped barking. It was not long before Torres heard their deep-throated growls. The two dogs were nearly on him. He took a deep breath. The DEA agent aimed his gun and fired.

CHAPTER FIFTY-THREE

BOOK COULD BARELY discern the outline of trees in the early morning sunlight. Most of the trees had been uprooted by the storm leaving several of the pines and hardwoods lying askew with one on top of the other. Book knew Panther was somewhere out there beyond the pile of fallen trees. By now he would have come out from underneath his canoe and set up behind the limestone outcroppings waiting for better light to pick out his target.

The Seminole would be unaware that during the night Book had crawled through sloshing rain and heavy mud and a pelting wind to get behind him. It had left the army ranger captain's body bruised and hurting. Before leaving the safety of the overturned canoe, Angela had wrapped Book in the white nylon netting while allowing openings for his eyes and mouth. What served as a wrapped-mummy look had forestalled even greater injury. The wind-swept branches and debris, for the most part, had glanced off the nylon mesh but some had fallen hard across Book's back and legs. It had left him questioning his ability to react and move effectively in the upcoming confrontation with Panther.

Gripping the three-pronged spear in his right hand, Book crawled in the direction that he hoped would bring him to the Seminole's hiding place. He had not gone more than a few yards when a rifle shot shattered the early morning stillness. Its origin seemed to be somewhere on the other side of a stand of fallen trees. Apparently, Panther was not wasting any time before beginning his attack. Book knew it would not be long before the Seminole started a flanking action against Angela. The army ranger captain quickened his pace. He had to reach Panther before the Seminole left the limestone outcropping. If not, Book's element of surprise would be lost. And that meant giving up the last hope remaining for him and Angela. Two more rifle shots resounded in the early morning air.

****

Panther raised the deer rifle and fired again. He directed another round into the section of rocks where he knew Book and Angela were hiding. The ricocheting bullets would keep his quarry pinned down while allowing him time to circle the limestone section of rocks. Then it would be just a matter of picking out his target and ending the hunt. First Angela and then Book. A couple of more well placed rounds should do it. The man and woman would stay low behind the rocks and not see him moving to his left. They would end up being easily outflanked. Panther would then kill each of them with a head shot. The Seminole felt the burst of adrenalin inside him. It was a good feeling. He knew that the final moments of the game were at hand.

Panther had seen Angela's head come up a couple of times. And quickly duck back down after he started firing. But not Book. The Seminole had not seen the army ranger captain's head yet this morning. Why not? Panther wondered. He had seen him yesterday just before the storm had struck. Then it became too dark to see anything. But why not now? Book had to be with Angela. He would not have survived going out in the storm. No man would have survived.

Uneasiness gnawed at Panther. He turned around to look behind him. But what if Book did go out in the storm? And he survived. And he was behind him at this very moment with the Glock gun in his hand. Panther brought the deer rifle up pointing it toward the trees. His dark eyes searched for any sign of movement, anything that might betray the presence of a man holding a gun. But there was nothing, not even a hint of someone. All that Panther could see and hear were rain and the sound of wind as it blew through the pine trees. The Seminole smiled. It was not like him to feel this way. He had allowed Book to cloud his mind, to touch his inner self. It was the trap laid with the cottonmouth. That's what bothered him. And the photograph left on the tree. It served to reveal the heart and mind of the man. Such a man could be capable of almost anything. But not surviving outside in a hurricane. Panther came back around with the deer rifle. Two more shots, he told himself. He would then move off to his left and circle the limestone outcropping. Book and Angela would be there waiting for him. The army ranger captain had not left the limestone rocks. He was only keeping his head down. The Seminole readied himself for two more shots.

The sound came from somewhere behind him. It caused Panther to turn around. The Seminole froze at the sight awaiting him. Appearing like some fiend out of hell, Book stood wrapped in the mud-cached, white nylon netting holding a three-pronged fishing spear in his upraised right hand. The army ranger captain was no more than fifteen feet away. Panther hesitated. His eyes stayed focused on the wrapped mummy-like figure with only its eyes and mouth showing. For a brief second, the Indian froze. His hesitation cost him. Book let fly with the fishing spear just as Panther's deer rifle came up.

****

Angela heard the rifle shot but nothing more. The unmistakable whine of the bullet ricocheting amongst the rocks that always preceded the shot was conspicuously absent. Then she heard Book calling to her. He was calling from somewhere out by the trees. It was in the area where she knew Panther was holed up behind the rocks. Gripping the Glock inside her right hand, Angela rose up and ran quickly across the open ground toward the trees. Approaching the grove, she heard Book calling to her again. But his voice sounded strange. Angela found him behind a pile of limestone rocks. The army ranger captain was lying on his back with his left hand pressed against a bloody right shoulder. And Panther was only a few yards away from him. Also on his back, the Indian had both hands wrapped around the three-pronged fishing spear's wooden handle. The spear's six-inch prongs were buried deep in Panther's chest. While his two dark eyes stared up at Angela. In addition to the pain, they held disbelief. She could see that he was trying to say something. Panther's lips were moving, but there was no sound. Then she heard him.

"Angela, your man has won. He can give you back your prize. Tell him for me, *'Este-catet ometskes'.*" Angela observed a pain spasm take over Panther's face. Then both his eyes closed.

"Angela, here's the prize he was talking about," Book said holding up the gold bracelet for her to see. "I took it off his wrist with him watching me."

"Frank, how badly are you hurt?" Angela said to him before she set the Glock on the ground and dropped down to him. Book held up the gold bracelet. Angela pushed it away. "The bracelet can wait, let me first take a look at your shoulder."

"It's shattered, but I think the bullet went straight through. I thought you'd be thrilled to have your mother's bracelet back."

"I am," she said to him while commencing to remove the nylon mesh from around his shoulder. "But right now I think your shoulder is more important than my bracelet. Frank, it is badly broken but there's not a lot of blood. We're going to have to get you to the hospital. The ranger station is less than a mile from here. Do you think that you can walk? How bad is the pain?"

Book told her, "It's numb right now so I don't feel much but the pain will come once the shock of it wears off. Angela, I've been shot worse than this before and I've survived. If you can help me take the rest of this nylon netting off and get me to my feet, I'll be fine. But before you do anything take your bracelet and let me see you put it on."

Angela took the gold bracelet from him and fastened it to her left wrist. She then held it up for Book to see.

"Frank Book, I don't think that I will ever understand you. You nearly get yourself killed going out in a hurricane and then shot with a deer rifle that's left your shoulder smashed to pieces and the only thing you can think about is seeing me putting on my mother's bracelet."

"It means a lot to me," Book said while leaning over to kiss her. "I'm the one who made you part with it back there in the swamp. I'm just glad to see you wearing it again."

"Thanks," Angela said allowing a smile to appear on her face. "Let me get the rest of this nylon mesh off of you so we can get going. By the way, I should tell you what Panther just said to me in Creek before he died. It was something that he wanted me to pass on to you."

Book showed his surprise. "What could Panther want me to know? I'm sure it wasn't anything good."

"But it was," Angela said, shaking her head. "It was the highest praise Panther could have given you."

"I can't see him doing that."

"Well, he did. He said for me to tell you, *'Este-catet ometskes'*— You are Seminole."

CHAPTER FIFTY-FOUR

GABRIELLA HEARD THE sound of streaming water before spotting the river. Hurriedly, she waved both her hands in an effort to entice the women to leave the path they had been traveling on and move toward the sound. The Mexican women were tired, close to total exhaustion. There was no clear path leading to the river and the tall saw palmetto plants along with an assortment of hardwood trees blocked the way. The women refused to go. Some dropped down onto the ground shaking their heads. Gabriella was beside herself. They had to keep moving. She yelled to them in Spanish that men with guns were not far behind. Then she brought up the Dobermans. And if Joe Torres did not kill them, they would be here at any moment. The fear of the dogs is what brought the tired women to their feet. Gabriella pushed and shoved trying to hurry them. Her sister Aleena, to Gabriella's surprise, joined in to help. The young girl took the lead by walking into the heavy undergrowth while looking back to cajole the others to join her. Soon all the Mexican women were filing behind Aleena toward the river.

"Aleena, stay on this path until you reach the highway overpass," Gabriella told her sister after they had come upon the narrow path paralleling the river. "Wait for me there. I'm going back for Joe."

A frightened look took over Aleena's face.

"You can't go back. It's too late to help him," Aleena screamed at her. "There have been no more gunshots for a long time. If he hasn't caught up to us by now he's not coming. Gabriella please don't go back. I couldn't stand the thought of losing you, especially after all we've been through."

Gabriella ran to Aleena and embraced her.

"I have to go back for Joe. I just have to. But Aleena, you've got to stay strong. You have to get these women to the highway overpass because there's no one else. Will you do that for me, little sister? Look at me and say you will."

"Yes," Aleena said while nodding her head and wiping the tears out of her eyes. "I'll get them to the highway overpass, Gabriella. I promise you I will."

"Good," Gabriella said before kissing her sister's forehead. She then turned and ran back in the direction of where she had left Joe Torres alone to face the two Dobermans.

****

Nearly exhausted from running, Gabriella slowed to a fast walk before heading around the bend. She prayed that Joe Torres would be on the path walking towards her. And that he would be displaying the same smile and look of confidence that she had come to expect from him. Torres was her hope. The only person Gabriella could honestly say that she trusted.

And when he was not there, Gabriella could not help but fear the worst. Panic set in. Torres should be on the path. He should be walking towards her at this very moment. He should be taking her into his arms and kissing her. Something must have gone wrong. The Dobermans. They must have been too much. Taking a deep breath, Gabriella started running again.

Gabriella found him where she had last seen him at the top of the knoll. Torres was lying on his back with one of the dead Dobermans resting on its side next to him. The other Doberman had never made it to the top of the knoll. It lay dead ten to twelve yards farther down the path. Covered in his own blood, Torres was conscious. Both his eyes were open and looking up at Gabriella.

"You should never have come back here," he said to her. "Those men can't be more than a few minutes away. Get going before they see you. There isn't anything you can do for me. This one chewed me up pretty good before I was able to put a bullet in its head."

Gabriella dropped down to him. Gingerly, she lifted Torres's lacerated right arm. It brought a grimace of pain to the DEA agent's face. His wrist and elbow were nearly crushed while the upper arm had strips of bloody muscle hanging loose from it. She heard a loud groan suddenly come out of him. Immediately, Gabriella lowered the arm before going to Torres's right leg. The pants leg had been ripped away exposing deep lacerations. She could see that both the knee and shin bone had been badly splintered. Gabriella fought back the tears forming in her eyes. Now is no time for him to see me crying, she told herself.

Gabriella said to him, "Joe, I'm not leaving without you. The women made it to the river and are on the path leading to the highway overpass. Now it's just you and me to worry about. I can help you to the river and then we'll make it the rest of the way to the overpass."

"It's too late. I'd only slow you down and make it easy for those men to catch up to us. I've got an extra ammo clip in my left pants pocket. Load it into the gun for me and put the gun in my left hand. Then get out of here. I can hold them off for a little while. It should give you enough time to get away."

Gabriella reached into Torres's left pants pocket and removed the ammo clip. She then picked up the Beretta and loaded the fresh magazine into the gun. He watched her set the gun down on the ground well out of his reach.

"What are you doing? Give me the gun," he said to her.

"Either you let me take you away from here or I stay with you. Joe, it's up to you. It's your decision to make. We go together or we don't go at all."

"Gabriella don't do this. Get out of here while you ..."

"Make up your mind, Joe. Are we leaving or are we staying."

"We're leaving," Torres said while extending his left hand to her. "Help me up and let's get moving." She took his left hand and pulled him to his feet. Torres let loose with a loud groan. He nearly fell back down onto the ground. She saw him close his eyes and shake his head in an attempt to rid himself of the dizziness.

"Are you alright?" she asked him.

"No, I'm not, but what difference does it make? We've got to get away from here and fast. Let me lean on your shoulder. And don't forget the gun. We're going to need it if we hope to get out of this thing alive."

Torres placed his left arm on Gabriella's right shoulder. The two started walking down the path slowly toward the river. Gabriella could hear him taking deep breaths. She felt the tremors caused by the pain shooting through his body. They were not moving fast enough. She knew at this pace they would never outdistance the men coming up behind them. He must know it as well, she thought.

And as if knowing her thoughts, he said between heavy pants of breathing, "Once we find a place where the path narrows, that's where we're going to make our stand. We can't outrun them so we're going to have to kill them."

Gabriella turned her head to look at him. Torres's face showed pain covered in sweat. Every step the DEA agent took was nothing less than a herculean effort on his part. She could not help but admire him all the more.

"How are you going to kill them? You couldn't even aim a gun in the condition that you're in."

"You're right. I can't. But you can."

Gabriella observed Torres show a smile in spite of his pain.

"Somewhere up ahead we're going to find a good place to stop. And there Gabriella you're going to kill these guys."

****

Torres knew that he could not go much further. His head was spinning. It took everything he had just to place one foot in front of the other. And he was thirsty. Torres could not remember being as thirsty. Neither he nor Gabriella had any water since leaving the concrete building earlier that morning. And they would not be getting another drink anytime soon. Not until they reached the river. But the men coming up behind them would have to be taken out first. Torres knew that he could not do it. To hold the Beretta steady long enough for him to aim and shoot was out of the question. Gabriella was their only hope. She was a police officer trained in shooting a gun. But could she face armed men who would be shooting back at her? How good was Gabriella? That was the unknown plaguing Torres.

"This place is as good a spot as any," he said to Gabriella before slumping down onto the ground off to one side of the path.

"Joe, are you sure? Five men with guns coming down this path. How do you expect me alone to face that many guns?"

Torres looked up to see Gabriella standing over him with the Beretta in her right hand.

"There'll only be two of them," he said to her. "It'll be the big black guy and the skinny white one. They're the ones in charge. The other three men are just rummies hired to babysit the women. Once they see the dogs dead and that they're up against somebody with guns they'll back off. The salt and pepper duo will keep coming because they know that they'll catch hell for losing the women. They'll want to get them back."

"Deek and Oil Can," Gabriella said. "Those are their names. I heard them calling each other by name yesterday when they were walking us around. Deek's the skinny, white guy and Oil Can's the big black man. They're both trash if there ever was any. How do you want to do this?"

"We lay down here this side of the path until they walk up on us. It narrows right here so one of them will be in the front and the other behind. Oil Can will probably have the lead with Deek directly behind him."

"Why do think Oil Can will be in front?" Gabriella asked.

"Because Deek's the smart one. I watched them for hours yesterday. I figure Deek will lag behind and wait to see if someone starts shooting. And if they do, he'll let Oil Can take the bullet instead of him. Deek's the one I'm worried about. We won't catch him by surprise."

"You're going to have to walk me through this," Gabriella said while not attempting to hide her apprehension. "I've never shot anyone before. The only shooting I've ever done has been on the gun range, and frankly, I'm not a very good shot. Joe, are you sure …"

"Yes, I'm sure you can do it," Torres interjected not wanting to give Gabriella time to question herself. "When Deek and Oil Can are in position, I'll tell you to stand up. Then just like on the gun range bring the Beretta up to eye-level with its barrel centered on Oil Can's chest. He'll be caught by surprise and stop right on the path. Shoot three rounds just like you've done when you had a silhouette target hanging in front of you. And after Oil Can drops watch out for Deek.

He'll be stepping off to the side. Point the Beretta at Deek's chest and don't stop shooting until you see him falling down."

She saw Torres reach out and touch her on the right leg.

"Gabriella, Deek will be firing back at you. Come to grips with it now and not later. All of his shots should go wide because he won't have time to aim his gun. Once Deek goes down keep an eye out for Oil Can. If the big, black guy tries to get up, if you see any movement out of him at all, shoot the gun until there's no more bullets left to shoot. Do you have any questions?"

"Joe, what if I don't hit both of them? What if I miss Deek?"

"You won't. I'll be right next to you making sure that you don't miss. Once the Beretta is empty drop it and help me to my feet. Then we get away from here as fast as we can."

"What is it?" he asked her after seeing a worried look suddenly appear. Torres observed Gabriella's upper body start to shake.

"They're coming. And you were right about it only being Deek and Oil Can. I don't see anyone else."

"Quick get down," he said grabbing her right leg. "Gabriella, you can do this. I know that you can."

She looked into Torres's brown eyes now only inches away from her face. Gabriella stared into them seeing her own reflection. She was inside him. And in a strange way a part of him, she thought. It sent a warm feeling throughout her body.

"Gabriella, are you alright?" he asked her before bringing his left hand up to her face.

"Yes, Joe. I am," she said staring back at him.

Torres told her, "Whatever happens in the next few minutes, I just want you to know that I love you, Gabriella. And that I've been in love with you ever since that first night we met at the restaurant in Laredo when you told me what you were willing to do to save your sister, Aleena. I only wish that now it was me doing the shooting and not you."

"Joe, it's okay. I'm not scared anymore. I know you're here with me and that's all that matters. But we better get ready. I see Oil Can coming down the path. And I'm sure Deek is right behind him."

Torres waited until Oil Can was within fifteen yards before he nodded to Gabriella to begin shooting. She stood and fired three rounds. Oil Can immediately fell back clutching his chest. Deek quickly stepped to the left side of the path. He began firing an assault rifle spraying the ground to the right of Gabriella. She continued to fire the Beretta. One of her bullets struck Deek in the throat. It brought the skinny man to his knees. Another bullet tore into Deek's face. Oil Can attempted to rise up. Gabriella shot the black behemoth twice in the back.

"Gabriella, drop the gun and help me up," Torres shouted to her. She did as he told her while pulling him to his feet. "Let's go," he said after placing his good arm onto her shoulder.

They were well away from where the shooting had taken place when Torres asked to stop and rest. He was breathing heavily. Dehydration was taking its toll on him. Gabriella lowered the DEA agent to the ground before sitting down next to him.

"Did you really mean that back there when you said that you love me," she said to him while searching his face for the answer. Torres's mouth was so dry he found it difficult to respond.

"You know that I did," he finally was able to get out.

"Then tell me. Tell me the way that I want to hear it. Use the words that the singer at the Café Monte sang when warning me to get ready for the kidnappers who were coming. Do you remember the words?"

Torres nodded his head while a smile came to his face. The DEA agent knew the words all too well. It was he who had chosen the song to be sung that night. They were the words that he had wanted Gabriella to hear.

"Do you want them in Spanish or English?" he asked her.

"Both."

"Very well," he said. "I would sing them for you but my mouth is so parched I can barely talk."

"Saying the words while you are looking at me is all I want," she told him.

"Eres la chica que me encanta—*You are the girl I love*," Torres said to her while gazing into Gabriella's large brown eyes. He leaned over and kissed her. "Now do you believe me?"

"Yes," she said. "Now I do."

Gabriella stood and reached down to help Torres to his feet. Taking the DEA agent's left arm, she placed it onto her right shoulder. Torres noticed the happy glow on Gabriella's face. A shining brightness lit up both her eyes.

"And I love you, too, Joe," Gabriella said before starting down the path towards the river.

CHAPTER FIFTY-FIVE

THE RAIN HAD stopped. A hot sun appeared in a clear sky making travel even more difficult. Angela and Book spent the entire morning hiking over soggy, rain-soaked ground littered with remnants of Hurricane Ruth. Uprooted trees littered their path in addition to the broken off pieces from residential houses and pleasure boats that had been snatched from somewhere miles away and discarded in the Everglades. The earlier numbness Book had experienced in his right shoulder was no longer present. It had been replaced by a throbbing, ever-consuming pain that continued to drain the army ranger captain of his physical vigor. It made even a slow walk excruciatingly troublesome. Book felt wave after wave of delirium coming to his head. He attempted to focus on the arduous task of placing one unsteady foot in front of the other.

"There it is," Book thought he had heard Angela say. And then he was certain of it. "Frank it's the ranger station. We made it."

A beige-colored concrete structure with pillaring columns supporting it came into view. Located on the highest ground for miles around, the government ranger station had been built solely for the purpose of detecting and observing brush fires occurring in the Everglades. The building existed ten feet above ground supported by six concrete columns. An observation platform encircled the exterior with sliding glass doors on opposite sides of the building. Book noticed a green-colored government jeep parked underneath. Close to the jeep was a stairwell leading up to the ranger station.

"Angela wait a minute, not so fast," Book said after seeing Angela starting for the building.

"Why? What's wrong?" she asked him before turning around.

"I don't know but something's not right. After coming this far, I think we can wait a couple more minutes to be sure, don't you?"

"Frank it looks all right to me. The hurricane shutters are off the windows and the ranger's jeep is parked underneath. He must be in there. I don't see any other cars around and the road leading up to the station doesn't have any cars on it."

"No, not any that we can see," he said while his gaze stayed fixed on the beige-colored building.

"Then what's bothering you?" she asked him. "We have to get whatever is on the flash drive to Jim Garrison as soon as possible. And your shoulder is not getting any better with you standing out here in this hot sun."

"The flag pole," Book said walking toward the ranger station. "There's no U.S. flag flying. No park ranger worth his salt would forget to raise the U.S. flag. It would be one of the first things that he'd do in the morning."

"But the storm snapped off the top portion of the flag pole. He's probably just letting it go until the pole is replaced. Frank, you can't read anything into that."

"Maybe you're right, but I don't think so. If it were me, I would have raised the flag anyway. That said we have no other choice but to go and see. Angela, have the Glock out and be ready to use it. My gut tells me something is wrong and it has never failed me yet. Come on and stay close to me."

****

The jeep doors were locked. And there was nothing showing on the front seat. Book stepped around to the set of aluminum stairs. He saw that they ran up to a closed metal door. The army ranger captain hesitated before climbing the stairs, turning back to face Angela. She was standing with the Glock in her right hand resting at her side. Her green eyes looked up at him questioningly. *Well, are we going up the stairs or aren't we?* Book could not shake the uneasy feeling consuming him. He wished that Angela was not there. That he alone was going inside.

"Maybe you better give me the gun," he said holding out his left hand.

"What? Don't you trust me?"

"No, it's not that. It's just that I want to go first. And without the gun, I wouldn't be doing much good. Besides I can shoot almost as well left-handed as I can with my right."

She gave him the Glock.

Angela told him, "I don't care about the gun. I just want to get in there and find a computer. Right now that's all I care about."

Book started up the stairs. Angela was close behind him. After reaching the top, Book held his right ear up to the door. He heard no sound coming from inside the station. He kicked the bottom of the door three times. There was still no sound inside.

"Try the doorknob," he told Angela. She turned it and the door opened.

Book stepped into a large, open room with the only light coming from two sliding glass doors off the observation deck. The lighting was poor at best in what appeared to be the office. He flipped on the wall light switch next to him. Nothing happened. Carefully, Book's eyes scanned the room. Tables and chairs occupied the middle, while a long counter with file cabinets lined up behind it, taking over one wall. Book felt Angela touching him on his left shoulder. He turned to see her pointing to what looked like two computers located on the far side of the room. They walked towards them.

"I'll try this light," Angela said flipping the switch on the wall closest to the computers. There was still no light. She went to the computers. "Frank, the keyboards have been smashed and the monitors broken."

"And the overhead lights have been shattered," Book said back to her. "I just stepped on some pieces of broken glass. Angela get behind the counter right now and stay there."

Book watched Angela run to the counter. The army ranger captain then directed his attention to an open door leading to another room. He started slowly towards it. Angela's scream stopped him.

"Frank, it's the park ranger. He's been shot in the side of the head."

Book hurried over to counter. He found Angela standing looking down at a dead body. There was enough light from the sliding glass doors for Book to see the bullet wound in the right side of the man's head. He appeared to be an older man in his early sixties wearing white undershorts and no shirt. Two glassy eyes stared up at Book and Angela.

"He was dumped here after someone shot him. Probably while he was sleeping. That's why the flag wasn't raised. Whoever did it removed the hurricane shutters from the windows and made the place look like everything was normal. They wanted us to come in. Let's get out of here while we still can."

Bullets tore into the wall next to them. The loud sound was deafening inside the room. Book had no idea from what direction the bullets had come. But he did know that they had been fired from an automatic rifle.

"Drop your weapon Captain Book or I will immediately kill both you and Agent Valadez."

Book could not see him. The man had to be inside the room with the open door. And it was too dark in the room to see anyone inside. The army ranger captain knew that he had no other choice but to drop the Glock. He let the gun slip out of his hand. It fell heavily onto the wooden floor.

"Now kick it away," he heard the man say. Book complied, kicking the Glock with his right foot.

"That's better. Now we can talk."

"Bernardo," Angela gasped upon seeing the dark face coming out of the room. Holding an assault rifle, Colonel Hosseini had the gun pointed at Angela and Book.

"Yes, Agent Valadez. But Colonel Arash Hosseini of Iran's Ministry of Intelligence and Security would be more precise. And don't look so surprised Captain Book. You didn't think that I had forgotten about you and your brother's flash drive now did you?"

"You're the one who murdered Andy," Book said staring hard at the man walking toward him.

"Yes, the pleasure was mine. He broke into my computer and stole some very valuable information from me."

Hosseini continued walking. His eyes were on Book while taking in Angela as well. A smile precipitously crept across the man's dark face.

"Since in a matter of moments you both will be dead, I might as well tell you what the flash drive in your possession contains. Today's date is July third. Tomorrow, July fourth, is the day that your country celebrates its independence. But instead of a celebration there will be much wailing and gnashing of teeth. Every major city in your country will experience massive death. Thousands will die. The exact time and location of each bombing is on the flash drive as well as the safe houses where my soldiers are waiting. That is what your priest brother stole from me. That is why I killed him a little bit at a time until I ended it by driving the point of my knife into his heart. He was stubborn. Your brother would not give up the flash drive. Yes, Captain Book there was screaming. I heard your brother's screams. And I relished them. They brought me great joy. Now hand me the flash drive or I will make things very unpleasant for you and Agent Valadez."

"Go to hell you bastard." Book started toward the Iranian colonel. The gun instantly jumped in Hosseini's hands. Bullets tore into the wooden floor at Book's feet stopping him.

"Captain Book try that again and I will take your legs off. Now give me the flash drive."

"I don't have it. Before leaving Gator's Pond, I mailed it to the Florida Attorney General's Office. By now the attorney general and his people know the location of every one of your terrorist cells. No matter what you do to us colonel, you've lost your war."

"Captain Book, I am not a fool. You never had the opportunity to mail anything to anyone. Now give me the flash drive at once or I will do to Agent Valadez what I did to your brother. And you captain will have the chance to witness it."

Book knew he and Angela had nowhere to go. The Iranian colonel was not going to be put off much longer. But what could Book do? The man was holding an AK-47 assault rifle. One pull of the trigger and Book's legs would be instantly severed from the rest of his body. Then the Iranian colonel could follow through with his threat of torturing Angela in the same manner as he did Andy. That would be too much to bear, Book thought. While his handing over the flash drive meant instant death for the two of them. A quick bullet shot into each of their heads. But not without a fight, the army ranger captain told himself. He would not die without fighting.

"All right, Colonel, you win. I'll take you to where I hid the flash drive if you let Agent Valadez walk out the door right now," Book said hoping to buy time. He saw immediately that Colonel Hosseini was not going to give him anymore time.

"Goodbye, Captain Book," Hosseini said taking a firm grip on the AK-47.

Book gritted his teeth. The army ranger captain knew that he was about to die. The sound of the gun discharging surprised him. It did not seem as loud as it had before. Then he saw that Colonel Hosseini's lower jaw had disappeared. The man was falling to the floor. Angela let out with a loud gasp. Book next heard the sliding glass door being opened. And he observed a man holding a handgun in his right hand stepping through the opening. Book also took notice of the fresh bullet hole in the glass door.

"Captain Book and Agent Valadez, I'm sorry for being so late but I had a hell of time trying to find this place."

"Cornelius Jackson," Book said seeing the black, leathery face and grayish, white hair belonging to the clerk of the Gator's Pond Inn.

"One of my many names," the man responded while walking over to Book and Angela. "I'm with the CIA and, as you can see by looking at me, very close to retirement. But I wasn't going to pull the pin and retire until I finished with the Black Spider."

Cornelius moved over to Colonel Hosseini who was lying on the floor looking up. The man's eyes were open. The Iranian colonel appeared to be conscious, cognizant of what was going on around him. Cornelius pulled up the shirt sleeve covering Hosseini's upper right arm. The tattoo of a black spider showed prominently on the man's dark brown skin.

"Just wanted to leave no doubt in my mind," Jackson said with a chuckle. "I've been following this bastard for over three years from one country to another. And I've been waiting to kill him ever since I first laid eyes on him. By the way, before I forget. Colonel Hosseini, Jack Ross told me to tell you that he sends his regards. You remember him, don't you?"

The Iranian colonel stared back at Jackson unable to answer.

"He said that I should remind you before I killed you. It was about twenty years ago that you two first met in Lebanon. You cut off his right arm with a chain saw. He said that I should help you to remember."

Jackson pointed his pistol and shot Hosseini in the right elbow before firing a second bullet into the black spider tattoo on the man's upper right arm. The Iranian colonel's body writhed in pain.

"I'm sure that helped you to remember," Jackson said with a hard look on his face. The CIA agent then shot Hosseini between both eyes. Placing the handgun inside his waistband, Cornelius Jackson turned to Book. "My boss, Jack Ross, and Agent Valadez's boss, Jim Garrison, are waiting impatiently in Miami for the information that's on the flash drive you have in your possession. Captain Book, I have a computer in my car and I'll be sending it to them as soon as I get it from you."

"Frank, we have to give it to him," Angela said stepping forward. She was reaching into her front pants pocket for the rosary beads.

Book was not sure what to do. His reluctance in turning over the flash drive to Jackson was not lost upon the CIA agent.

"Captain, I see that you hesitate when it comes to giving me the flash drive. Jack Ross anticipated that might be the case so he contacted your commanding officer Colonel Henry Blake at Fort Benning. I was instructed to tell you that 'God, family, and country in that order is how you should place priorities in your life.' I hope that helps you in coming to a decision."

"It does," Book said prior to his turning to Angela. "Remove the crucifix from the rosary beads and give it to him. I'd like to keep the beads. It's all that I have left to remember Andy by."

Angela did as Book instructed before quickly handing the crucifix containing the flash drive over to Jackson. The CIA agent took it from her while at the same time a white-toothed smile formed across his black, heavily-lined face.

"Thank you Captain Book and Agent Valadez for your service to your country. As soon as I get back to my car I'll be sending whatever is on the flash drive to Jack Ross and Jim Garrison. And I will also request that a helicopter be sent to transport both of you to the hospital. We will probably never meet again so this is goodbye." Laughing, he added, "Perhaps the two of you should pretend that we never met at all. And that nothing out of the ordinary took place here today. I think that would be for the best."

Book and Angela watched the DEA agent leave by the same way he had gained entry, through the sliding glass door opening.

"Frank, is it really over?" Angela asked before placing her head onto Book's left shoulder. She felt his arm coming around her.

"Yes, it's over," Book said while he directed Angela toward the door and the stairs going outside.

CHAPTER FIFTY-SIX
(JULY FOURTH)

"BADGER ONE. THIS is Papa Bear how do you read me?"

"Papa Bear. I read you loud and clear."

"Good Badger One. What is your 10-20?"

"Papa Bear. I am on a Brazilian beach with a dry martini in my hand watching the sun going down while at the same time contemplating my retirement."

"Badger One. Nonsense. You are not retiring any more than I am. There is a situation in Prague that calls for your immediate attention. Certain people there do not have the best interests of our country in mind and you must rectify the problem."

"Papa Bear. May I finish my martini first?"

"Badger One. Finish your martini. But I want you having breakfast in Prague tomorrow morning. Do you read me?"

"Papa Bear. I read you. And by the way Papa Bear how did your excursion with Jim Garrison work out. Did the information on the flash drive prove useful?"

"Badger One. Extremely so. All the terrorist cells across the country have been eliminated in the same fashion as the one in Miami. The threat to America, for the time being, has been removed. You are to be commended for a job well done."

"Papa Bear. The credit should go to Captain Book and Agent Valadez. They are the ones who secured the flash drive and survived the Everglades to reach the ranger station. I only swatted the mosquito that was trying to bite them. Will Captain Book make a full recovery from his shoulder wound? And how about the Mexican women in Operation Rescue? Are they safe?"

"Badger One. Both Captain Book and Agent Torres were flown by helicopter to the Mayo Clinic in Jacksonville, Florida. They are expected to make a full recovery and return to active duty. And referencing your inquiry into the Mexican women, they are all back in their home country. DEA agent Torres and Laredo police officer Lopez were able to rescue the women from their captors and successfully escort them to safety. While Cash Wiley and the Thompson twins have been arrested by the DEA and are awaiting trial. Badger One, your mission was a complete success. I only hope that you do half as well in Prague."

"Papa Bear. So do I. In the meantime I have the rest of the evening to enjoy this beautiful sunset along with my dry martini. I will make contact with you tomorrow shortly after my arrival in Prague."

"Badger One. That is affirmative. Over and out."

"Papa Bear. Over and out to you."

EPILOGUE

VINCE DEWITT COULD not have been happier. He had done it. All his scheming and hard work had paid off. Within minutes, two armed security guards would be coming to escort him down to the convention center. And after reaching the podium at center stage, DeWitt would then show his trademark smile to the thousands of people jammed into the Miami Beach Convention Center, not to mention the millions who would be watching him on television. The former U.S. Attorney for the Southern District of Florida had won handily the Democratic Party's nomination for governor of Florida. His acceptance speech was only minutes away.

The knock at the hotel suite door set his heart racing. Dewitt looked one last time into his hand-held mirror. The beaming smile was perfect. The people were going to love him. He would win them over like he had won over everyone else. The Senate Committee on Homeland Security had given him and the U.S. Attorney's Office full credit for the successful completion of Operation Silverback. Cash Wiley and the Thompson twins had pled guilty in federal court to what ultimately would be a lifetime behind bars for each of them. While the U.S. press just adored DeWitt. The Miami Herald ran a headline, *U.S. Attorney DeWitt Saves Abducted Women*. CNN ran complimentary stories on the famously rich and politically connected

DeWitt family. Vincent DeWitt was touted as the rising star in American politics. The Democratic Party and its East Coast power brokers were quick to seek him out to run for governor of Florida. DeWitt was only too happy to oblige.

There was another knock at the suite door. This time harder. DeWitt put down the hand-held mirror. He went to the door and opened it. What he saw left him feeling weak in the knees. The DEA Head of Special Operations Jim Garrison was standing in the doorway.

Garrison's first punch broke DeWitt's nose. His second punch fractured the left side of the former U.S. Attorney's face sending him to the floor. Dazed and hurting, Vince DeWitt looked up at an angry Jim Garrison.

"I warned you not to put any of my people in jeopardy," Garrison said to him. "If you want to file assault charges against me go ahead. Then I will tell the American public how you got your best friend Casey Blurmeister killed and how you lied to the Committee on Homeland Security so that you could become governor of Florida. You're nothing but scum, DeWitt. If you ever jeopardize any of my people again, I'll kill you."

Garrison walked out and slammed the door shut behind him. He nodded to the two security guards who were getting off the elevator that he was getting on. Exiting the elevator on the first floor, Garrison walked through the expansive convention center. The place was humming with excited people waiting to hear the acceptance speech from the Democratic Party's nominee for governor of Florida. Garrison hated to be the one to disappoint them.

The warm, night air greeted Garrison as he stepped out of the convention center. His car was parked on the other side of the parking lot. While walking toward it the CIA Head of Special Operations thought of Angela and Book. They were getting married tomorrow morning and Angela had asked Garrison to give her away at the church wedding. He would be driving to Fort Benning, Georgia, directly from Miami.

The thought of seeing Angela again brought a warm feeling to Garrison. She and Book were two of the good people in this world. There were plenty of bad people like DeWitt and the Wileys and Colonel Hosseini. But few of the good ones. And then an idea came to Garrison. Maybe people like Angela and Book along with people like Joe Torres and Gabriella Lopez are put here to make up for the bad ones. They are God's way of evening things out. In some crazy way that is how it all worked. Shaking his head, Garrison smiled to himself. This world was far too complicated to figure out. Besides he had a lot of driving to do. Fort Benning, Georgia, was miles away from Miami, Florida. And he was not getting any younger.

THE END

ABOUT THE AUTHOR

J.C. Quinn resides in Florida. Besides *Dead Priest at Gator's Pond*, he has written *To Kill A Fox*, *Triple Murder*, and *Heroes: Stories, Letters and Thoughts of a Catholic Man*.

CPSIA information can be obtained at www.ICGtesting.com
Printed in the USA
LVOW13s2342210114

370319LV00001B/2/P